EVENT 2012

Adapted from the book "Warp Factor II-Titanic II"
by Curt Morelock and co-author, Ray Burke.

TITANIC II

What really happened?

First edition written in 1987 and published in 1996
Rewritten in 2002 for adaptation to screenplay....

Order this book online at www.trafford.com
or email orders@trafford.com

Most Trafford titles are also available at major online book retailers.

Print information available on the last page.

ISBN: 978-1-5536-9528-8 (sc)
ISBN: 978-1-4122-0015-8 (hc)
ISBN: 978-1-4122-4767-2 (e)

Trafford rev. 10/18/2018

www.trafford.com

North America & international
toll-free: 1 888 232 4444 (USA & Canada)
fax: 812 355 4082

Dedication

I would like to take this opportunity to dedicate this volume to these fine people. First of all, my mother, who gave me a solid love for God and always encouraged me in the accomplishments of my youth and beyond. My love for the great ship also came from her and my forth grade teacher.

Secondly, my sister Gin, who constantly kept after me to complete this effort. She told me that all authors felt inadequate at times. I owe the finished product to her and her faith in me. I wish my mother and Gin were here to enjoy the final curtain.

Then there is Ray Burke my mentor, who saw in my work a moving love story. I am not a writer. I don't even know where the coma's go nor do I know what an adjective is. Worst of all is my spelling... Thank the Lord for spell check and even that is not to be trusted fully. Ray took the bull by the horns and helped me finish this rewrite so we could adapt it for the silver screen. Ray said something once that made my day, "Curt, there are no perfect books – they all have mistakes!"

I want to tell you about Don Carbon of Buchanan, Mich., who had faith in my work to the point of having my Titanic story published. The black, gold embossed hard cover, library edition competed well with 39 other books (by authors from around the world) at the Florida International Museum during the Titanic display. 894 were sold during the short engagement of 26 weeks. They're now being sold at the "Ship of Dreams" display in Orlando, Florida and several other Museums around the country.

Last, but not least, God the almighty who is the reason for it all – thank you. ---- curt morelock

About the Author

He was born in Hagons, Virginia to poor farmer parents. His father helped his father run a country store until the elder Morelock went broke. His family moved to Michigan looking for a job. Just after his father was hired the bottom fell out of the economy (1929). John Morelock was retained all through the depression and was promoted to a better job in 1934 within the Clark Equipment Co.

Curtis (nicknamed Curt) graduated in 1946 and volunteered for Army duty that same year in Alaska before it became a state. He was honorably discharged in 1948 and reentered Seminary that same year. He was ordained to the ministry in 1950. 1970 -1975 he was attached to the U.S. Air force as a Chaplin and rose to the rank of Captain.

He wrote the original novel in 1987, but it was not published until 1996 by Moellerhaus Publishing Company. During one of the author's book signing trips he met Ray Burke, another author, who purchased a copy and was impressed by the story. Ray agreed to take on the job of adapting the book to a rewrite for the purpose of making it into a screenplay.

The original plan in 1985 included having the story made into a motion picture. This dream could still come true even though the author will be 74 in July of 2002. He believes there is someone out there that will believe in him and the novel.

The volume you are about to read is the work of both Curt and Ray Burke. Enjoy!

About the Author

Chapter 1

The call

Randy, still in his reverie, gazes at his high tech computer screen in awe of a ghostly young woman, walking across the water, holding her hands out toward him. As pale as death, her long dark hair spills over the high lace collar of her long white Victorian dress. "Save us!" pleads the frail voice of this beautiful young creature.

She comes ever closer, her eyes were so penetrating he becomes spellbound. His eyes finds her lips, his heart, his manhood and his curiosity are immediately aroused. She, with arms open wide to receive him, made him burn with desire. He could not wait to hold her and comfort her. With feelings never felt before he reached out to take her in his arms, closed his eyes and was about to kiss her .... "Mr. Kaplan, are you still with us?" interrupted Dr. Dateless Devant, Webster Institute's somewhat eccentric Mathematics professor. He had been teaching here for many years and was well respected in scientific circles for his papers on time and light. (He considered himself to be one of the few members of academia who fully understood Einstein). Established in 1893, Webster Institute of Engineering is a small school in Glen Cove, N.Y. with emphasis on Marine Engineering.

Everyone was quite familiar with Randy's constant daydreaming. Matt shook his head while Roxanne rolled her eyes in recognition of another such episode. She was trying to ignore the fact that Randy, in anger, had just thrown his pen across his desk and onto the floor.

Randy mumbled, "Ah - sorry. I was just...about to kiss her." The class broke out in laughter with a few oohs and uhs. He looked at his computer screen and it was blank. The young woman had vanished. "Never mind!" His voice was always full of excitement but now it had changed to resolve.

Smiling, Professor Devant turned to his class and said, "Good! Now, pick up your pen and then we can get back to our discussion–'the feasibility of time warp equations'. Class, please click on your virtual museum."

As the class clicked on their computers, a virtual museum of time travel appeared on every screen. A talking head of Einstein, against a background of stars, turns 180 degrees as he lectures on his Theory of Relativity.

Professor Devant joined in, "Relativity - Einstein's view of time and space. If it's true, time travel should be not only within the realm of possibility, but within the realm of probability! Now, if you will click the next page..."

The class, as one, touched the screen. "Perhaps the answer to time travel," said Professor Devant, "Can be found in Spectrum analysis. Einstein used bands of light in his famous experiment. He theorized riding a beam of light across the universe would slow down the present- while time continues in the future dimension."

As Professor Devant spoke, a picture of the sun appeared opposite a prism while computer calculations analyzed each band of color in the spectrum and its wave-length. The professor then lined this up with the bands of light from the sun. and clicked on a chair, moving it between the sun and the prism.

"Computer calculations indicate," continued Professor Devant, "that if we harnessed enough energy, perhaps the white light from the Sun, separating it into wavelengths through the optics of a prism and at the same time projecting a focused laser toward the invisible, ultra-violet end of the spectrum, from the opposite direction -- we might in fact, cause a rent in time and space, an implosion, as it were, traveling counterclockwise through a parallel dimension backwards through time."

The professor concentrated the light from the Sun through the prism into a single laser beam and aimed them directly at each other. The two lights met in the center, over the chair and prism. A violent flash of light - a spark - and then - nothing! The chair was gone! The class applauded.

Randy smiled, looked up and said quietly, "Wow! Cool! Would you be able to travel anywhere you wanted? Any time? That **is** the question.

"Anything's possible, Randy, but true bi-location is really a prospect for the future. For now, it's only a theory--alternate dimensions, wormhole and black holes in space, experiments with light and prisms--but, who knows?" responded the Professor, looking off into space. "One day! (Pausing)......I like to think it's only a matter of time....so to speak." The professor paused, began to laugh. As they each caught the connection, they laughed along with him. Holding up a finger, he admonished, "But, a final warning and another question. When science finally discovers a way to travel in time, could we, in fact, have it within our power to change the course of history? If so, what will happen then? Could wars be avoided, or could the game of chance become extinct? Confuse events to the point of chaos?

At this point the bell rang, catching Randy still staring off into space, visualizing the application of these time-travel principles to more than just a chair on a computer screen. The rest of the class turned off their computers and left. Only Matt remained to find out what was going on in that genius brain of Randy's.

"Matt, I talked to Prof De Vane, did you know his dad was a scientist? He told me about his dad's experiments, that's the reason Devant believes in this stuff. Put that together with what we learned today and I know how it works....I'm telling you Matt....I know!"

"Come on, Randy! He may be the best teacher in school, but---you don't really think.....?" queried Matt. Randy, wearing his Titanic T-shirt, turned to Matt. He was being challenged on one of his two obsessions--time travel and the Titanic.

"I just know we can make it, I'm not sure about the year, though!

"Where? When? What are you talking about? And who's 'we'?" Matt challenged. Although blessed with as great a measurable IQ as Randy, Matt was more world-reactive, less imaginative and continually amazed at both the extent and the product of Randy's dream world.

Then Randy told Matt about the girl in his dream, all of it, he didn't leave out a thing, "I was almost kissing her when it was interrupted by

Devant. I'll bet she's there in 1910. I've got to find out!"

"Are you talking about going back to.....?" Matt doubling over.

"1910," replied Randy, his expression becoming more serious.

"The Titanic again!" said Matt, almost yelling.

Randy nodded his head, "Yes. We'll go to the lab at school early!"

Matt shook his head and said, "Randy, now I know you're crazy!" then calming down a bit, Matt asked, "Why is it so important? I mean, what's so important about cobwebs, sunken ships and dead people?" He had never seen Randy so serious before.

"It's a long story, Matt." Randy said, wondering if his friend could grasp the full impact the Titanic had made on him. "It hurts me to think that intelligent people like those engineers could have been so careless. I mean, they were downright sloppy. Maybe you can understand it all when I get through telling you."

"Try me!" came the blunt reply. "I'm trying to get it all straight in my mind."

Randy paused, thinking of the right place to begin.

"When I was in the fourth grade, I had a teacher by the name of Fuller. She made me love the Titanic as much as she did.

Randy stared off into space for a moment, then continued, "Since then I've had this thing about the great ship, and other things like that in history. With this time business -- in reality, **now** is forever. Everything is happening at the same time--all at once, at this very moment. Time is just a divider--a measuring device. It separates **events**. Some day everyone will understand that. When you remove the dividers, what you have left is the eternal **Now**! That's why we're told to 'live in the present moment,' because that's all there is. Doesn't that just blow your mind?"

"Right," came Matt's uncertain agreement. "But our chances of ever doing anything about it are next to none. It's already history." With a puzzled expression in his light blue eyes, Matt took off his dark-rimmed glasses and pensively rubbed the side of his nose with an ear-piece. Randy knew he had, or was about to have, Matt's full attention.

Randy said as he walked off. "Don't forget! Early at the school lab. Remember, tomorrow at dawn I'll be there. I leave with or without you!" He turned on his heel and walked away, leaving Matt dumbfounded.

Chapter 2

"Time to get going. Don't want to miss those first direct rays," he murmured to himself. Dressing quickly, he grabbed his bag and ran out of his room, headed for the school lab. When he arrived, he entered by using a credit card to open the lock. Everything was as he had left it the day before. The wall clock read 6:21 A.M. He raised the blind to find the sun just peeking above the horizon. He turned away from the window as Matt entered.

"Right on time, traveler," Randy welcomed him.

From one side of the lab, a laser shone through a huge prism, casting a rainbow band of prismatic colors across the floor, up the wall and across the ceiling. The sun's rays seeped through another prism, breaking apart the color bands, channeling the wavelengths into a narrow laser beam toward the optical master prism at the other end.

Holding a spiral notebook, Randy said, "Professor Devant told us it would take a lot of energy, right? The sun produces one phase and the optical master produces the other from the opposite plane. When the two meet...WHAM!" Randy clapped his hands for emphasis.

"You're serious," Matt concluded, "I just came to make sure you didn't do something stupid like blowing yourself up. You say we're going back in time? You and me? You want me to go with you? I must be dreaming!" He picked up the notebook Randy had been holding and began to read out loud,

"The prism is the key to the whole thing. It acts as a collector. The implosion originates in the center, stimulated by opposing penetrations of light.... Matt stopped reading, "Where did you get all this stuff?"

"From Devant, remember...I told you about it...I bet he'll wish he was here!"

"Yeah, right," Matt continued. "The sun produces one phase and the Optical Laser produces the other by entering the prism from the opposite plane. When the concentrated rays of light meet, the time reversal reaction begins." Matt heard Randy chuckle..

Matt looked up from the notebook "What's funny?"

"It won't be exactly pleasant, but we will survive." Randy's dark eyes shone. "I can't wait for it to happen to us! With a setting of point 63 intensity, we can regulate how far back in time we will travel, I think"

"I don't believe I heard you say that," Matt groaned as Randy's intentions penetrated his understanding. "This is our Last day on earth."

Ignoring Matt's comments, Randy said, "The way I got it figured, when the implosion occurs, anything within twenty to forty feet of the prism will enter time warp with it. Just like the chair!

Randy walked over and stood in the center of the room as the two opposing beams of light narrowed. "Come on, Matt. Time to go," instructed Randy.

Matt stood, unsure of his next move. He had brought some things with him in case Randy talked him in to this crazy trip, but he was not enthused. "And just where are we going-- besides straight to a mental institution? Oh, God! Let me guess! I can't believe I'm doing this!"

"I programed the equations on the computer and set the time period selection factor for about the same day in 1910. With any luck we should come close," Randy assured him.

"Oh, great!" was all Matt could say. "'With any luck...,' And if our luck doesn't hold....my God we're going to die!

"Oh, ye of little faith," Randy said, as he watched the two beams of light meet at the huge prism. One from the laser the other refracted rays of the Sun. As the two met, Randy, his eyes shining, was encompassed in a almost supernatural white light, swirling counterclockwise. Matt, standing stationary, couldn't believe his eyes as the clock on the wall spun counterclockwise.

"It's working! Randy said, "I hope we will be OK!"

"You're crazy!" retorted Matt. His words were lost in the maelstrom.

Professor Devant and Dean Reynolds hurried down the hallway with the custodian jangling his keys.. "Got a call from Security. Said someone's in the lab--caught it on video. What would anyone be doing here at this hour?" he asked.

They walked up to the door and, as the custodian was about to put the key in the lock, an implosion rocked the hall! A pulse of blinding light flashed through the door amidst the sound of broken glass. It was as though a full-blown tornado had erupted in the lab. Loud screams and several thunders unleashed their roars within a split second, sparks shooting in every direction.

They looked at each other--the custodian, fumbling with the keys, finally opened the door. When the smoke cleared, the lab was empty. Only those things anchored down remained. "Where'd they go?" he asked.

"My word, what a mess!" Professor Devant opined, as he stood in the doorway, confounded.

At this point, Ms. Johnson, Dean Reynold's secretary, entered the scene running. "Is everything all right?" she asked.

"Call the police! No, call an ambulance! No, call the coroner!

"Did someone vandalize the lab, Dean?" asked Ms. Johnson.

"Go, do what I told you!"

Professor Devant stared thoughtfully into space. As the sun continued to rise, he entered the lab, walked around the semi-empty room. But he noticed a small prism left behind on the windowsill. Picking it up, he turned it over in his hands, seeking clues as to what might have transpired. Then, smiling enigmatically, he rejoined the others.

"Your lab was involved, Devant. What do you have to say about this? asked Dean Reynolds.

"The only thing I can contribute is that Randy Kaplan and Matt Miller demonstrated extreme interest in an experiment we'd been working on yesterday. If they had gone further with it on their own, they could have run into an unexpected explosive force. Why they or their bodies are not here, I have no idea." He was understandably reluctant to introduce time travel as a factor in their deliberations.

"We'd best call their parents, find out if they're at home and, if not, at least prepare them for the worst," Dean Reynolds conjectured.

Blue lights of police cruisers flashed against the buildings. TV & radio vans maneuvered for strategic parking space on the Webster campus or along the street. Students and local residents, obviously awakened by the blast, gathered in clusters, waiting for news of what had happened,

Reporters managed to identify and seek out Randy's and Matt's parents who had just arrived. Since Mrs. Kaplan was crying, reporters sought her out for the 'human interest' angle.

"How could this happen to my baby?" cried Mrs. Kaplan.

Sticking a camera in her face, a reporter asked, "Where do you think they are?" Mrs. Kaplan answered, "I don't know. I only hope he comes back to us......soon." Mr. Kaplan put his hand on her shoulder.

Another reporter approached Dean Reynolds with a camera. "We are speaking now to Alan Reynolds, dean of Webster Institute, trying to make sense out of an evident tragedy. Dean, could you please tell us why, after an explosion like that, there were no bodies, no explosive materials, nothing found on the premises?" Looking straight into the camera, Dean Reynolds said confidently, "I have no idea, but I'm going to find out and heads **will** roll."

Chapter 3

The Crossing

A meadowlark warbled cheerfully, presenting his morning concert. The soft Autumn breeze waved the branches of the tree where the feathered soloist perched. Although it had not fully risen, the sun was bright and warm. A beautiful Indian Summer day, so characteristic of October in New York. In a flash of light, Randy appeared on a hill whose location was not immediately evident. Another flash and Matt appeared next to Randy. They opened their eyes, not knowing what to expect. Slowly they became conscious of their surroundings. They were lying in a field with the larger prism and the pedestal nearby. Within a 30-foot area, hundreds of scattered papers and other small items, evidence of the scope of the implosion.

"No! Don't tell me we're....," pleaded Matt.

"In 1910?"

"I told you not to tell me that!" Closing his eyes with all his might, he continued,"I'm gonna wake up any minute now."

"Well," said Randy, "it looks as though we've gone somewhere, but where are we and what's the date?"

"What about the people we left behind? They'll never know what happened to us!"

"Matt, chill out and listen!" insisted Randy. "We've just accomplished something the world's been dreaming about for centuries. We are definitely not in our own time, and should be somewhere south of our hometown, Glen Cove. The experiment certainly worked, and that's enough to convince me we're on the right track. We're on a mission."

"But, do you know just where we are? We can't see either the campus buildings or the town from here. And what mission--the Titanic? Randy, have you flipped? You can't change history!" He was hoping he had misunderstood Randy's intentions, or that he could dissuade him from this craziness. "Anyway, it's too late and I think I'm going to get sick!"

Almost completely ignoring Matt's concern, Randy said, "Well, let's get going so we can find out where we are in time. Construction on the

Titanic began in 1908 in Belfast. She didn't leave Southampton until 1912...Hopefully my data entries dropped us in 1910, enough time to accomplish the necessary changes. If this is Long Island, we've still got a long way to go to get to Belfast."

"Well, I guess I have no choice but to go with the flow. Hey, man, we can find out what year it is in a hurry!" Grinning mischievously, Matt pulled a two-inch TV from his back pocket and pulled out the antenna.

"Pizza-brain! That won't work!" said Randy, obviously irritated.

"Oh, that's right, no TV stations then...I mean now. No pizza yet either, I'll bet. Now that does it! How can anyone exist without pizza? Well, TV and pizza isn't all we haven't got," Matt went on. "We haven't got a laser to go back with either."

"Good grief, Matt, that's right, we didn't bring one along!"

"Does it bother you, Randy? I didn't think it would, but I guess it does. I mean--we may never get back," Matt stated.

Randy, knowing the far-reaching effects of Matt's abilities, felt somewhat relieved. Not being able to return hadn't actually crossed his mind. He was like a man possessed.

"I wish I had memorized the schematics for the laser," whispered Matt.

"You astound me, Matt. You've got a great deal tucked away in that genius brain of yours. I can't understand why you would worry about this mission," Randy responded. "Well, we better get going. Chances are if we head West we'll run into the Long Island Railroad tracks coming out of Glen Cove or the Glen Street station itself. In any event, we shouldn't have trouble finding out where we are and the date." Maybe the best thing to do is to keep going toward the Sound. You know how many Yacht Clubs there are in the Glen Cove area. If we do get that far, we might be lucky enough to run into a sailing yacht heading toward the City, or, better yet, across the 'Pond' to Southampton or Belfast or some other port in Britain. We could serve as crew--what with school in session this time of year, it may be difficult to find people to crew," Randy speculated.

They calculated they were just a few miles south of Glen Cove, they were probably even with the southernmost of Glen Cove's yacht clubs. Of course they couldn't be sure which, if any, existed in 1910. But if they couldn't find what they were seeking there, they reasoned they could easily walk back to Glen Cove and take the train to New York City, or come up with some other plan.

Continuing on, they came upon the Harbour Cliffs Yacht Club first. The office was closed, but aboard one of the larger yachts tied up to the dock, a gentleman was overseeing the caulking of nail holes in his decking.

"Good afternoon, sir." called out Matt, "We're students at Webster planning to take the rest of the school year off and travel to Ireland and England. It's in connection with an engineering project we're working on. Is anyone here headed that way who could use two crew?....Oh, excuse me....I'm Matt Miller and this is Randy Kaplan."

"Welcome aboard. I'm Cornelius Graham. I don't know that anyone is today. Jim Barker up at Gull Harbor was talking about it. We've been sailing buddies for a long time. Jim is somewhat abrupt and cantankerous. But lf you can make the grade with him, you'll have a friend for life and learn more about sailing than you would from anyone else in the harbor. Tell the old goat hello for me and that 'Corny' sent you. He'll get a kick out of that."

"We will. Thank you, sir. By the way sir, do you have a calendar? A calendar? Sure, I got one right here in my pocket book. You can have it, it's from last year." "You've been a big help," Randy said as they turned to leave, wondering what they may be getting themselves into now. Randy handed the pocket calendar to Matt...Matt smiled as he handed it back and said, "1909. Wow!

Chapter 4

Just north of Harbour Cliffs Y.C. a high cliff, dropping straight into the water, provided a view of the whole area. They jogged up the hill toward it with enthusiasm--things seemed to be going very much their way. Upon reaching the top, they threw themselves on the grass panting. As they regained their breath, they sat looking toward the north, viewing the scene in silence. Randy was quite pensive, and seemingly upset.

From the brow of the cliff they could see the large GLEN COVE water tower off to the northeast and the distinctive roof of the Institute reflecting the afternoon sun. The cluster of businesses forming downtown appeared much smaller than in 2010. It was good, nevertheless, to see something of "home."

"What's going on in that mixed up head of yours, Randy? Having homesickness problems already?"

"As a matter of fact, I am."

Masts of many sailing vessels could be seen clearly to the north. Anxious to meet the "Captain Bligh" who might take them to Belfast, they walked quickly in that direction.

When they reached the Gull Harbour Yacht Club, they were greeted at the office by the club's manager.

"We're looking for Jim Barker," said Randy. "We understand from a friend of his at Harbour Cliffs that he's planning to sail to Europe soon. If so, we hoped he'd need crew. Can you clue us in on that?"

"Can I 'clue' you in on that? That's a new one on me. Where you boys from?" asked the manager.

"Oh, we're from quite a way west of here. Sort of a local expression back home. Sorry. What we meant was, can you tell us if that's so," Matt explained.

"Oh, sure. 'Captain Jim' Is sailin' to the other side, the only trouble is, He left yesterday."

"Oh man!" cried Matt. "Now what are we going to do?"

"I don't know, we'll figure something out."

"What!"

"Great Balls o' fire Matt, how am I supposed to know."

"Well, you better come up with something and quick!"

"That's you - gettin' spastic will take care of everything. The last time I checked we weren't in any hurry - right?"

"Well, no, I guess not....I'm just upset. I'll live."

Chapter 5

Belfast, Two Months Later

Nearby they found a tavern with a sign blowing in the wind and rain. It said "The Skiff." From the sound of it, it was a pub for old salts. Seventeen days at sea, a brutal nor'easter and compliments from the captain made them think they could fit in anywhere. Upon entering, it didn't take long to find out they'd made a bad mistake. The place was jammed with rowdy sailors, each trying to outshout the rest. Women of the night were blatantly plying their trade in loud voices. The result was chaos But it was dry! Randy and Matt took a good look around. Up on a balcony a man in long-johns came out of an upstairs room with a mug of grog in his hand, singing a sailor song they hadn't heard before. Nobody joined in.

They noticed two chairs by a window and, while walking toward them, began to ask questions about the big ships under construction. Nobody responded.

"Are these two seats occupied?" Matt asked. One of the two men at the next table shook his head and, as he gestured toward the chairs, gave a knowing wink to his companion.

"We're shipbuilders, uh, engineers," Randy blurted out, "and we're looking for a big one to work on." As Randy was talking, a waitress set two glasses of something in front of them. Trying to act nonchalant, they took a few swallows and went on pushing for information. Whatever was in those glasses tasted bad!

Matt wondered why Randy was acting strange, and realized he couldn't see too well himself. Things began to blur---.

Early the next morning they awoke in an alley next to the pier, still soaking wet and feeling very sick. They had been robbed!

A local police officer, following his morning routine, was clearing out the vagrants who slept there regularly. Having no identification, Matt and Randy were hauled down to the station house. Here the Chief of Police spent most of the morning asking them questions: "Who are you? Where did you come from? Why are you in Belfast?"

Randy was more than a little upset. "Drunken sailors drugged us, took wallets, our money and our pride," he protested.

The Chief had them recount their story of how they were seeking jobs working on a big ship, and had worked their way from the States to Cork on a sailing yacht. The captain could verify this, but he had left two days ago for France. They hoped to take care of everything in Belfast on their own. If it were absolutely necessary to call on him, they would.

At this point the chief's wife entered to pick him up for lunch. She was sister to the head superintendent for Harland and Wolff Shipbuilding. Fortuitously, she worked as secretary to Alexander Carlisle, designer and Master Builder for the King's Royal Navy. He had been assigned to coordinate all elements of Titanic's design.

"I'm sorry, but waiting outside I couldn't help but overhear your conversation. White Star Line has plans to build three monster ships," she said. "Two, the Olympic and the Titanic are already under way. The third, the Gigantic, will be soon. Olympic will be first out of the gate in seven to eight months, followed by Titanic."

"Who's doing the building?" Randy asked, trying not to appear too anxious.

"The company my brother works for--Harland & Wolff has built 65 of the 96 registered British ships He's heard rumors concerning two foreign lads claiming to be shipyard staff, hanging around the docks last night. The rumors persisted throughout the night shifts with the help of the overtime crews. By this morning, it was the talk of the yard. You two would not, perchance, be the subject of these notorious rumors, would you? The company is looking for skilled employees to complete the office staff," she continued, glancing at Randy with a curious smile.

"The rumors you heard were true alright. We are marine structural engineers," Randy offered.

"Well, chaps, there's nothing to substantiate your claims, and you are without passports," said the chief, "You are obviously Americans. I'm sorry, but I must turn you both over to higher authorities. I hope you realize that I don't want to do this, but I have no choice."

"Randy, I told you this would happen over here!" Matt was getting wound up.

"What could happen? Over here? What is all this?" The chief spoke with renewed interest as Matt's outburst piqued his curiosity.

Laughing, Randy quickly covered Matt's tracks. "Nothing. Nothing's wrong. He's just mad because he lost a bet. He's just talking; it's not important." The chief became confused, but was tired of pursuing it.

Irish jails were a true phenomena---more like concentration camps than prisons---no game rooms, outings, movies, day rooms, etc. The walls were musty and damp, spider webs hung from the corners. The mattresses were thin and hard. If you looked closely you could see footprints of the jail's more enterprising rats on them. The mattresses rested on cots of knotted ropes. Guards screamed continuously at the inmates, venting their spleens even in the middle of the night! It was next to impossible to sleep. Such was the case in Belfast that second night.

Early the next morning, they were brought to the chief's office. "Sit down, lads," he began, with a serious expression on his face, "My wife, Regina, came up with a compromise. I wasn't in agreement at first, and I'm still having trouble with it. She seems to like the idea so much, however, that I said I'd explain it to you this morning.

"Here's the deal. Since all your papers were stolen, along with your money, she thought we should allow you to work while we investigate your claims. She also wanted me to give you the equivalent of your twenty dollars to help you settle in. The best of it all is, you are now temporary employees of Harland & Wolff. I think you'll be sweeping floors or something like that. Report to Adam Boyle's office at 11 A.M. this morning." Scratching his head, he continued, "Now get out of here! By the way, that money is a loan."

Randy stared at Matt and said, "Put that down in your little black book. We'll have to get you a new one." Randy turned back to the Chief and said, "thank you, and your wife, sir for giving us a great day!"

Matt joined in the thanks and assured Randy he'd find a black book.

The chief's wife was a key player in the roles these daring young men would be playing. Their presence in another dimension required that they use every option available to them. This wonderful lady had provided one leading to their employment at the shipyard. She had told her brother they were strong young men looking for work. The upcoming meeting would be the product of that conversation.

"Janitors!" cried Matt to Randy as they emerged from the police station, "We can't offer changes of any significance as janitors!"

"I know that! It's all wrong....maybe she didn't explain it right or something. We'll just have to play it by ear. Come on, let's get out of here."

Since they had several hours before the meeting at 11 A.M., they began looking for a place to live. They started a few blocks from the shipyard and walked in a square pattern away from it. A few For Rent signs were posted, but none suited them. Finally, they spotted a sign advertising a third floor flat in a row of houses, neatly kept and on a tree-lined block.

They found the flat adequately furnished and reasonable. One strong point was its magnificent view of the harbor with the gantries in the background An efficiency arrangement provided a large sitting area with a somewhat worn but comfortable couch, two side chairs and a large, solid oak table.

While walking around the city Randy swore up and down he caught a glimpse of the beautiful girl of his dreams.

"Matt! I'm telling you–I saw her–she's here in Belfast!

All Matt would say was, "Yeah, right."

Chapter 6

Randy and Matt arrived at Adam Boyle's office promptly at 11 A.M.

A tall, well-constructed receptionist with brown hair greeted them, and round wide, hazel eyes that seemed to smile continually. She introduced herself as Emily O'Rourke. Matt rolled his eyes and pretended to faint.

"Don't pay any attention to him. He'd fall from a twenty-foot roof if he could get a laugh. Matt, cool it." Randy was a bit upset.

Matt was fascinated with the way she looked at him over the top of her tiny glasses. He was even more fascinated by the way she walked toward the office with her hips swaying. It reminded him of the opening sentence in one of Mickey Spillane's mystery novels; "She came toward me with her hips waving hello."

"Please follow me, gentlemen," she directed, and upon entering his office, introduced them to Adam Boyle.

"Good morning, chaps. I'm glad I can provide you with some good news to offset the wretched night you must have had in the dungeon. Apologies on behalf of Harland & Wolff.

"Mr. Carlisle, Chief Designer for the Titanic project, thought your background might be better used as assistant engineers rather than janitors. I certainly agree with him, and I've taken the liberty of making an appointment with him for you. It's at 1 P.M. this afternoon. His office is straight down the hall. Emily, we'll have the boys meet you here, then you can show them to Mr. Carlisle's office.

"Assuming Mr. Carlisle does not change his mind, I would like to have my assistant, Kevin O'Malley, take you on the 'Visitor Tour'--now, if it's convenient for you." Two nodding heads concurred "Emily, please take Randy and Matt to Kevin's office. When you come to work Monday morning, I'll go over the construction prints with you. That should catch you up in a hurry. I'll have a lot to catch up on myself after the weekend, so it may be best to get here at about 10 A.M. When you arrive, have Kevin give you your H & W. badges. Then you can wander the yard at your leisure."

"Thank you, sir. We're really looking forward to this." said Randy.

As they left Adam Boyle's office, Matt whispered to Randy, "Gee, I'd hate to have to watch her walk down the hall."

"Matt, will you get a grip! This is serious business we're about. Now just chill out! "Forgive us, Miss O'Rourke. We didn't bring Matt's cage along with us today. Certain precautions may be necessary to bridal the desire to have the world notice him."

"Oh, I think I can handle it," she assured Randy with a hint of a smile.

She motioned them to follow her, which was what Matt was waiting for. He seemed to float down the hall after her. When they reached O'Malley's office and, after due introductions by Emily, they thanked her and headed off on the tour. Matt waved to Emily as she left and followed it with a wink. The wink seemed to noticeably increase the size of her smile..

"Follow me, gents," said O'Malley, "I've got something to show you." As he moved through all the steel and machinery, it was evident O'Malley knew what he was doing and where he was going. Matt and Randy were amazed at the numerous industrial tools and equipment in use at that time, especially the pneumatic hammers.

After a few minutes, the three men stood on the edge of the assembly basin called "the slip." One end was open and a huge ramp ran down into the channel that led to the sea. There, before them, was an awesome sight. The bottom third of Olympic had row after row of gigantic ribs. The stern included some of her double-sided coal bunkers. Titanic's keel had been laid on March 31, 1909, which put the Olympic's construction well ahead.

Their amazement and awe continued as they saw thirty towers making up the great gantry on both sides of the ships. A huge gangway went up through the towers from the floor at the bow to crane height--one-fourth of the way back from land side toward sea side. Thousands of skin plates were stacked on the floor in front of the developing liners. They were leaning on each other from opposite directions and resembled a field of large army pup tents.

Randy and Matt were stunned. Years of pictures, hundreds of books, even the National Geographic reports hadn't prepared them for this.

"I feel a little dizzy," said Matt, his eyes glued to the panorama of human endeavor before them.

"They're almost 900 feet long," Randy said softly, shaking his head. "Can you believe what we're looking at?"

"Nope," was the supporting reply.

"Well, men," Kevin O'Malley said. "I'll take you back to Adam Boyle's office. I understand he wants you to see Mr. Carlisle."

"Right," said Matt, "Thank you for showing us that fantastic sight. It's like it's from some other world--so huge!"

"It's all of that and more. It is the largest single object mankind has ever conceived You'll get to see it on your own. If you have any questions, let me know. Good luck."

"Don't have any questions now, but we'll probably bother you with them once we get our feet wet. Thanks for the tour. Matt and I really appreciate how we've been accepted by the company. You people have treated us like we're going to be worth something to you on this project. Thanks again," Randy said. His comment could not have anticipated the lack of acceptance they were to confront almost immediately from antagonists within the company.

With the tour completed, they found their way back to Adam Boyle's office. "Hi, Emily, we're back. What an operation you guys have going out there! We're ready to do our part, so take us to your leader!"

"Follow me," Emily countered with a smile, as she started toward Carlisle's office.

"My pleasure, Ma'am. I'd follow you anywhere!"

Feigning disinterest, Emily pointed her nose toward the ceiling and emitted a muffled "hrrumpf."

Chapter 7

Alexander Carlisle wanted to finalize Randy and Matt's upgrade in employment by asking several questions to test their knowledge of shipbuilding technique. He had asked his secretary, Sandra Collins, to take notes during their meeting. Ms. Collins had been with the company for over twenty years. Matt, as a result, was less distracted here.

"Mr. Carlisle, never have we been more impressed. Mr. O'Malley just took us on the tour. No one can be prepared for what is there--it is absolutely overwhelming! We feel privileged to be part of it." Randy effused.

"Yes, we are very proud of the project. Hopefully we are contributing to an era of great ships that will change the travel habits of the world." Carlisle responded. "As you know, our principal competitor, the Cunard Line, has recently introduced a ship with a narrower beam which generates 24 to 26 knots. Olympic and Titanic are designed to attain 21 to 22 knots. We will attempt to match the speed of their ships, but also provide some of the most luxurious accommodations ever seen."

"Well, sir, we hope we can be of some help in that effort. It's a tremendous responsibility," offered Randy.

"I hope you can, too. To determine where we might assign you, I would like to ask you a few questions." When he began to do so, he was amazed at the answers he received. Probing even more deeply, he presented questions to them that only accomplished engineers could fathom. Their responses convinced Carlisle that these Americans should be hired for his staff.

He then formally offered them positions as Assistant Engineers, indicated they would draw the equivalent of thirty dollars per week, and that their hours would fluctuate according to workload.

"I have directed Adam Boyle to give you access to the construction prints when you report for work on Monday morning. I believe you will be very impressed."

They talked for over an hour concerning company policy, which allowed Randy to drop the first hints of the fate of Titanic.

"Sir, we are looking forward to seeing the prints. We've been concerned about several aspects of the ship's construction and outfitting, and the way they might impact its ability to withstand North Atlantic icebergs.

The prints should either confirm these concerns or put them to rest."

"Are you suggesting that elements of our design and construction threaten Titanic's integrity and safety? Where in the States would you have been exposed to confidential company information? You haven't been here long enough to have picked it up. He was confused and, a growing redness in his face indicated he was more than a little piqued at the temerity of these young men.

"We can understand your surprise, sir, but our interest in the success of Titanic and her sisters is no less than yours," concluded Randy. Bear with us, as I've said, and allow us to discuss these concerns with you after we've reviewed the prints."

Taking a big chance, Matt added, "One thing we should warn you about now is the selection of Captain Smith for Titanic's maiden voyage. We are aware of his popularity with Society. His tendency to use excessive speed, however, will not do her well. This will be confirmed when he meets with an accident on another vessel prior to taking Titanic's reins."

Carlisle's immediate reaction was one of disbelief.. "Mr. Ismay has not, himself, made a decision on who will take Titanic's maiden voyage. How could you possibly know that--clairvoyance?"

"No, sir, 'deduction'." Matt interjected. The confidence with which they both had spoken tempered his reaction,

"Well, now, I'm not sure I am willing to...." he began to protest when he was interrupted by the entrance of the same beautiful girl they'd seen on the dock. Randy did a double take as his jaw dropped. Her long black tresses hanging loosely, her tailored, dark green dress and ivory complexion created a true work of art. Randy once more was overwhelmed by this gorgeous image. A vision of his grandmother's Dresden doll passed briefly through his mind as he tried to regain his focus.

"....Sarah," said Carlisle. "I've asked you not to interrupt me when I am in conference. But, since you have, I would like you to meet two American boys who will start work with us Monday. This is Matt Miller, and that is Randy Kaplan. This angel, gentlemen, is my daughter, Sarah."

"Father! Please! Hello, Randy and Matt. Wasn't it the two of you we bumped into on the dock last night? I know I have seen both of you before.

Randy seems even more familiar. Why is that?"

With great effort, Randy spoke. "I believe we did bump into each other yesterday during the rain. And when I say 'bump' I mean 'BUMP'." Matt joined in the ensuing laughter, while Carlisle seemed a bit non-plussed.

"Please excuse me from this gala reunion, but I've got some work to do. You fellows, report to Adam Boyle at 10 A.M. Monday. This will give him a chance to assign his people for the week. Following that, he will be available to you for as long as you need him.

"I have directed him to give you access to the construction prints when you report for work Monday. I believe you will like them very much. You will work in his office to begin with. If you confirm any of your concerns, contact me. In the meantime, I suggest you keep the matters we discussed and your divinations to yourselves."

Amidst farewells and assurances by Randy and Matt, the three exited the office and continued their "reunion" at Ms. Collins' desk. Randy was still in a state of paralysis, but was startled into awareness by Sarah's "Goodbye." She was to take a piano lesson in an hour and needed to practice--"You know how that is--" As she walked down the hall, she turned back to Randy and said, "Perhaps we can meet here for lunch, . Monday--noonish," and she was gone. Sarah, seemed to Randy to be a bit forward for the times.

Emily O'Rourke had come to Ms. Collins' desk upon hearing the laughter. "I'm amazed at Miss Carlisle's openness with you, Randy--may I call you that?" Randy nodded his head vacuously, as she continued, "She's usually shy and reserved, and doesn't open up like that. Somebody's made a hit!"

"It was a union made in heaven or, at least, in that somebody's dreams," Matt explained. "She's one of the reasons we're here. Don't ask why, Emily, 'cause nobody knows the rest of the story."

"Matt, knock it off. Let's go. Excuse us, Emily, I don't mean to be rude, but we've got lots of work to do this weekend.," Randy asserted.

"Yes, sir!" saluted Matt, as he winked at Emily and confirmed the noontime luncheon date. "Where Randy goes, there go I."

As they left the shipyard, Randy waxed philosophical once again. "Matt, I'm in love! Did you hear me? I'm in love! I had no idea it could happen here, but it did. Wow!" Matt just stood and stared; not convinced of the possibility of "love at first sight." But then maybe this wasn't first sight, what with the dreams and all.

"How can this girl from Ireland communicate a future need of hers through a dream to me, separated as we are (or were) by one hundred years? Why am I selected to receive the message from among the millions born since 1912? No time restraints seem to exist in such a communication.

"Is that how prayer works--prayer for each other, prayer for the world, a specific situation, the past, the future? Is prayer the generator, love the resulting spiritual power that transcends time and space, connecting all mankind and all creation? Maybe we're supposed to meet those people and undergo those experiences---some pleasant, others not—at least for those that love Him," Randy finally concluded.

"Is this Dissertation #2 of Kaplan/Miller's Theo-Chronology 101, first revealed by Doctor J. Randolph Kaplan to a worshiping world in Glen Cove, New York, U.S.A., sometime between the twentieth and twenty-first century?" asked Matt.

"Randy, for the love of mike, can't you just fall in love without analyzing or justifying it philosophically? Just go with the flow; relax and enjoy. She's is beautiful! It doesn't take a super-philosopher to reach that conclusion. You'd better be careful, though. If this gets serious, you and Sarah will be faced with a difficult decision the likes of which any century has never known. Family friends and acquaintances in both centuries might have some thoughts on that decision."

"Yeah, I suppose you're right," Randy agreed despondently."

Since they weren't to report for work until Monday, at 10 A.M., the boys were looking forward to a tough working weekend consolidating their presentation and gathering facts and figures to back their recommendations. Best not to be disturbed by leaving the flat to eat, so they stopped at a local grocer's to pick up some cheese, bread, wine, milk, eggs and butter. Once again they were amazed at what a dollar bought..

Upon returning to the flat, they each made up a snack, sipped some wine and relaxed. One or more attempts at discussion of the project in general fell flat, sleep came early.

"Maybe it would be best for us to be clear-headed tomorrow by getting to bed early. I don't know about you, but I'm beat. These Irish jails don't pride themselves on nightly beauty rests."

"O.K., said Randy, "I could use a solid night's sleep, that's for sure."

On Saturday morning, after she'd heard the boys stirring about, their landlady arrived at the door with breakfast. Knocking softly, she entered and placed it on the table. "Aye, and I thought you might could use a little nourishment. Just leave the dishes in the hall and I'll pick them up later."

She left as quickly as she had come.

"We didn't have a chance to thank her. We sure picked a great landlady," observed Matt.

"We'll thank her later. Right now all I want to do is fill my empty stomach,": Randy said, as he began the early morning taste test.

After eating to the full a very well prepared offering, they settled back in their chairs and relaxed. But they had a hard time keeping their minds off the tremendous task before them.

"I think we'd better review our game plan," Randy proposed.

"Which part?" Matt was still relaxing.

"I don't know exactly," he admitted.

"Well, let's make a listing of all the mistakes that were made with the Titanic. We'll change as many as we can," Matt suggested. "After that, we will mark them off as we go along, and put them in the recycle bin, as it were."

"Matt, I do believe time travel has actually unscrambled your brains. It's exactly what we will do," Randy said approvingly. "Let's see how much of the list we can remember."

That Saturday seemed the longest day in their young lives! They worked late into the night. Listing all the facts from memory was a tough assignment, but necessary.

"Not enough lifeboats," Randy commenced.

"Not enough lifeboats," Matt repeated.

"Communications inadequate. You know, I believe almost 90% of the world's major accidents could be blamed on communications, or lack thereof."

"Communications inadequate. Check! Randy, I know you'll have trouble believing this, but I have never been involved with a think tank before. Doesn't that appear to be a waste of I. Q.?" Matt bragged.

"Come on, Matt, get serious. We don't have time for nonsense!"

"Hey, man, my brain's on fire!" Matt insisted, clowning around just to aggravate his partner. I think it's cooked!"

"Jerk!" Randy said sternly as he threw up his hands, "I guess I'm the only one who cares about this project!"

"Give me a break!" Matt snapped back. "Are we partners in this or not? I presume we are."

"O.K., fine! Let's just get this list completed tonight. Do you want to go on working for a while longer?" Randy was beginning to soften. "I think we have spent so much time doing this, we're getting edgy."

They got up from the floor and walked around the room stretching. Matt started yawning and seemed unable to stop. Randy came back from the kitchen where he'd gone for a glass of water.

Matt yawned again and said, "One more thing we should mention--no sonar or radar exists in 1910. But it doesn't matter, since I've memorized the schematics on both of them plus the laser machine. They were in my Advanced Electronics Made Easy magazine back at school.

"A bit more bragging, Oh, Prince of mine? Are you serious? Memorized the schematics? I can't believe it! Matt, you are either a genius or a nitwit, and I don't know which. One thing I do know, if you can build that laser, we are out of here!"

"I know, I know," said Matt trying to sound humble.

"You're a trip. Do you know that, too?

"Yep," Matt couldn't be moved.

"Well, grab the pad and write this stuff down. I've got another thing we don't want to forget." Randy wanted to get back to work.

"Matt, do you remember the trouble created by compartments being designed too short? There were sixteen of them. They reached up only to decks 'D' and 'E', which allowed water entering through the holes in the hull to fill up, spill over the tops of the compartment bulkheads, and flow backward toward the stern, much like a tilted water-filled ice-cube tray.

When the forward compartments were filled, as the bow went down, the water began to flow rearward, thus filling compartments previously unaffected by the damage."

Way into the early morning hours they discussed, at length, various solutions to this and other listed design problems.

At about 1 A.M., Matt stretched and yawned, then fell back in his chair. Rubbing his eyes, he said, "We'd best quit now," and fell sound asleep.

Sunday morning they slept refreshingly late, catching up with some of what they'd missed the past few weeks. After dressing, they both sat briefly reviewing their files and concluded that they could take a few hours off, have breakfast, get some air and see some of Belfast. Perhaps a few more hours of preparation in the evening would suffice.

Leaving the flat, they rapped on the landlady's door to thank her for her thoughtfulness and to inquire if there was a restaurant nearby open on Sunday. She referred them to "Margaret's Cafe" just beyond the wharf area, one of few open to attract churchgoers on the Lord's Day.

"Margaret is an institution in this part of town. One minute she might be telling a funny story, the next reading from the Bible. She means well, and has customers from every persuasion enjoying her stories and readings"

Although most restaurants and cafe's were closed on Sunday, Margaret's remained open to cater to those attending the Cathedral masses and other church meetings. Her encouragement of fellowship was accepted as more than sufficient justification for her violation of the so called 'Sabbath'. Her bulging doors and short line outside them attested to this acceptance. The quality of her food added further justification.

They found the cafe easily and, after a short wait in the cool morning air, were seated. Before they could order, Margaret appeared with an enormous bible. Everything stopped. Only the sound of coffee percolating in the kitchen broke the silence. A dropped teaspoon sounded like a bomb.

Pulling a stool up to the breakfast bar, she said, "Since this is Sunday, I've chosen a reading from Matthew's Gospel, chapter 7, verses 7 and 8.

It concerns:

'The Power of Prayer.'

"Ask, and you will receive. Seek, and you will find. Knock, and it will be opened to you. For the one who asks, receives. The one who seeks, finds. The one who knocks, enters."

Silently, the two young men absorbed the message and were astounded at how appropriate this reading was to their situation. It seemed to tell them that persistence in the face of adversity was necessary, and the strength to maintain this persistence was available. All they had to do was ask, of course, if God approved.

Filled both physically and spiritually, they walked back to their flat What role they might personally play while intruding into time and eternity, was a subject discussed with reverence and humility. Recalling the words of the Lord's Prayer which his Christian cousin Rachel often prayed, Randy said,

".....and forgive us our trespasses....for messing around in your territory."

"Amen to that, brother!" said Matt.

Arriving at their flat, they brought out the growing list of projects to be fixed. Hard at it until supper time, they finally finished the list and their position on each, to their satisfaction.

Matt wasn't ready for another heavy discussion that day, but Randy's expression suggested his degree of readiness was irrelevant. "O.K., Randy. Let's have it. Something else has your cerebral cortex energized."

"Well, Matt, I think it is something we need to come to terms with."

All right! All right, already! Let's get on with it. But that's IT!"

Randy tried to explain it in the simplest terms, not because Matt would have difficulty comprehending, but because of its complexity to himself.

Holding out two charts, Randy began, "Matt, these are calendars for the years 1910 and 2010, taken from a Perpetual Calendar I found in the school library. If you'll notice, in 2010, today, September 26th, is Sunday.

In 1910, on the other hand, September 26th is Monday.

My digital watch displays today as:

Sun ' 10
9 - 26
11:49.35

The day is right, but the date is wrong.

"It happens to be programmed to provide the proper day when the date is entered for years 1990 to 2029. That's why. At the turn of the century, I had no Y2K problems with the watch. Other problems, yes, but not with the watch. Most digital watches don't display the year, since our activities mostly concern the time of the day or day of the week, but seldom the year.

"The digital without the year provide separate adjustments for day and date. Ours do not. The day is slaved to the date, and you can't find the date by using the day. The technology to program a Perpetual Calendar into the watch was available before we left, but no prototype was on the shelves. Since our watches don't have that, we're stuck with improvisation.

"So here's my proposal. You turn your watch back one day, making it the 25th, which today is. I'll leave mine alone, which will give us the right day--Sunday.

"You'll be 'lord of the Date', while I'll be 'lord of the Day.'

"Do you comprehend, Oh, 'lord of the Date? If not, just check the 1910 calendar on the wall each day upon arising."

"Tell me, Oh, 'lord of the Day', will I lose a day of my life when I turn my watch back?"

"No, Oh wretched One, we will give you back your lost day upon your return to 2010. It's the same as our Daylight Savings time, in which the hour you lose in the Spring is returned to you in the Fall.

"Actually, the 'time' we perceive as moving through our days and years and lives, is only a chronometric device to maintain order in our universe. It's based on the earth's orbit around the sun, and its rotation around its own axis. Since all that exists is the present moment, you can readily see that nothing we do chronometrically can change a single moment-

--of eternity. "You might even say, 'Time is that which is measured by chronometric devices'."

"Feels like time for dinner, Randy. We haven't had much to eat over the weekend, and, God knows, we need it!"

After resting for a while, they asked the landlady to about another reasonable restaurant. They thanked her when she did, and commented on how much they liked the flat. She was very pleased with these new tenants.

They found the restaurant a few blocks away, and enjoyed a delicious corned beef and cabbage dinner.

"I can see why that's the Irish national dinner on the world menu. The Irish should be proud of that contribution," observed Randy. As they finished, Matt grabbed the guest check and stood up quickly. "That sure is a reasonable meal. A twenty dollar bill goes a long way at these prices. But it'll be touch and go making it until the first paycheck. "

"Why are you in such a rush! Hold on a second!" snapped Randy, taking one more sip of tea.

"C'mon, let's go home. I'm tired and I'm through talking." Matt stifled a yawn as he walked to the cashier. "We've got some more junk to squeeze from our brains yet tonight."

Chapter 8

Walking up the street laughing about something the cashier had said, they didn't notice the two men following them.

Somehow the two, employees working on the ship, had heard enough about them, or overheard Randy and Matt speaking to each other in a manner and accent that aroused their suspicions. Rumors started as the boys met, first with Boyle, then with Carlisle. A date of 2010 had somehow gotten loose in the yard, and fanned by ignorance, the rumors spread to the point where at least these two felt compelled to take action.

The older of the two was saying to his companion, "Something is wrong here, these blokes are up to no good, I tell ya. That strange talk about the future and all. They spell trouble, and are probably here to do our ships 'arm." Slipping back and forth through the shadows, they stalked their prey, listening to every audible word.

Matt was saying, "I can't wait to finish what we came for and get back to 2010."

"Well," Randy observed, "it will be good to get back to the fast lane." As they laughed, Matt finally noticed the two men following them.

"Hey, can we help you?" he shouted.

The taller and younger of them, waving his arms wildly, ran toward Randy and mumbled, "You're dead, ya bloody aliens!" His intention was to smash Randy's head, but Randy ducked and the sudden change of direction threw the assailant to the ground. Matt jerked his head around just in time to take a crushing blow to the side of his face from the smaller man. He fell to the ground writhing in pain and bleeding from the mouth. Bent on making sure a thorough job was done, his attacker kicked Matt in the side. He screamed so loudly, his assailant became frightened and fled.

The initial confrontation evidently failed to cause them the serious bodily harm their assailants had intended.. Randy ran to Matt to check on his condition and assist him. The man who tried to hit Randy took off up the alley following his friend. The angry Americans were left frustrated, and yelling at each other. Chase seemed pointless, since they weren't familiar with the alleys and Matt wasn't in any condition to run. They returned to their flat helping each other along.

Back in the flat, Randy cleaned up Matt's blood and treated his cuts, which turned out to be less serious than his blood-spattered face and clothing implied.

"Those guys were trying to kill us. What do you suppose they were after?" asked Randy.

"I don't know, but in the future, when walking in dark alleys, maybe one of us should walk forward and the other backward. That way they won't be able to sneak up on us," Matt suggested. "Whatever we do, we'd better keep a close eye out for them. I don't think they accomplished what they were after."

"Stealth is the only characteristic I can detect they share with those 'time troopers' of my dreams," said Randy. They're probably just hotheads with short fuses."

"Wake up, Matt, wake up!" urged Randy. It's Monday and time to save the ship."

Mumbling to himself, Matt rolled over and looked at his watch. It read Sun 9 - 26. What're you bugging me for, Randy? Let me sleep, it's Sunday."

"It's not Sunday, it's Monday! Recall I said I would be 'lord of the Day'. My watch says it's Monday, so get your butt out of the sack! UP!"

Progressing toward wakefulness, Matt still maintained his prone position. Sometimes Randy couldn't tell if Matt was kidding. After a few more exchanges, Matt finally broke into laughter, saying, "I know, I know. Just funning' ya, your lordship."

As they walked toward the shipyard, they were still sore from their nocturnal combat. It wasn't all that bad, compared to their experience in the storm---there had been many bruises beyond Randy's shoulder dislocation.

It was a bit warmer than the day before. They were fascinated by the early 1900's traffic where horses outnumbered automobiles and the streets seemed more suited to them. Mud and ruts made driving an auto an adventure and walking in the streets a true challenge, particularly after the recent heavy rains. The drivers of "horseless carriages" were an amusing sight. Wearing goggles, gloves and long trench coats, they seldom exceeded twenty miles per hour.

An even more interesting sight was that of better dressed women trying to cross some streets holding the hems of their long Victorian dresses above the mud. Matt, never one to miss an opportunity, picked out one of the more attractive damsels in distress to carry across the street. With arms outstretched, he leaned forward to pick up the lady of his choice. With a polite squeal, she responded to his effort, and collapsed into his grasp. Upon reaching the other side, Matt tripped on an unseen cobblestone and lurched forward. Fortunately, Randy had crossed ahead of them, and was able to arrest their fall and keep her upright. An even louder squeal accompanied her rescue.

After setting the lady down, Matt hastened to apologize for his clumsiness. Before he did, however, he took one step backward, tripped on the same stone, and sat down hard in the mud. Trying, but not succeeding, to stifle his laughter, Randy said, "Despite appearances to the contrary, ma'am, this is not a circus, nor are we a comedy team. Carrying ladies across the street is my friend's attempt to outdo Sir Walter Raleigh. Unlike Sir Walter, however, he needs rescuing himself now and then.. I trust you are all right, and no damage was done."

"Oh, no sir, I thank him for his gallantry," she said with a coquettish smile. "Good day, gentlemen." And off she went.

Before Randy could begin, Matt said, "I know, I know--now you say, 'Matt, when are you gonna quit?' Never, my friend....'in the beginning, God created man....et cetera, et cetera, et cetera.' Help me up!"

"Matt, you're sure having a time of it. First the blood; now the mud. We'd better stop and take care of that mess before we go any further. Oh! wait a minute--I feel a limerick coming on.....it's coming....ah, here it is--

"There was a young man name o' Matt,

In a puddle quite clumsily sat,
Last night he'd lost blood,

Today sat in mud,

He'd be smart to stay home in his flat."

"Cute, very cute!...Don't just stand there, limerick-brain! Help me up!"

After rendering Matt presentable, they headed for the shipyard. As they mounted the stairway toward Kevin O'Malley's office, Matt asked,

"Hey, Randy, do those two guys over there look familiar?" Randy looked where Matt was pointing, straining his eyes to make sure.

"Yeah,! Those are the two who followed us last night! I think."

Since they were close to Kevin O'Malley's office, they stopped in and asked if he could identify the two workers. He quickly responded, "That's O'Brien and McCarthy---two fine lads, I might add Do you want to meet them?"

"No, not now," Randy answered, playing it cool. "Thanks for the tour, yesterday. That was really impressive."

With that they headed for Adam Boyle's office, where Emily greeted them warmly. "He's waiting for you, gentlemen, I'll announce you.

"Mr. Boyle, here are your two American engineers."

"Welcome, fellows. Please call me Adam. Mr. Carlisle asked me to provide you with the blueprints for Titanic. If you'll step into my workshop, we will put them at your disposal."

"Thank you," said Randy, "We really appreciate how cooperative you've been. We've heard that the plans are magnificent, easily read and followed."

Chapter 9

The construction prints were as advertised. One, or the other of the boys, could frequently be heard uttering one-word expressions of awe. "Unbelievable!" "Magnificent!" as they leafed through the many large pages.

Boyle seemed to radiate the proud feeling of the company. They were calling the ships, "Our Three Sisters," even though the third one had not yet been started. Each employee felt he or she had an important part in this fantastic venture.

"Men, what we have here is a set of the most valuable working drawings in the world. Your job is to study them extensively and make recommendations on things that need to be improved. You bring them to me and I will submit them through Mr.Carlisle to the Board of Designers, who will make the semi-final decisions.

Mr. Ismay, representing White Star Line, for whom the ships are being built, of course, has the final say-so. He respects the Board's expertise and seldom counters proposals they approve. I want to tell you right up front that Mr. Ismay and the Board are hard-nosed, so do your job well . They may not adopt a single thing. But you do your best, because a lot of lives are at stake. Incidentally, Mr. Ismay has a temporary office on the premises to assist him in staying on top of things. So, you see, he knows the ropes." Matt and Randy exchanged knowing glances. They said volumes without opening their mouths.

"What you're saying is we are to make them safe for travel, but not to change much; right?"

"No! I didn't say that." Boyle corrected. "Just have solid reasons for each suggestion."

"That sounds reasonable," Matt said in deep thought.

"Let me show you your office. As Mr. Carlisle said, you'll be with me for a while, then move to a separate office out in the yard."

By the time Randy and Matt finished, it was lunchtime. Emily ran to

intercept them as they left the office, saying, "Sarah will be here shortly for lunch, as promised yesterday, Randy. She usually brings something from the Carlisle larder which beats any other food in town. Only a Dummkopf would leave at a time like this."

"Und zo, fraulein, Du bist sprecht ein Deutsch as well?" Matt responded in deep, guttural tones.

"Nein, but you don't have to be a linguist to recognize a Dummkopf, Dummkopf!" Emily retorted. Matt turned a bit red in the face, while Randy observed that it should be fun to watch the sparks fly between these two.

At this point, Sarah arrived with the promised luncheon. "Can we sit in your office, gentlemen, or do you have plans more exotic?" she asked.

Once again Emily was amazed at her openness with the boys. There has to be a lot behind it, she thought.

Once again, also, Randy went into his jaw-drop, stammering a shy hello, completely overwhelmed by Sarah's beauty. She was wearing a long dark dress, white lace collar and blouse, and a white picture hat festooned with red rosebuds. It was almost unfair to expose him to such loveliness.

The four retired to the office of the new assistant engineers, where Sarah presented them with a small platter of cold steamed shrimp and a block of excellent Gruyere cheese. Biscuits and jam, and tea topped off this unusual lunch.

But Randy was not seeing or enjoying what he was eating. He just stared at Sarah in such a way and for so long, she became embarrassed.

"Randy, did I forget to put something on this morning?" she asked.

"Oh, I'm sorry, Sarah, uh....I was just thinking that there is something between us that is beyond our understanding. What's happening? One hundred years between.....whoops," he muttered as Matt elbowed him.

"What Randy means is that he believes that time is illusory, and that we may have been, or are, in time together, perhaps at differing points, but still within the same eternity. Does that about sum it up, professor?"

"Yeah, Matt. Sounds like you almost understand it." Then, turning to Sarah, he said, "Sarah, we have time for a short walk before lunchtime is over. Care to join me?"

"I'd love to, Randy. We have to get to the bottom of this relationship, according to Randy."

"Great! While we're gone, Matt, maybe you can exploit Emily for what she knows about the politics of this organization. Particularly as it pertains to those two creeps we've been dealing with."

"O.K. Randy, but don't get lost. I'll wait here with her."

Randy and Sarah walked off the shipyard property with heads down, sensitive to the stares of many workmen. Among them, McCarthy and O'Brien, who said, "Now he's got the boss' daughter fooled--if we let them get away with it, they'll probably mess up the ships. They've got to be stopped!" They walked toward a local waterfront park hoping to take advantage of the sunny day. It was all Randy could do to keep from taking her hand as they walked. He felt as though he'd known her all his life. Before he could make such a move, however, she took his arm and, looking up to him, said, "I hope that doesn't bother you. Randy. I just don't want to fall in the mud. Do you mind?"

"Do I mind? Do the flowers mind the sun? Now where did that come from? I know! From months of seeing you in my dreams."

"But, Randy, how could it have been me? We hadn't met until yesterday."

"That may be, but it was surely you. Even your voice is the same. That's why I did a double-take and was rendered speechless when we bumped into each other on the dock, and again when we met in your father's office."

"If you recognized my voice, I must have said things in your dreams. Do you recall what they were?"

"Well, it wasn't much; you said the same thing over and over---it was 'Save us'!"

"Save us? Save us from what? How can you, in New York, save anyone from anything here in Belfast? Is this what Matt was trying to say before. He was suggesting that we are always close to others because we are all one in both time and space. I think I understand the concept, but why are we--you and I--thrown together this way? Why me? Why you? Why am I in your dreams and no one else's, at least as far as we know?"

"That's why we're here, Sarah; because of my dream!" Randy explained. "Our finite minds aren't expected to understand all the mysteries that surround us. All I know is that my strong feelings for you preceded our meeting by many moons. So, there, I've said it and I'm glad!"

As she unconsciously moved closer to him, she said,

"I'm glad too, Randy. There must have been two sparks looking to start the same fire."

With that, they walked in silence to the park where they found a bench in the warm sun. "Randy, I know we have to learn more about each other,

but at this point, I can safely say that the future could be ours together, if we take it. I've been engaged to the son of a friend of my father's for the past two years. You 'bumped' into him on the dock your first night in Belfast. I know my father would be disappointed, were it to be terminated, but I also know that he has considerable respect for you already. When the two of you get to know each other better, I'm certain he will understand."

"Well, Sarah, let's take our time--we're talking about a lifetime here. Are you ready to make that kind of decision so soon? Even if you were, and I were, other considerations might interfere."

"For example?" She said softly, staring at his lips for the reply.

"Well, where we each come from, for instance. Cowboys and Indians as compared to Lords and Ladies. Victoria had little influence on the Colonies. Which do we choose, and how will the displaced one adapt to a new way of life?"

"Now who's jumping ahead? My feelings haven't settled down yet, and you have me choosing jodhpurs or evening dresses!"

After some minutes of thought in silence, they both suddenly tried to fill the void. In chorus they said, "We'd better start back!"

"Thank you for walking with me, Sarah. I really enjoyed it."

"I would very much like to be a part of your world, Randy. But you seem to be very nervous and cautious."

"Sarah, maybe if we were to go out together some evening next week, we could get ourselves on the same track, and really enjoy ourselves."

"That would be wonderful, Randy!" Sarah replied.

"Perhaps our first date should be a double-one. Matt could ask Emily. They make a fiery team, and should be a lot of fun. Your parents might feel better about that than if we went out alone before they really got to know me."

"Agreed! I'll really look forward to that. Besides, I think the world of Emily."

They returned to Emily's desk, where Matt was debating with her about something else they didn't agree on.

"Welcome back, lovebirds? Don't fight against it. You both look rather - moon- struck." Emily trying to shift attention away from Matt.

"We have a date for next Friday. Emily, would you and Matt care to join us?" Sarah asked. "It should be a lot of fun, if you two can get along for more than five minutes."

"I won't answer that now," retorted Matt. I'm not sure Emily and I could make it through the evening. I'll let you know."

As the two boys made a move to return to the prints, Emily blushed and said, "Well, I never!"

Sarah put her arm around Emily's shoulder and said, "They're really not all that bad, Emily. They're the best thing to come out of the Colonies in a long time. With that, she waved to Randy and left.

They returned to the flat, fired up by their own aggressiveness with Carlisle. "That may be the only way to sell our package to the Board, i.e., without enthusiasm, but with confidence and examples of success," Matt interjected.

Chapter 10

The first few weeks on the job the two boys familiarized themselves with every part of the ship. Armed with prints covering a given section, they would check every detail, ask questions of the workers, and even bring lunch with them to become more familiar with the work gangs.

Occasionally they would hear grumbling, and were certain it was envy over their sudden arrival and access to the inner sanctum. Some had heard rumors that they were from some other world. The hope among a small number of workers was that Matt and Randy, whoever they were, would give up and leave--back to wherever they came from. O'Brien and McCarthy seemed to be behind a good deal of the suspicion and gossip.

It was during one of these forays onto one of the gigantic slips that they met Reggie. Reggie was, apparently, the only black man working in that area of the project. He was handsome, tall, quite light-skinned and wore a finely trimmed thin mustache. His accent was similar to that found in most British colonies in Africa and the Caribbean--obviously Oxford English, his speech gave evidence of a some higher education.

They found Reggie to be a very straightforward individual who, though in what was really a foreign country, carried himself as a man quite sure of himself.. He was quick to laugh and responded with considerable humor appropriate to any race. Amusement filled his eyes as he described his job of "Gopher." "Go for this and go for that, is what it amounts to."

Reggie was to become both a good friend and a source of much technical know-how. Their relationship with him grew stronger as time went on.

Matt was making considerable headway with his project of recording the three schematics from memory. Sonar and Radar could make or break their mission--the laser their ability to return to the 21st century. Trial and error created a vast wasteland of paper covering the floor under the dining table.

The same scene was taking place in the bedroom. Randy was working on the extension of the sixteen watertight compartments. Instead of ten feet above the waterline, he had concluded that they should have been thirty feet, and needed to be pulled from "D" and "E" decks up to "C" deck. Then he had to figure out a way to cap them off without losing much room---

creating a form of longitudinal bulkhead. He also wanted to work on the double bottom problem. It should be brought up to and past the waterline.

"You know, Matt, I wonder if the ship's rapid sinking was due less to the tears caused by the iceberg in the underwater compartments, and more to the water pouring from this tears into the opposing coal bunkers. Only twelve square feet of hull was penetrated, horizontally for almost 200 linear feet along the hull beneath the waterline. But a small amount of water hitting the coal bunkers would have caused an explosion. And the way the bunkers were built, the explosion would have blown out through the outer plates. What do you think?"

"Yeah, that could be the reason she sank so fast, but that was just one of the theories we read about in those books you had."

"Well, just in case, we'll recommend they triple the outer skin portion of the bunkers. I wonder if it would work to keep the coal damp all the time? That could keep a fire from breaking out in the first place. We can use that as a fall-back position if they don't buy the triple skin." Randy had shifted into high gear in his "think-tank" mode.

"Good idea," Matt responded.

"I know!" boasted Randy.

"Hungry?"

"No. I don't want to interrupt my progress. Things are really beginning to shape up."

"Well, I need something to keep me going. I'd really rather be back home in 2010, kicking back with a 'cold one' and watching an NBA or college basketball game on the tube."

"Better stay with the program or I'll have you fired," Randy jested.

"Please do, my man. I'm ready for the grand return. Can I take Emily with me?"

"I shouldn't dignify that question by responding to it. Maybe you could round up a whole bevy of beauties and bring them all back with you. Just think what a 21st century harem-master you would be with a bunch of Victorian ladies."

"Why didn't I think of that, Randy. What a brilliant idea!"

"I knew you'd think so, you pervert," retorted Randy, "but enough about temptation; let's get on with the homework. First, I want to make a decision on when we hit Ismay with the advantage of calling the ship Titanic II. I think we should do it as soon as possible, so he knows we're going to be making reasonable and appropriate recommendations. Let's do it tomorrow," said Randy.

"Well, we don't want to overwhelm him with the two of us there, so why don't you take this one yourself.."

As soon as they got to work the next day, Randy sent a memo requesting a short conference with Bruce Ismay. It was going over Adam Boyle's head, but they were concerned about the time frame involved and did not want to delay things with inter-office red tape. Once the name was painted on the hull, it would be difficult to convince anyone to change it."

After about two hours, he received a response to come to Mr. Ismay's office immediately. His impatience propelled him up to the third floor, hitting every third step on the way. He hesitated before Ismay's door, straightened his clothes, regained his composure and tried to knock in a casual manner. This would be a barometer of how his and Matt's suggestions might be received, and just how much they could expect to impact the operation; maybe even whether they would be able to save Titanic.

"Enter!" was the abrupt command from within. He had a hard time making his legs obey, but managed to open the door and step into the room. Ismay smiled and waved his hand forward,

"Have a seat, son, and tell us what's on your mind."

Randy was glad to see Mr. Carlisle standing by the window. Randy nodded and said, "Hello, sir." He took a deep breath, then voiced his concern, "Because there are so many skeptics today and so many horrible stories about monster ships---Titan, for instance---that have met with unthinkable disasters, we've just got to fight fire with fire!" He paused for a moment, assembling his thoughts internally.

"Yes, yes, go on," Ismay probed, impatiently.

"If we add one simple change to the name, we can let nature take its course."

"And then," Carlisle injected, "people will ask why we changed it."

"Then, being human, they will have their own answer," Randy assured them.

"Wait!" Ismay raised his hand to stop everything. "What change are you proposing?"

Add the Roman numeral II after Titanic," Randy's face took on a definite glow of expectation.

"What on earth for?" Ismay became practical with a look of dismay.

"Think it through!" Randy commanded authoritatively.

Ismay looked at Carlisle with raised eyebrows and silence ensued. After a minute or so, Ismay explained,

"No, we couldn't do that. The people would infer that we claim it to be the second Titanic."

"That's it!" Randy's tone smacked of victory.

"You're really confusing me now," said Ismay, staring at the floor.

"I see it," said Carlisle, catching the obscure logic. "The public forms bad opinions about those horror stories. Then when they see Titanic II they will subconsciously ignore the first one. Obviously no one would think of naming a ship after a loser. Like the Titan for instance. That bit of psychology will set the second one free to be whatever she can be."

"Exactly! No more stigmas on board and it will confuse the media," Randy nailed it down, "and.. they will forget about the "II" part."

"It's good, very good," Carlisle was staring straight ahead, "It's nonsense -- but it may work. What do you think, Bruce?" Ismay got up from his big black leather chair, walked over to the window, and stood there in silence. Some moments later the number one man turned and spoke.

"I don't know, Alex." The weight of the decision was taking its toll. Randy thought at this point he had lost the battle. It seemed like an hour went by as this great man pondered the options. Finally, he turned abruptly and said with borrowed conviction and obvious reluctance ...

"Let's go for it!" Randy watched them shake on it, as if they had come up with the original idea. He could now relax his jaw that had been clenched since he came to the meeting. He had never known such tension in any job before. A prayer of thanksgiving was in order and came forthwith. He whispered softly, "It's coming together."

"Pardon me?" Ismay asked as he turned to shake hands with Randy.

"Oh, nothing. I was just thinking out loud," Randy replied, smiling.

"Mr. Kaplan, it will be done when the hull is ready for it. Thank you for coming," Carlisle said kindly.

"Thank you." Randy said as he closed the door behind him. He began wiping his brow and blowing out a long breath. His relief concerned more than just the "II" question, but the fact that Carlisle did not expose any of their previous conversation, or their claim to knowledge of the future.

Returning to the office, Randy was walking on air as a result of this early victory. "Matt," he called as he entered, "you won't believe how it went between Carlisle and me, Ismay broke under the pressure and agreed to add the II to Titanic as we suggested."

"Great! But let's hope we can sell our more important recommendations as easily," Matt retorted. "Let's face it, a couple of numbers on the stern is good psychology, but costs a lot less than a lifeboat or bulkheads!"

"Yeah, you're right, Matt. Well, as Boyle told us, we'll have to include much detail and persuasive arguments if we expect to make marks on the 'win' side of the ledger."

Chapter 11

During the week following his walk with Sarah, Randy had great difficulty concentrating. Whenever he paused in his work, her face appeared before him--her soft voice assuring him of her feelings for him. He had never felt as consumed by anyone or anything as by Sarah, but always haunted by the thought of what the future (or past) might hold. Since Randy and Matt were as busy as they were, Randy had little opportunity to spend even a few moments with Sarah. But passing by Emily's desk each day gave Matt the chance to come to terms with her.

"Emily, maybe we should sign a cease-fire agreement," suggested Matt, his smiling eyes betraying his serious demeanor. It would forbid you to call me 'Dummkopf' or other insulting names, and forbid my mentioning your physical attributes (of which there are many.) Does that pretty well cover it?"

"I'm sure we'd need an escape clause, so that violations can be appropriately dealt with," Emily responded, "but we can try it."

"Well, then, that does it. I'll tell Randy and Sarah we'll go out with them Friday. O.K.?"

"Agreed."

Friday came quickly. Randy, in anticipation of being with his new-found love, was highly nervous. He and Matt had purchased stylish suits, shirts and ties. Unfortunately, the style called for a profusion of buttons, which were giving Randy a great deal of trouble.

"What's the problem, 'punk'?" asked Matt, "Sarah got you all a-twitter? You're acting like a 16-year old on his first date."

"So would you if you knew this was the love of your life, and so much was stacked against it--100 years, for starts."

"Where's your Theo-Chronology theory now, my friend? If this is a love for eternity, won't your theory take care of it?" prodded Matt.

"Tonight's not Eternity, Matt! It's one bit in a programmed schedule of chronological time. Tomorrow depends on how things go tonight. In which century's tomorrow will we wind up, mine, hers, or will it be none at all?"

"Wow! Am I glad I haven't been smitten like that--that ain't no fun. Now you take Emily and me. All we concern ourselves with is who's going to make the next dig or faux pas.".

"O.K., Matt, but some of us can't go through life with such a devil-may-care attitude. I envy that trait, I guess. Give me a hand with these danged buttons, Matt, or we'll never get out of here."

Early December having arrived, it was no surprise to have a dusting of snow in the late afternoon. Their whole world had turned white, sounds of even the big ships' horns were muted. Sarah could almost hear her heart-beat in the silence.

To make it easy for the boys, Emily had arranged to meet them at the Carlisles'. As they arrived, Sarah's father was leaving for a dinner meeting with most of the Board members to discuss problems they had been encountering. He stopped momentarily and, with a facetious grin, assured Randy and Matt he was not likely to mention Captain Smith's future to the Board.

"It is somewhat premature, Mr. Carlisle, You'll still have time to take corrective action following his accident," Randy countered confidently.

"I'll believe it when I see it, and when I do, I will list you two among the prophets of the ages. Have a good time tonight and bring my angel home at a reasonable hour, Randy." With that he donned his goggles and, with his rear wheels skidding in the snow, was off in his brand new "horseless carriage." A loud backfire penetrated the cool, damp silence, announcing his departure and shaking the snow from adjacent trees.

Sarah and Emily met the boys in the Carlisles' two-story entryway, which led into a large reception room. A glass cupola formed the entryway ceiling, contributing to the impression of spaciousness. Vaulted ceilings in the reception room towered above the room's massive dark and exquisitely carved antique furniture. Large oriental rugs, contrasted against the white marble floors, defined seating areas. A baby grand Steinway piano in dark, carved wood stood near the entrance to the dining room, tempting all who passed to stop and listen, even at times when it was not being played. Museums in the States in 2010 would be proud to provide space for rooms of this magnificence.

"Hello Randy. Seems like ages since we've seen one another," Sarah said, "but it's actually been only a week." She reached up to him, kissed him on the cheek and brushed the snow from his shoulder. "My, how handsome you look"

Recovering from his surprise, Randy responded, "Thank you. I'm not sure I can stand another week like it. You look smashing."

"Well, I was hoping to work Emily out of my system over the weekend, but I guess that'll have to wait, maybe a hundred years or so from now." Jested Matt with a quick glance at Randy.

"Right! It's almost sadomasochistic, the way we torture each other. The only problem is, that the Dummkopf doesn't know when he's beaten," Emily jibed.

"Now, there you go, violating a clause in our cease-fire. It seems to me your failure to remember our agreement indicates that your cognitive gifts just don't match your physical attributes," Matt retorted.

Everyone joined in the laughter, after which Sarah moaned, "Randy, it looks like we're in for a rough evening."

As the laughter died down, Mrs. Carlisle entered the room. One could readily see the source of Sarah's beauty. Statuesque, with dark hair beginning to grey, and Sarah's soft, white skin, she was dressed as if she were going out.

By 2010 almost all the class in clothing extant in the early 1900's had disappeared. Sports attire and relaxed, tie-less dress seemed to be bringing everyone to a middle-class level of conformity, rendering one person or group indistinguishable from another. But here the class of the period was manifest in this handsome woman.

"Mother, I would like you to meet the new engineers working with Father, Randy Kaplan and Matt Miller, from the United States."

"Welcome, gentlemen, it is a pleasure meeting you whom I've heard so much about. Randy, are you certain you and Sarah have not met before?"

"I know it seems that way, Mrs. Carlisle, but in view of where Matt and I are from, it would have been highly unlikely for us to have met."

"Do you mean in the States, or is there some other consideration that causes you to be as certain as you are?" inquired Mrs. Carlisle.

"Please, Mother, no further inquisition!" appealed Sarah.

"Well, I wouldn't have pursued it this far if your father had not mentioned that at least Randy, if not both of you boys, seemingly have been blessed with gifts of prophecy or clairvoyance. He cited some examples which, though not as yet confirmed, you presented with seeming confidence."

"Mrs. Carlisle, I know your husband was shocked to hear us allude to things of the future I can understand his reaction. Actually, it is simply a matter of playing the game of chance at a sophisticated level," Randy assured her, "Determining the likelihood of an event occurring in a given set of circumstances. This is particularly true in our concern for certain elements of the ship's design."

"I can follow that, but how do you arrive at the conclusion that Captain Smith is to experience a minor accident?"

Matt, feeling that he was responsible for this one, jumped into the fray by saying, "Well, ma'am, it is a slight variation on the game of chance. You bet on your horse to win on the basis of his past record and his present physical condition. Similarly, we take Captain Smith's record of employing excessive speed, factor that with how his acceptance by Society may have rendered him overconfident and reckless and, Voila! He's a good bet to experience at least one speed-related incident."

"That sounds very interesting but, whether you are clairvoyant or very advanced in analysis, something of a mysterious nature is involved here," Mrs. Carlisle revealed, "which doesn't bother me, but arouses my interest. By the way, how do you do at the races?"

"Oh, Mother! You're not a betting woman!"

"No, but with what they have, I'd likely become one. The 'Sport of Kings', is it not?"

"Well, enough of that," Sarah stated, "My mother, the 'wagerer', has made dinner reservations for us at the Captains' Club. Later they have dancing, and, if it's not too cold, we can watch the boat traffic from their dock."

"Sounds terrific!" Matt stated, "Thank you very much, Mrs. Carlisle."

"You are welcome. Be home early, Sarah."

As they left in the Carlisles' second horse and carriage, Matt started singing "Jingle Bells," expressing how a ride of this kind at Christmas time touched him. "Boy, does this make me homesick!"

"Oh, thanks a lot, Matt," Emily said firmly, " Forgive me for intruding on your reverie, but where do I fit in to your Christmas melancholy?"

"Poor little fella is away from home for the first time, He's looking for a mother, not a girl friend," Randy chided.

"Now look here, Randy, I've given up a lot to follow your escapade, and I think I deserve at least a bit of understanding, if not sympathy."

"All right, boys, let it go. We're here to have fun and get to know each other better," countered Sarah.

"Well, I'm learning a few things about Matt, all right," said Emily.

Matt returned to singing "Jingle Bells," in a melodious voice to stifle the barbs.

"We've never heard that song. Is it strictly American?" asked Sarah.

"Yes, it is. The author was a man who, no matter what occupation he tried, failed at it. Salesman, preacher, businessman, whatever--he failed at them all.. Then one Christmas he wrote the song for his 7-year old daughter, and over the years it became the number one secular Christmas song. He hadn't failed at it, but he wasn't alive to appreciate its ultimate success and popularity."

Arriving at the Captains' Club, their horse and carriage were taken by a valet, and they were greeted warmly by the maitre-d'. "Good evening, Miss Carlisle. A table has been reserved for you and your guests. Follow me, please."

They were led to a secluded table on the second floor with a beautiful view of the waterfront. Tall plants separated them from other diners and the dance floor. "This should minimize the rumors," Sarah thought.

Lively banter and a sharing of each one's history and hopes filled the spaces between courses, which were excellently prepared. Randy and Sarah sat so close together, though, they had trouble eating. Eyeing a chance to even things up, Matt said, "If you lovebirds eat many meals together, you'll starve to death."

"As long as we're both doing the same thing--eating or starving--it's all right with me," Sarah said through a look of rapture. Randy blushed a bit.

Despite the extensive kidding that occupied most of the meal, they had
many laughs, while discovering things about each other. The band had not begun to play, so they ordered after-dinner drinks and left the dining room to sit in the glass-enclosed room overlooking the port. Here Randy and Sarah were able to discuss their situation more privately.

Once seated, Sarah said, "Randy, I would like you to meet my chosen fiancé. You'll find him quite likable, if a little stiff. My father suggested having you and Matt and Emily for Christmas dinner. There you could meet Richard. He is the son of Lord Summergill, whose estate he will inherit.

"One attribute in his favor is his ability to provide me and my family with security and considerable comfort. I'm not sure it is Father's intention to compare you two, but it certainly will provide him an opportunity to do so." "Sarah, I've never been much of a stage presence. Maybe, if I behave myself, say all the right things, he'll come down on my side of the chart,"said Randy in a somewhat acerbic tone.

"Oh, come on, Randy, you can handle it. Just be yourself. Being able to do that would be a plus, since Richard is a bit pompous."

At this point, in the semi-darkness of the room, Randy reached for Sarah's hand, not knowing how she would react. It seemed to be a meeting of hearts, since she responded by tightening her fingers through his.

"You know, I've never known a girl like you," Randy spoke out boldly. "In fact, I didn't know there were girls like you. Most of the ones I know try to impress the guys. You don't try to impress anyone, you're just you and I like that."

Each time they were together, which was often these days, Sarah sensed a quiet tension between them. It was not openly discussed. She knew she had fallen in love with this handsome American, and she felt helpless in its progression. It was happening in spite of the unknown factor. Her eyes followed him as he moved; she listened to every word he spoke with anticipation. She hoped to catch a glimpse into the dark secret that haunted and inhibited him. Somehow she knew it would be resolved, and some day her dream would come true. It would just take time.

A boat whistle echoed over the harbor. When silence returned, Randy said, "As far back as I can remember, I would try to imagine what kind of girl I would fall in love with---tall, thin, short, plump, rich or poor," he chuckled. "Do you know what I mean?"

"Yes. Go on."

"I know you think I'm forward, but I really feel great when I'm near. you. My feelings for you are strong. That's what I'm trying to say."

"Are you really?" she asked, smiling.

"Yes, I am. We've got to speak the truth between us," he affirmed. "Something special is happening here."

"I know," she agreed, her voice quivering. "Do you want it to happen?"

"I do and I don't," he answered thoughtfully. "The reservations have nothing to do with you. It concerns a job I have to do. In fact, it's a tremendous challenge. When it's finished, maybe then would be the time for something to happen."

"I think it's too late already," Sarah whispered softly. They were very close now, watching each other's lips. Would he dare? Randy leaned closer and still closer. He kissed her gently, then they embraced. Her softness pressing against him aroused feelings he had never experienced before. He could easily imagine them in a life together. Words were no longer needed as their continued embrace assured hope for the future.

As Sarah looked over Randy's shoulder, she sat back and said,

"Oh, look, Randy! What a beautiful sight!" He thought she was referring to Titanic, and responded by saying,

"She sure is a beautiful ship."

"No! No! Look....in the sky, it must be a comet."

"I read in the London Times that Halley's Comet would be visible for several nights this week. That must be it. The last time it was observed was in 1831. Sarah, it must be a special gift to us. Call the others so they can see it too."

Amidst much oohing and aahing, they all expressed themselves concerning the beauty of the long tail following it. One was heard to say,

"What a wondrous universe."

The first notes from the band brought them back to reality. Neither wanted to leave the feelings they were sharing with each other.

"Let's dance!" yelled Matt. "We'll see how intercontinental dance styles mesh."

The four returned to the dining room and joined in the dance. A waltz was being played, which was not something the boys enthused over. Willing to follow, however, they listened as Emily said,

"Just count, 1, 2, 3 - 1, 2, 3. There's nothing to it."

"How does one pursue his romantic interests while counting aloud?" inquired Matt. "And when do you get to hold your partner when you're dancing at arm's length?" Despite their comments, they were soon in the rhythm and enjoying themselves.

After a few more dances, they decided to return home, and called for their carriage. Randy and Sarah were quiet on the way, but Matt was teaching Emily the complete "Jingle Bells" softly now.

Arriving at the Carlisles', they said their goodnights without embracing. Four was a crowd, and hugging in a crowd didn't suit either of the boys.

Chapter 12

"A and "B" forward decks were taking shape. The excitement of completing their job was overwhelming them. Eating properly was not as it should have been. Long hours with little food sooner or later took its toll. While down on one of the lower decks checking rivet sizes, Randy became ill. He broke out in a cold sweat, was sick to his stomach and, without warning, collapsed. Two cleanup men working nearby came running to him. One of them turned Randy over on his back and told the other one to go for help.

"Hey, Mr. Kaplan, you O.K.?" the man asked as he shook him gently. Not a sign of life came from Randy. The rescuer was scared, but kept calm. Reaching over the lunch boxes, he picked up a flask of water and poured some on Randy's face. There was a grunt and his eyes opened. The concerned laborer sighed with relief." I think he's O.K." he yelled.

Hearing the disturbance from his work area, Reggie sprinted to the scene, to find the attention focused on his good friend Randy. Stepping through the circle of workers, he scooped him up with little effort and headed for the sick bay. While being carried Randy once again lost consciousness.

When he awakened later that day, Sarah was sitting in the room close to the bed. The hospital room was dim and she was waiting patiently for him to see her there. "I wanted to make sure you were in good hands, " she said softly when she noticed he was awake. I love you, you know."

"What happened?" he asked with obvious difficulty. It was the end of a long vigil. He had been unconscious for several hours.

"What happened?" he repeated, becoming more cognizant of his surroundings.

"Sweetheart, you are going to be all right?" she whispered. "The doctor said a lack of nutrition caused your fainting, but it may be an ulcer, brought on by your poor diet and stress of the job. He prescribes rest and a regular eating schedule. If you can't take enough time for sit-down meals, at least have some snacks. I need you back on your feet, my lovely man."

"I know, Sarah, and I think just a few days rest will do it. Could you drop by each day to see what may be needed? I'll also need some T.LC."

"T.L.C.?"

Tender Loving Care, ma cher. A popular acronym back in the States."

"You know I'll be here for you, Randy, with as much TLC as you'll ever need. You definitely need a stress-free environment to fully recover. Don't worry about the ships. It's in God's hands, and you can't beat that kind of help."

Randy grew stronger each day and actually beat the doctor's target date for release. Being able to watch the ship's progress from his room was sufficient motivation for a speedy recovery. His relationship with Sarah blossomed as they spent time alone together. Sarah and the kind landlady got along very well and divided the chores associated with Randy's confinement. A regular fare of Irish songs, limericks and riddles from the landlady cheered things along, taking Randy's attention away from the forthcoming presentation. Meanwhile, work on the Titanic edged closer to the time when Randy and Matt would have to make their pitch to the Board. If they waited too long, those portions of Titanic II involving the most important changes might already be completed. Any hope of getting Board approval then would be gone. Work had already begun on "A" and "B" deck levels aft.

Randy's absence from the work scene caused Matt to request temporary help in the person of Reggie. Adam Boyle approved the assignment. Reggie turned out to be a rapid learner, and was able to relieve Matt of a great deal of fact accumulation and blueprint assessment. Matt had him stop by the flat each evening, share whatever repast might be offered, and assist Randy and him in analyzing the day's facts.

Their respect for Reggie and his abilities grew with each day. He absorbed ideas and concepts like a blotter and contributed to a technology which would dazzle most sophisticated scientists or technicians of the early 1900's. As a result, they were well prepared to make their presentation to the Board when Randy was physically ready.

During this period, they had made it clear to Reggie that they did not see color when they looked at him, but saw a person with considerable talent and self-respect, who could hold his head high in any gathering. To assure him of their sincerity, they asked him to join in their presentation to the Board, to act as a reference source. They had no idea what prejudice they might stir up by doing so, or what effect it might have on the Board's acceptance of their recommendations. They believed, however, that their mission was not restricted to technological considerations. Even a minute change in the attitude of such an August body might have its own rippling impact on the future.

Randy had inquired as to Reggie's marital status. He was single, but had a beautiful girl friend, Olivia, whom he intended to marry. Randy had suggested that he bring her to the flat one evening when he worked with them, and when Randy was well enough, they could all go out together.

Reggie did bring Olivia to meet the group. She was almost as tall as Reggie, slightly darker skin, regal in her bearing. Her soft voice and gentle nature were perfect complements to Reggie's more aggressive approach to life. Sarah and Emily accepted her without question, and perceived her as presenting a great opportunity to discover more of the world. Her presence seemed to blunt the sharper edges of his reaction to local and world prejudice. As it would turn out, however, these edges were to reveal themselves at a most inauspicious time.

At one point during their working together, Reggie protested that they may be trying to make a white man out of him; pushing him into the white man's world. Randy was quick to disabuse him of that notion.

"We're not trying to make you a white man, we're trying to help you become a better black man--I mean Negro--unh, colored, or whatever it is you want to be called! I'm Randy, not a 'White Man'. Reggie was so stunned he didn't move a muscle. He couldn't believe Randy was talking to him this way.

Matt put his two cents worth in. "Just suppose your native country was an industrial giant, taking great pride in their technology. If you were part of all this and knew that we had the ability to share in it, would you help us or let us stay the way you found us?"

Reggie sat very still, his eyes glued on Randy. Not a finger moved, not a word was said. Matt's breathing penetrated the silence. Reggie looked down at the floor and mumbled a few words too soft to hear.

"What?" Matt asked.

"I said," clearing his throat, "I'd try to help you improve yourself, to be like me." That word hit the mark and he smiled.

"All right!" Randy held his hands up in simple praise of his friend's new comprehension. They hugged one another, easing the tension. An honest relationship that gave birth to trust was formed in those trying moments.

"I really appreciate the way you have accepted me. You know, some times you feel like a freak out there when you're the only one of my color.

"Well, Reggie, we've been through a four-year civil war over this problem, you remember. Of course ours included one portion of the country in a master/slave relationship, the other with freedom for all, but not without prejudice. It would be a shame to have thrown that many lives away without some improvement in our race relations," explained Randy.

"It's been only forty-five years since the war, though--a short time to overcome two hundred years of an abhorrent relationship. We're working on it, but it's going to take a lot longer than forty-five years to really change it. We know we will continue to endure prejudice and discrimination against people that are blacks, at least in the U.S., for a long time.

"The British Empire, global as it is, should have had sufficient exposure to race relations (brown, black, red, yellow?) to have made some progress. But then, as colonies under the rule of Britannia, perhaps the problems are as difficult, if not different."

"Well," Matt jumped in, "enough of solving the world's problems, let's stick to our own here in the magic world of unsinkable monster ships. Besides, it's been a long day and I'm shot."

"I know you can't speak of what's going on in the inner offices of H.& W. while you work and eat with the crew," Reggie stated, "But, is there any way I can help, either directly or indirectly, with the projects you are involved in? Maybe I can even help with your problems with O'Brien and McCarthy. That's getting nastier every day."

"No, Reggie! You stay away from that battle. They know we are friends and between that and your significant minority position, you need to be very careful with these crazies. Stay away from them! You can help in other ways, but just don't go near them, OK?" cautioned Randy.

"I understand, Randy. I'll play it "cool," as you put it.

"I want you both to know how comfortable I feel with you, and I want to thank you for it."

"That's very interesting, Reggie," began Randy, "Is it possible that your feeling of comfort with us is not generated by us, but from deep inside your sense of self.? I mean, comfort or discomfort is what we feel inside--emotions arise when our inner needs react to outside stimuli. How we react is determined by the experiences of our lives---the love we received, and our emotional, physical and spiritual deprivations as a child and other phases of our maturation.

"So you see, Reggie, you can take the credit for the comfortable feeling you have. Don't blame us!" If you feel uncomfortable with others, take control of it and change it!"

"Thank you for that, Randy. But you will never know what it's like to be a speck of pepper in a barrel of salt. They never let me alone or forget it. I guess I will always be different.

"Well, I'll be leaving now. It's been a great night, but there isn't much of it left for sleep. Thanks for the encouragement. I'll see you in the morning."

After Reggie had left, Randy and Matt discussed how they might best utilize him in their preparation.

"Matt, before we commit Reggie to sticking his neck out, I think the least we should do is to let him in on our mystery. All of it!"

"O.K. Let's bring him over tomorrow night and fill him in, Randy. I think he can handle it." But could they tell him the real reason they were here? Could they risk telling anyone their secret? Should they put that much trust in Reggie?

The following evening Reggie arrived ready to spend as long as necessary to get ready for Monday.

"Welcome, Reggie," Matt began, "just leave your coat on the chair and have a seat.. Since we have asked you to become a member of this 'Save the Titanic' team, and face the 'Awesome Foursome (Ismay, Andrews, Carlisle and Morgan), along with the other scowlers on the board, we felt we should tell you all there is to know about us and the project. What you are about to hear must be kept absolutely confidential. It can never be repeated to anyone, ever! Do you understand? When we are through, it will be obvious to you why we must keep it that way."

"Yes, sir." was Reggie's solemn pledge. The look on his face indicated sincerity. He was sure they were about to tell him what all the hubbub in the yard was all about. His pulse rate went up and he began to sweat.

Randy, then, meticulously explained the events concerning their journey back through time from the year 2010 to the present. He then described how they had arrived at Belfast. The lengthy explanation took over two hours and left them all the more exhausted.

Reggie sat quite still, squeezing his lips tightly together, listening intently as Randy spoke. His jaw was moving back and forth, betraying his mixed emotions. They were waiting for Reggie to say something--- anything. Silence reigned. It was nerve wracking. What would he do? Jump and run? Tell the police? Worse yet, tell everybody. Maybe he would just laugh.

"Would you please make me a part of all this?" Reggie finally asked humbly. "It's great, really great!"

Relieved, Randy assured him he was already an important part of it.

"Reggie, by now you can understand the enormity of what we're doing, and the hazards accompanying it. In my dreams, dark angels are telling me that we can't change history. Maybe I'm being a bit arrogant and stubborn in not taking them seriously, but other visions counteract them, and drive us on. Can you imagine the power our knowledge of Titanic's fate brings to bear? I hope it is enough to convince our board that their rejection of our recommendations will leave Titanic in jeopardy. Your participation will expose you to the inherent dangers of pursuing the course we're on. Will you take that chance?"

"Yes, that doesn't phase me. Life without risk can get pretty dull, and being a 'gopher' is definitely risk-proof. The only thing I'm having trouble with," Reggie went on, " is your trip back through time. That's eerie! How could you be certain of where you would wind up in time.?"

"Reggie, there is nothing my genius time traveler friend can't do if he puts his colossal brain to work on it." Randy finally ended his speech.

"Thank you. Thank you. You are truly good friends." With that, Reggie stood up to leave. "I'd better be going; I've got to work in the morning. What time is it?"

"Almost midnight.," Randy answered as he opened the door. "See you at the yard, Friend. Good night." Closing the door, Randy leaned back against it and smiled. Matt clenched his fist, punched it in the air and said, "Yesss!"

By the afternoon of the next day, Randy felt up to leaving the flat to get some air. He was not prepared for the drop in temperature that had occurred during his confinement. They had been so busy they had forgotten Christmas was only a week away. When Sarah arrived, he asked if they might go shopping and take in some of the decorations on homes and shops. She agreed to go if he took it easy and didn't overdo it. One other condition was put forth–Matt wouldn't sing "Jingle Bells." He had exhausted their appreciation of it on the last date by singing it continuously.

Laughing as they left, the loving couple rapped on the landlady's door yelling, "Merry Christmas." From in her flat she wished the same. Hastening to her front window, she waved as they climbed into Sarah's carriage. "Yes, Sarah, this is going to be a wonderful Christmas," said Randy.

As evening came, they stopped the carriage and walked. through a city park. The only sound was their heels on the sidewalk. They seemed to have reached a level of maturity in their relationship that did not require continuous sound. Their love was strengthened by the silence, a silence that made them feel as one, together and united with all creation. Both were thinking of this when Sarah broke the silence.

"Randy, each day I know we feel closer to each other. The way we can walk in silence and really feel each other's presence through it; the appreciation we have for each other's needs; the joy we feel when we see each other; these and so many other things convince me that we are meant to be together forever.

"When we have Christmas dinner with my family, the Summergills and our friends, I'm certain my parents will see this love between us--I've certainly told them enough about it. As I've told you, John, the one chosen to be my fiancé, will be here with his parents.

"I would like to get together with Father, John and his father, and you, so that we can end my forced engagement to John and look to our becoming engaged. I don't believe Father will object to doing this. If this were other than a brokered engagement, I would take care of telling John myself. It was, however, an arrangement supposedly in the best interest of both families. Love was not considered an essential. If it happened, so much the better."

Almost immediately Sarah noticed the familiar blank, gray look in his eyes signaling full retreat. She'd seen it on several occasions before, and prepared herself for his withdrawal from the scene.

"Randy, what is it? As soon as I mention anything of permanence associated with our relationship, you leave me, at least emotionally. What is it?"

"I can't tell you--you'll have to wait until things settle down, as I've told you before."

"Randy, here comes the ultimatum I 'd hoped I wouldn't have to voice. If you can't tell me what the problem is before Christmas day is over, and if and when you plan to include me in your life, I will cancel the meeting with John and his father concerning our engagement, and ask you to leave me out of whatever you're doing. Maybe that will speed up your casual approach toward me."

"Please, Sarah. At least let me get the presentation to the Board behind me before we deal with the future."

"When do you expect that to occur?" Sarah asked.. being a bit cool.

"Your father is pulling it together. I hope it's Monday or Tuesday, because the Board members will be leaving or too involved in Christmas, to sit still for our presentation "

"That may get you through Christmas dinner at the Carlisles', but you are skirting the edge of my abyss of former loves if it goes any further."

Brought back to reality from the dream world they'd been in all day, they headed back to the carriage and rode toward home in a different kind of silence.

"Good night, Randy. Please understand that I do still love you."

"I thank God for that, but am I hearing the final bells toll?"

"Perhaps, Randy. Perhaps," came the last words he could hear as she took her seat in the carriage, snapped the reins and turned toward home.

Chapter 13

It was getting late in the week when Randy arranged with Carlisle to have the Board of Designers meet for his and Matt's presentation on Monday, December 19th at 2 P.M. Members were to be informed of the starting time and the fact that it would last no longer than an hour. Randy also advised Carlisle that Reggie would be assisting them, perhaps even explaining the detail of certain recommendations. Carlisle suggested that the Board be advised of the cast of characters prior to the meeting so there'll be "no surprises," as he put it.

"You know there are so few Negroes working on the Titanic, that having one that close to the action may take a few minutes to get used to."

Randy thought to himself, "Something's better than nothing--even a small step in the right direction."

"Thank you, Mr. Carlisle. I know you're concerned about our coming on like prophets. We'll keep the future out of the presentation unless it becomes evident that nothing else will persuade them to take the recommended action."

"Well, Randy, you're not likely to be stoned by the angry mob, as were the prophets before you, but you'll have a tough time convincing them of your gifts. Of that I am certain. I have enough confidence in you to not be overly concerned."

"Thank you, sir. We need a boost like that now and then. I hope we live up to your level of confidence."

"We're on, Matt! Next Monday at 2 P.M. we shoot the rapids!" Randy yelled as he burst into the flat. " Let's get together with Reggie, lay out the structure of the presentation, and get our exhibits and ducks in a row. We'll need to anticipate every possible reaction so's not to wind up on the rocks---or should I say, 'on the icebergs'?"

Back at the Carlisle's, Sarah had become somewhat apathetic, speaking very seldom and staying in or near her room most days. It was obvious to her younger sister Hannah that Sarah was either broken-hearted or severely depressed. Christmas seemed a difficult time to experience emotional upset. Depression was at the year's high during this season; without introducing additional problems.

One quiet afternoon, Sarah began to play somber classical pieces on the reception-room Steinway. The longer she played, the more her tears flowed.

"What's wrong with Sarah, Daddy?" asked Hannah, Sarah's 14-year old sister.

"I'm not quite sure, Hannah. I know she feels quite strongly for Randy, and probably is frustrated because I arranged her engagement with John Summergill. I told her that just the other day his father and I were saying the time was right for a wedding and a bouncing baby or two. Sarah exploded, saying, 'I couldn't! Not now.' She started to cry, covered her face with her hands, dashed from the room and up the stairs. I rushed after her, and asked 'Don't you love him?' There was no answer.

"Hannah, why don't you go sit on the piano bench with her and see if you can get her to talk."

It seemed that Sarah didn't want to notice Hannah as she sat down, so involved in her thoughts was she. Her fingers flew up and down the keyboard as though on their own, while tears continued to flow.

"Sarah, do you need someone to talk to?" Hannah asked quietly. Still no answer. "Sarah, Daddy said he would willingly cancel the engagement arrangement if you were in love with someone else. Even more willing if it were Randy Kaplan." At that, Sarah stopped cold...

"Did he really? Did he really say that?" she asked, almost in disbelief.

"Yes, he did, and I know he means it because he loves us both and can't stand the thought that either of us is unhappy because of something he did a long time ago.

He was too upset with himself to sit down and talk to you about it."

Hearing this, Sarah pushed back the bench, jumped up and went to find Daddy. She found him in the kitchen, where she hugged him tightly and kissed his wrinkled cheeks. "Daddy, I am so happy, my heart is dancing!

Hannah told me what you'd said about my engagement to John."

"Yes, Sparrow, I should have been more sensitive to what was happening around me. I'm sorry for having caused you such pain.

"Daddy, you know I love you. You are always there when I need you most."

"And I always will be, dear....So, tell me, Sparrow, who's the lucky boy? It is Randy Kaplan?" her father asked.

"Yes, Daddy, it is. It seems we have known each other forever. He told me he saw me in the same dream every night, and heard me say, 'Save us! Save us!' over and over again."

"Sarah, my sparrow, I've come to respect Randy and Matt a lot. They are doing some important work for Harland & Wolff. Randy is brilliant and I like him. There's something very different about him, though, and that concerns me some. I'll talk to him about it Monday before the meeting."

"There's something in the way, Daddy. I don't know what it is. Every time I mention anything about commitment or permanence, he pulls away from me. He says he has something to accomplish before he can get serious about us."

The following morning, the master-designer awaited Randy's arrival patiently. "Randy, would you step into my office for a moment?" he called when Randy arrived. He used discussion of work as a pretext, but really wanted to observe Randy more closely and determine his intentions toward Sarah.

Randy was sitting in the big black chair, wondering why they were going over the lifeboat material again.

"Do you love Sparrow?" came a direct hit.

"I... I..." sputtered Randy, "don't know anyone by that name, sir.

"Oh.....Sarah. I mean Sarah."

Randy was surprised at the intimacy of his relationship with Sarah. "Yes, I do. I meant to talk to you sooner, sir. Our relationship has been honorable. I am sincere, but I can't marry her. Not yet," He swallowed nervously. "You see, I have a slight complication and just as soon as it's cleared up, I'll make my next move." The young man paused, thinking through his last remark. "Good grief! I mean...like I said, my intentions are honorable. I hope you understand."

Carlisle smiled. "Can I help you with the complication?"

"No, sir! It's my problem."

Carlisle frowned and asked, "Are you married? Is that it?"
"Who, me?" Randy grinned. "Oh, no! No previous involvements. I have a....a....let's call it a time problem, sir. I mean, it's just not the right time." Randy noticed the confusion in Carlisle's eyes and shrugged. "I wish I could explain, but there are things to work out. Please give me some time."

"Randy, I am most solicitous of my daughter's happiness. We will discuss this further after Christmas dinner." Then, reverting to his master-designer role, he said, "Return to the job, Kaplan," nodded once and dismissed him in a business-like manner.

Randy left feeling he hadn't made a good impression. He knew that one day soon he must return to his own time, and Sarah would probably fade into the mist of memory. What a mess! He loved this woman and wanted her as his wife. It was doomed from the start.

Back in the office, Matt was flirting with another blonde file clerk. He noticed Randy approaching with a blank look on his face. When he came through the door, Matt said, "I'm ready to make the inspection of those three 'C' deck starboard portholes. How about you?"

Noting the gathering of the better looking secretaries and clerks, Randy assumed that Matt was at it again. He was right, of course, and his critical expression prompted Matt to say,

"Just entertaining the troops, Randy. Emily understands. I'm here just to find out what Carlisle wanted with you. You know I never waste an opportunity? What did Carlisle say?"

"I'd tell you if I could get a word in edgewise," Randy sighed. But let's have some privacy first. It concerned Sparrow."

"Sparrow? Who in blazes is Sparrow?"

"Sarah. Sarah Carlisle," Randy explained. It's the pet name he's called her since she was a tot."

"The boss's daughter--I warned you to be careful. Fathers in this day are very protective of their little girls- you know, he could shoot you. 'Sparrow'....Hey, I think I like that name, how 'bout you?"

"It's O.K., but that's his name for her. I'll get one for her if I need it."

A hint of jealousy was heard in his tone. For the first time, he really thought about Sarah going back with him. "Wouldn't it be super?" he exclaimed suddenly, " My father would love her because she's just like Mom. She has that same smile that makes her eyes glow. Matt....if only I could take her back with me."

"Man, are you crazy? She can't go back with us!" Matt interrupted.

"I know it!," Randy snapped.

"Then don't even think about it!"

"Fine, Matt! I'm just day-dreaming. Let's change the subject."

Matt stared for a moment, then, realizing the extent of the frustration his friend was experiencing, he said, "Look, friend, I understand. Really I do. I may be an air head at times, but I do use my brain once in a while.

"I have an announcement to make. We may not be going back. Our trip here was fortunate, but what if we're trapped here? Suppose I can' t come up with a Laser that works? Then what?"

"Well, Matt, that certainly would eliminate my having to choose between now and then, wouldn't it? Sarah and I could live out our lives together. That ain't all bad. Besides, with what we know and could apply in this dimension, we could probably live in considerable comfort. Maybe even compete with the lure of the Summergill estate."

Chapter 14

Monday the 19th rolled around fast. The day dawned bright and clear. Somewhat unusual for this time of year. Matt and Randy had arranged to meet Reggie at their office at 1:30 P.M. A short review of their package was made, Reggie's exhibits and facts were checked, and handouts put together. Then they sat in quiet prayer. The whole purpose of their trip through time was on the line here.

At 1:55 P.M. the presenters took their seats at the dais along with Carlisle, and waited for the Board to arrive. First came Tom Andrews, chief designer for H. & W. Then came Andrew's assistant, Jeremy Murphy, followed by Sean Connelly of Lloyd's of London, and Lord Summergill, representing her majesty's regulatory commission for naval and commercial fleet construction, Lord W. J. Pirrie, Chairman of H. & W., and finally, J. Bruce Ismay, CEO of White Star Line.

Carlisle had been previously advised that J. P. Morgan would not be in attendance, since he was in South America. A quorum was present, however, and Carlisle kicked things off at precisely 2 P.M.

"Gentlemen, we have an opportunity today to listen to a presentation by our two new American assistant engineers. In assigning them to the positions they hold, I put them through a battery of questions that would be difficult for some of the most capable engineers. I was tremendously impressed, as I believe you will be.

"The two presenters are Randy Kaplan, team leader today, and Matt Miller. Assisting them is Reggie Sanders, a member of one of our work teams. He has been a considerable help to them in their preparation for this meeting." Each of them nodded as Carlisle mentioned their names.

"Randy, please take over," said Carlisle.

"Thank you, Mr. Carlisle. Gentlemen, we appreciate your busy schedules, particularly during the Christmas season. We will make our presentation as brief as possible, while hopefully allowing sufficient time for each item.

"We requested the meeting to review our recommendations, because we feel very strongly that the safety of our ships and the welfare of our passengers might be in jeopardy without them." Stopping to take a breath enabled Sean Connelly of Lloyd's to interject a question.

"Randy, before we get into the specifics, would you please comment in a broad manner on the statement that Titanic II is 'unsinkable'."

"There is no question, sir, that Titanic II comes as close to being 'unsinkable' as any major vessel built during this century or the last. Designers working both for Mr. Andrews and Mr. Carlisle should be congratulated for having seen to it. As we will explain later, however, three areas of the ship's design concern us. These are significant enough to render her somewhat less than 'unsinkable'. Use of the term for marketing purposes may be a bit premature, if not presumptuous."

"Just how perfect must a vessel's design be to qualify as 'unsinkable', Mr. Kaplan'?" challenged Jeremy Murphy.

"Mr. Murphy, much depends on the circumstances of the ship's use, the degree of safety its operators foster, weather, and so many other factors, that we do not believe any ship can be described as completely unsinkable. Our presentation will, hopefully, bear that out."

"We have divided our presentation into two major categories: first, three recommendations involving the ship's design; then four more of a non-design nature, but of equal importance. Each of these will be supported with facts, figures, cost estimates and analysis. We will provide each of you with this information in a comprehensive handout. For this reason, there should be no need to take notes, except for questions you wish to ask, or reminders you need to note.

"During our offering this morning, Reggie will draw attention to charts to help us focus on the area of the ship involved."

"BUT! Before we get to the details, we would like to prepare you for our presentation by taking you with us to New York on the maiden voyage of Titanic II. Hold onto your hats or whatever you find comforting--this. may turn out to be a rough trip.

"Matt, please take over."

"Thanks, Randy. Gentlemen, our scenario begins as we board Titanic II at her dock in Southampton. We will occupy a first-class stateroom on 'A' deck and avail ourselves of the incredible amenities offered us. She will sail to Le Havre, France and then to Queenstown, Ireland, picking up passengers as she goes. We are cleared for departure from Queenstown in the afternoon of Thursday, April 11, 1912. Our arrival in New York is scheduled for Tuesday, April 16th. Whatever else may impress us during our voyage, nothing will compare to the 'Grand Staircase' between 'A' deck and the boat deck, and its soon-to-be-famous clock.

"On Sunday, April 14th, we are two days out of New York. Some time after 11:30 P.M., Titanic II is steaming at the awesome speed of 22 knots through a large ice field, approximately 175 kilometers (95 miles) south of the Grand Banks of Newfoundland. Though skies are cloudless, it is a moonless night, and mist is rising from the ice. A brilliant array of stars typical of a dark night on the ocean is obscured by the mist. Within the field are a number of various-sized icebergs. An American vessel, the Californian, has sent wireless messages to ships warning them of the extent of icebergs in the area. It also has taken the precaution of sailing outside the perimeter of the field No acknowledgment from Titanic II is noted, because of a huge backlog of messages to be sent.

"At exactly 11:38 P.M., a lookout whose binoculars had dropped from the crow's nest earlier in the shift, suddenly sees an enormous iceberg one mile ahead, lurking in the mist directly in the ship's path. With panic in his voice, he yells through the voice tube to the bridge, 'Large iceberg dead ahead, less than one-and-a-half miles!'

Murdoch, 2nd mate on the bridge watch, immediately issues orders to the Engine Room:

"PORT ENGINE , FULL ASTERN"

MAINTAIN FULL FORWARD ON STARBOARD ENGINE

To the helmsman: "HARD 'a STARBOARD!'

Arriving on the bridge, the Captain is informed of the orders given, and countermands it, ordering the engine room to bring both engines to

FULL ASTERN

"The ship shudders as her engines struggle to move her from Ahead Full to Full Astern. The reversed propellers begin to change their thrust by 360 degrees, counteracting the ordered rudder setting.

Bridge personnel quickly calculate the time to traverse one mile at 22 knots--approximately 3 minutes! "Although we will begin to slightly decrease our speed, we will be unable to reduce it sufficiently before reaching the iceberg."

As the ship approaches the iceberg, every effort is made to bring the bow around to avoid collision. Our reducing speed has concurrently reduced the rudder's response capability. This combines with the opposing effect of reversed propeller rotation, to render rudder control difficult. Her bow begins to drift to port, exposing her starboard side to the wiles of this gigantic iceberg.

"A collision is inevitable, and we are left to speculate only on where we will be struck and how seriously. A sharp edge of the iceberg makes contact below the waterline, fifteen feet aft of the bow. For the first 15 to 20 feet (5 to 6 meters) following contact, it buckles hull plates and pops rivets. in #1 and #2 holds, skips a space roughly the same length, punctured both exterior and interior plates of #3 hold, and most damaging, skips to the 4th compartment (boiler room #5) where it punctured through to the fifth compartment (boiler room #6.) Water enters and fills the penetrated compartments (Reggie points to the area involved on display chart), then flows over the tops of the interior bulkheads in either direction until the undamaged bow compartments are filled.

As weight builds in the bow, it begins to slowly sink, causing intruding water to flow rearward over the bulkheads. Pressure on plates with popped rivets causes further flooding. Water flowing into the coal bunkers reaches the hot coal, causing an explosion which blows out plates surrounding the bunkers and hastens the ship's demise.

(Subsequent investigation determined that, although the punctures amounted to the equivalent of only 12 square feet altogether, during the first 50 minutes following the collision, 25,000 tons of water had been added to Titanic's gross weight of 46,500 tons. Also, investigators analyzing the composition of the hull's plates, determined it to be high in sulfur content, rendering it extremely brittle and unable to bend without fracturing.)

"Mostly unaware of the seriousness of the collision, passengers on the main deck step aside as the upper 20 feet of the iceberg scrape the rail, spreading ice on the deck. A playful ice fight begins, with great hilarity. In stateroom C-70, its occupant has left the porthole open, and is showered with ice as he sleeps.

"The bow continues to sink, raising the stern section upward out of the water. No longer supported by the sea's buoyancy, the weight of this 300-foot (90 meters) stern section causes it to split away from the main body of the ship. By 2:20 A.M., April 15, 1912, only 2 hours and 40 minutes after striking the iceberg, both sections of the invincible Titanic II have disappeared vertically into the 28 degree water, coming to rest 2 ½ miles (4 kilometers) below its surface.

Over 1,500 passengers and crew are without lifeboats and die jumping or falling from the almost upright section, being trapped below decks and drowning, or, as in the majority of cases, thrown into the frigid water, where they will die from hypothermia within the hour. The nearest possible rescue ship, the Carpathia, is now over two hours away at her flank speed of 17 knots.

"When Carpathia finally arrives at the macabre scene, they find considerable debris, hundreds of floating bodies and 16 lifeboats with anywhere from 12 to 64 survivors in each. Survivors in a few of the boats are looking for signs of life among bodies in the water. Somewhat more than 700 survivors are ultimately rescued--only those fortunate enough to have boarded lifeboats."

Matt stopped speaking and sat down. An awesome silence indicated the extent of the board's immersion in the story and all its ramifications. None of the team, nor Carlisle, chose to interrupt the silence. The board members had to go through the full gamut of emotions before responding to such a scene. Taken to the depths, they were finding it difficult to extract themselves from it. The monster ship which had been consuming them in her construction, surrounding them as they met and filling them with a creator's pride in her imagined "maiden voyage," was...GONE! As the seconds went by, the anesthetic effect of Matt's scenario was fading. Anticipating a barrage of questions and comments, Carlisle stood up and said firmly, "Randy, please continue the presentation with your ship-design recommendations?" said Carlisle, hoping to divert potential chaos.

"Yes, sir, of course," Randy replied. "Gentlemen, our scenario may seem far-fetched or an example of extraordinarily poor luck, but I can assure you that it is a real possibility to which you should give very serious thought.

"Apparently an American author by the name of Morgan Robertson, theoretically supported our scenario in a book published in 1898. entitled FUTILITY, or, 'Wreck of the Titan!' It described the sinking of a ship, in many ways the same or close to being the same, as our Titanic II. Even the name Titan! seems portentous. He goes so far as to state that the ship will embark on its maiden voyage in April of 1912! We have a copy for each of you. You should find it remarkably coincidental--at least exciting reading. You may not have seen this before, but it probably hit your desk before anyone even thought of Titanic..

"While some of us may still be searching for survivors in the North Atlantic, we will, nevertheless, discuss the design recommendations first. This, in order to allow for time to discuss the other recommendations.

"Our first recommendation calls for tripling exterior hull plates below the waterline from the bow rearward to a point 80 meters aft of centerpoint. This will effectively repel hit-and-miss penetration of her hull by any sharp element--iceberg, dock, vessel., etc.

As an adjunct to this recommendation, we suggest that the additional plates be fabricated from a lower-sulfur content steel than that used in the existing hull plates. Analysis indicated that had all hull plates been so fabricated, the iceberg might well have bent them, but not splintered them due to their brittle nature.

"Our second recommendation is to extend compartment bulkheads from 'D' and 'E' decks up to 'B' and 'C' decks. This will enable the compartments to contain the water without its running over the top and flooding undamaged compartments, aft of Boiler Room #6. We believe that both efforts should be undertaken, but if only one can be afforded, choose to bring up the interior bulkheads. This can be done more cheaply, with less redesign and less addition of weight. Our scenario suggested that with this redesign, the water might have been contained within the first four compartments, averting a major disaster. The term 'unsinkable' derived from the belief that no more than five compartments would ever be penetrated. This incident involved penetration of six compartments.

"Our third recommendation is to double the thickness of the plates around coal bunkers to avoid blowouts in the event of explosion. There is a way to overcome this need. That is, by keeping the coal moist and cool so as to avoid the explosion when water meets hot coal. The only problem with that is it relegates monitoring of coal temperature to human effort and attention and its accompanying potential for oversight."

Tom Andrews asked, "Assuming we approve the lifting of bulkheads to 'B' and 'C' decks and increasing plate thickness around the bunkers, what impact will that have on her max speed?"

"Mr. Andrews, we calculate that at about one-half knot loss. Of course, we have 900 feet (275 m.) of ship to find offsetting reductions without reduction of integrity. Our handouts will show some of the possibilities along with supporting data. Are there further questions? If not, we can get on to the balance of our recommendations. If some develop after we close this meeting, we will always be available to pursue them further."

"Sounds good to me, Alex. Maybe we can keep this to an hour meeting if we keep it moving," commented Ismay

Chapter 15

The first of our non-design recommendations is to install an additional 24 lifeboats, enough to take care of all passengers and crew.

"Lifeboats! Can anyone deny that the primary cause of the great loss of life in our scenario was an insufficient number of lifeboats? Without implementing any of our other recommendations, the addition of another 24 lifeboats would have saved the lives of all but those trapped below when water-tight doors were closed,--in boiler rooms or other such compartments. In two hours and twenty minutes, 40 boats would have been filled in an orderly fashion, lowered and away from the ship when she went down.

"The ship would still have perished, but those going down with her would be small compared to the 1,522 who actually did.

"Mr. Kaplan," asked Jeremy Murphy, once again in a challenging tone, "Are you aware that the 16 lifeboats to be installed meet the requirements of Her Majesty's Board of Trade? Lord Summergill, here, is her representative- tentative for fleet construction."

"Thank you, Mr. Murphy. Yes, we are aware of that, which causes us to wonder how the Board of Trade can find that number sufficient. Does a minimum complement of half-enough boats also apply to those ships not declared 'unsinkable?'

"I believe I can speak to that, Mr. Kaplan," injected Lord Summergill,

"The Board of Trade's assumption is that only in a rare situation would lifeboats be utilized to abandon ship. So why burden the ship operator with additional costs and weight, and less useable main deck area?"

"Well, sir, we've seen a number of 'rare' disasters along the shipping lanes recently, and we have just finished telling you of another. Their great loss of life seems to have had little effect on the Board's thinking. The only reference to these disasters has been included in our recommendation that the name of our ship be changed to Titanic II.

"The real question here is: are the lives of over 1,500 people worth the price of 24 additional lifeboats and their accompanying inconvenience? That is all this is about. If they are not, then I am fearful of the obvious indifference this position implies. Beyond our promise to the passenger of luxurious facilities lies an inherent commitment to provide him a high degree of personal safety. Leaving him bereft of such, we also leave him to swim for his life in sub-freezing water. Has ever-increasing emphasis on profit effectively eliminated respect for the lives of our passengers? It would seem so!" Surprisingly, Bruce Ismay had not uttered a word. But when he did, the walls vibrated, his subordinates came to rapt attention.

"Mr. Kaplan, it is evident that your brief exposure to business has not been enough for you to comprehend what the manager must consider in his decision making. He has no manual to cover risk taking, or a risk percentage versus costs graph to help him. He must make the best selection at the lowest possible cost, to satisfy its investors. We have no problem with taking the risk of shorting our lifeboats, since we have been advised that Titanic II, for all practical purposes, is 'unsinkable'."

"That being the case, Mr. Ismay," Matt joined the bout, "why have any lifeboats at all? That would reduce costs and weight and increase the main deck walk areas. As Captain, I would much prefer to have no lifeboats than to have half-enough. That way I don't have to play God--either they all drown, or none of them do."

"That would violate Board of Trade minimums. Try your criticism on Summergill!" Murphy offered.

"Our regulations may at times appear foolish or out of line." Lord Summergill responded. "The complement of lifeboats required for each ship is based on the ship's tonnage rather than the actual capacity of passengers and crew. If we can cover areas of greatest risk, we are satisfied. Our purpose in life is to see to it that outright recklessness is not tolerated."

"If I understand you gentlemen correctly," Randy responded, "you are ready to accept the risk that, on April 15, 1912, will cost Titanic II 1,522 passengers and crew.

"The immense cost of bad publicity alone will suggest our recommendations should have been accepted. White Star's reputation will surely accompany Titanic to the bottom."

"Mr. Kaplan," Tom Andrews inserted, "I'm getting the impression that you have no question Titanic II will sink on April 15, 1912..You speak of it as though it were in the past, you tell us what will happen, and at other times what is happening. You even refer to the results of a 'subsequent' accident investigation. Certainly you weren't on the scene when the purported accident occurred---or were you?"

"Mr. Andrews, one of the required courses at our engineering school was Deductive Reasoning & Analysis. This course taught us to reason from available facts to logical conclusions. We are simply saying that we have deduced from the facts on hand that she could sink on that date, with the loss of life mentioned."

"Well, I for one would be eager to take such a course. Where can I sign up?" asked Sean Connelly, derisively.

Ignoring Connelly's sarcasm, Randy continued, "In the interest of time, gentlemen, I suggest we move along to the second non-design recommendation. That is, to provide training for the crew and passengers in the calling away of lifeboats, including at least one lifeboat drill for all hands. When lifeboats are needed, the abandon ship command has been issued. The state of panic ensuing can be reduced if the boats are handled by people who know what they are doing. It will also eliminate calling away boats not completely filled, as was the case in our scenario. If there had been an average of 18 more people in each boat, we would have saved almost 300 more lives.

"Of course, you may find it awkward conducting a drill for 2,200 when there are only 1,100 seats. Perhaps you can hold fore and aft drills, training one-half the complement at a time."

"This recommendation makes a lot of sense, costs little to implement. I would recommend we adopt that immediately," said Carlisle.

"I concur," echoed Ismay. I'm not sure I am pleased with Randy's obvious effort to make sport of a decision to stay with 16 lifeboats."

"Our third recommendation is to train captains and bridge personnel in handling an imminent collision. Use of rudder and engines in combination to maneuver would be one item, particularly as they apply to collision-avoidance. In our scenario, 2nd Mate Murdoch actually ordered that combination of actions recommended by Knight's Modern Seamanship to most rapidly and effectively evade a head-on collision.

"The Captain's reversal of a portion of Murdoch's orders suggests that either he panicked, or he was unaware of the effectiveness of Murdoch's orders. His countermand slowed the ship, rendered a collision inevitable, and exposed the ship's most vulnerable sections to severe damage. A bow-on collision is much preferred to one in which the underwater hull is exposed to damage. "In 3 minutes, at 22 knots, there never was a possibility to stop or slow the ship sufficiently. The Captain's delayed effort to do so only compounded the problem. Had Murdoch's orders been carried out, the maneuver would have provided the ship with the best chance to clear the iceberg.

"I can readily concur with that recommendation," said Ismay, "although I'm having some difficulty accepting your implication that Captain Smith's 2nd Mate may be more knowledgeable than he in matters of ship maneuvering."

"Mr. Ismay, if you will permit me, that is the subject of our next recommendation. This one may slow us down a bit. That is, to assign captaincy of Titanic II's maiden voyage to a captain other than Smith. Although we realize that Captain Smith is considered the 'Millionaires' Captain' and has behind him over 36 years of experience, we also know that he has had incidents resulting from his use of excessive speed. His reputation with society is likely to create further overconfidence and recklessness which will do Titanic II little good. As you saw in our scenario, he also exceeded prudent speed in sailing directly through a known iceberg field."

"Now just a minute, Mr. Kaplan," Ismay exploded, "We listen to your criticism of our business practices. You accuse us of negligence in our responsibility for passenger safety, and now you have the temerity to suggest to us that our #1 Captain, reckless beyond tolerable limits, should be removed from Titanic II's maiden voyage. How do you conclude that your wisdom exceeds that of the most experienced board in all of Britain?"

"Mr. Ismay, I completely understand your feelings. All I can say is that Matt and I have seen it happen, learned from it, and now hope to convince you not to make the same mistakes with Titanic II as were made on Titanic. You see, as of April 15, 1912 Titanic will be found at the bottom of the North Atlantic at 49R 56' 49" W. 41R 43' 57" N.

Confusion registered on the faces of everyone in the room except the three boys and Carlisle, who said,

"Gentlemen, don't ask me to explain by what means the boys have been able to fathom this information. But, let me tell you my experience with their abilities. They are not yet aware of what I'm about to tell you. Two weeks ago, Randy told me that Captain Smith would experience a minor accident in a major port within two weeks. Today is the 14th day. This morning I arrived early and found a wireless message from our office in Naples:

'Early A.M., date, Oceanic, E. J. Smith command, demolished

2nd strbrd channel buoy enter Naples. Ship 8m. crease above

waterline. Prelim cause, XS speed. Handle local, no press

Galbreath 12/19

"Since it was a minor incident, and being taken care of by our Naples office, I chose to keep it to myself, for discussion here. What I mean to imply by mentioning it to you is that Randy and Matt are speaking from some source of knowledge which is accurate; a talent we should capitalize on and use to advantage. What brings it about or what you may call it is irrelevant--it seems to work!"

"'One swallow does not a summer make',"(1) recited Ismay. "And I'm not likely to swallow 'Management by Clairvoyance' as a way to run a business. Show me the facts, or that you can call them all right with no misses-- maybe I'll listen."

"Well, sir, perhaps I can add one more 'swallow' for your management consumption," Randy interjected. "Within the next ninety days, Captain Smith will experience another minor incident. This will happen as he enters the Sea of Marmara enroute Istanbul. Once again, excessive speed will be the chief cause. Captain Smith will be unable to stop as an Izmir-to-Istanbul packet boat crosses Smith's bow in an early morning sea fog. Fortunately, it will be shuttling to Istanbul with no passengers. The packet's maneuverability will be all that saves it from being fully broadsided and split in two. As it will turn out, the packet will require several thousand dollars for repairs. With passengers, the incident would have been a disaster."

"Randy, were your crystal ball to contain even more evidence of Captain Smith's recklessness, it would not likely displace his thirty-six years of excellent performance. He's our man!

Up to this point, Reggie had managed to contain himself. But combining the belittling of Randy and Matt's proposals with the Board's casual dismissal of the lifeboat question, he could contain himself no longer.

"Gentlemen, I was not on the schedule of speakers, but I must voice my opinion on what I see and hear from this August body. It is inconceivable to me to be hearing your general or tacit agreement with a decision not to increase the number of lifeboats. I propose an analogy--one that my skin color qualifies me to discuss.

"For 200 years prior to the Civil War in the United States, slave traders abducted natives of African tribes, put them aboard sailing vessels manacled to their beds, and brought them to the U. S. for sale to land-owners primarily south of the Mason-Dixon line. If an individual slave died or became seriously ill or beaten beyond usefulness, he was merely thrown overboard. If a storm caused a slave ship to founder, the manacled drowned. It was inconvenient, but there were many more where they came from, and the profits so great, the loss of a ship of little consequence.

"The bottom line thinking that went in to the planning of Titanic II, though differing in purpose, is not dissimilar to that which accompanied the slave trade--both consider the passenger expendable in the name of profit. The major difference is that the passengers on Titanic II are the captains of industry, the cream of society; graduates from the hallowed halls of Harvard and Yale, Oxford and Cambridge, financiers from the sheer canyons of Wall Street, internationally known artists--not primitive slaves from tribes of jungle Africa! The Titanic II passengers will receive more cordial treatment, but the result is the same--if you are lucky, you won't die.

"Has respect for human life and the Judeo-Christian ethic diminished to such a point? If so, stand by as the rush to profit sacrifices many more millions in war, even more perilous, unsafe operations and other conspired actions. God will seldom be consulted, as material gain drives all matters on earth. I suppose that kind of thinking will always prevail."

With that, Reggie sat down to await the blast. He did not have to wait long. Speaking for all the shocked board members, Ismay bellowed,"Alex, do you really expect us to sit here calmly and be castigated for the prudent exercise of management responsibility. This man of color chooses to compare us to the slave traders. I am insulted, and astonished at his nerve.

"Your people have not only challenged our decision on lifeboats and maligned our #1 Captain, you now go to the extent of challenging our moral values. Frankly, Alex, I'm surprised you allow thinking like this among your close employees."

"Bruce, I think what we're hearing is a reaction to, what seems to be, your callousness in considering your passengers as expendable. I believe we have reached an impasse here, and that further discussion will be useless. Randy, you and Matt and Reggie hand out the background package. Gentlemen, you all can review it at your leisure, if you are so inclined. We can meet again after a short time, go over the changes again, or provide you more information if you need it, after the Christmas hiatus. Please consider that our ship design recommendations are rapidly approaching their place on the construction schedule. If anything is to be changed, it must be done rather quickly."

"Alex, at this point, I don't think I can be receptive to any changes that increase costs or add weight. After all, we do have the benefit of this ship being declared 'unsinkable'. I'm not one for looking a gift horse in the mouth, or 'fixin" somethin" what ain't broke,' to quote from a plantation adage with which you boys doubtless are familiar. This meeting is hereby adjourned."

Their return to Carlisle's office with heads bowed communicated the results to Boyle and the others.

"Kinda rough, boss?" asked Boyle.

"And then some, Adam. The whole program went down the drain.

Reggie, I admire your spunk, and your analogy was crushing, but these people aren't used to being criticized or taken to task for an omission or faulted commission. I wouldn't be surprised to have Ismay in here looking for your black hide first thing in the morning."

"Mr. Carlisle, I appreciate the support you gave me--letting me sit in at all--but also supporting my comments," Reggie responded.

"Reggie, I am very pleased with the way things turned out. We have a significant period to work on them before she is launched."

"You were really up against it in there, Mr. C., and I, too, appreciate you taking the lumps for us." said Matt. "They apparently just don't want to accept anything."

"I'm pleased to see that you are still in there fighting, but it looks like we've hit the stops on this one. If what you say about Titanic II actually occurs, White Star will have significant problems," opined Carlisle.

"Somehow, Mr. Carlisle, Matt and I, and now Reggie, will do all we can to render her as safe as possible within the allowed budget. It is still more than a year until her launching. Some good should come from it. Time to fall back and regroup, as they say," Randy concluded.

"I don't know how you do it, Randy, and I actually don't want to know.

The identification of what's past, what's present and what's future has become so confused in my mind that I'd rather not be involved. Of course, it doesn't bother Bruce--his feet were planted firmly in mid-air today! He'll deal with the future when it gets here. That might not be so bad. He stays focused, if less flexible, gets things done on schedule, if not ahead, and sleeps better without nocturnal juggling to keep all those balls in the air. Successful managers don't all succeed the same way. You may not like certain of their tactics, or them personally, but you have to stand proud for having participated in their achievements."

"While we still have our momentum going, if somewhat slowed, I'd like to do as Randy has suggested--fall back and re-group. We have the whole holiday period to do our own cogitating, but a few ideas exchanged between us tomorrow may help to keep us all headed in the same direction.

"Can you all make it tomorrow morning? I know you've had little time for shopping, but a few early hours should shake some time loose for it"

With that, they disbanded and headed for home, carrying with them the positive attitude Carlisle had demonstrated.

Chapter 16

Having had time to think about the Board meeting, Bruce Ismay came to see Alex Carlisle early the next morning to discuss what had transpired. He was in a considerably less defensive frame of mind, but still seriously questioning what Randy and Matt had introduced.

"Good morning, Alex. Do you have a minute to go over what went on Monday afternoon?"

"Certainly, Bruce. Have a seat. I'm winding down toward Christmas, so there's plenty of time for kicking the problem around."

"First, I want you to know how much I appreciate what you and the boys have gone through in the interest of safety. Please pass that along to them. That young fellow, Reggie, got to me a bit, but I can understand where he's coming from. He feels the need to stand up for anyone he believes is being maligned or demeaned. That would seem natural to anyone in a minority position. My angry reaction was to the combination of things for which the Board and I were being taken to task. Although young people may have some new slants on things, they have not reached that level of wisdom which permits this kind of criticism. Am I off base thinking that, Alex?"

"No, Bruce, I can understand where you were. I'm sure you felt the need to defend your management capability. The only concern I have is that we may be overlooking a few very serious deficiencies in our ship's integrity which could result in the scenario described. It's all a matter of how much faith you put in these two fellows......

"Certainly, if after having the media announcing her 'unsinkability' to the world, a minor collision with an iceberg sends her to the bottom, White Star will be hard pressed either to make amends or recover from the adverse publicity that would obviously result -- particularly with the internationally known people who will be aboard."

"Then you are accepting what they say as truth? I have difficulty with that. But, maybe lack of faith is a big factor in all aspects of our lives. I seldom bring in to deliberations the help of anyone I can't see, talk to, or have confidence in."

"One can always change, Bruce." Said Alex, in a firm, soft voice.

"Thank you for taking the time both for the presentation and for your thoughts here and now, Alex. Have a Merry Christmas."

"You too, Bruce," replied Carlisle.

"Oh, incidentally, would you have Randy and Matt develop a training outline for lifeboat handling and collision avoidance, based on the recommendations of "Knight's Modern Seamanship," Not just for Titanic II, but for all our ships. We should be able to do that without too much additional expense."

"I'll get them on it right after Christmas, Bruce."

. Making up for lost time, Randy and Matt wandered through the shops of old Belfast, intrigued with the many handmade gifts to be had....and very reasonable. They could afford some excellent items for a mere pittance.

"I hope you're not going all out for Sarah, because I'm going to be there with just a few meaningful gifts. I'm sure we'll find what we're looking for in these shops," said Matt.

"I'm really looking for a good painting and some jewelry. I'll know it when I see it."

Christmas day arrived. Randy and Matt had exchanged gifts with each other and with Reggie and Olivia on Christmas Eve, so as to clear the day for dinner at the Carlisles'. Sarah and Emily had left gifts for Reggie and Olivia at the boys' apartment, and had received what had been left for them.

Due to Sarah's ultimatum, Randy was not to be in touch with her until Christmas dinner. For this reason, Matt suggested to Emily that they wait until then to share Christmas. Now Randy and Matt were both wrestling with wrapping paper and ribbon, fighting the clock.

"How did people back in these days live without rolled wrapping paper, scotch tape and tags?" Matt wondered.

"Guess they found it necessary to be creative, without having everything done for them like we have," Randy responded.

"We'd best get it together, Randy, or we'll miss the dinner of the year."

When the foursome arrived at Carlisles', Sarah greeted them at the door, and announced that Mrs. Summergill had come down with influenza and, so as not to spread it, the family had decided to remain at home.

"Come in and warm yourselves by the fire. You look like you can use it, advised Sarah. "Matt, would you help my father make some punch while I talk to Randy for a moment? Thanks. Randy, please come into the sun room for a minute."

"I didn't even say hello to your parents, or the other people here. This must be pretty important," observed Randy.

"It is, Randy, it most certainly is! Before we go into meet everyone, I wanted to make sure we were not putting on an act to impress everyone as to how in love we are with each other. We may very well be, but you know what I said about your answer today."

"Yes, I do, and the first thing I want to tell you is that I love you more every day, and I have sweated out these past days thinking how I may lose you today."

"Randy, I want to become your wife, spend the rest of my life with you, but we have to come to some understanding of what it is that's holding you back. I really love you, and I don't want to lose you, either."

"Sarah, I promise I will tell you all about it, but I don't think this is the place or the time. We can get together tomorrow, maybe go for a buggy ride, and I will tell you everything. You won't believe me, but I'll try to convince you to the best of my ability. Can you agree to that?"

"I had hoped to have the engagement taken care of today--that's not going to come about. Now you want to postpone our discussion until tomorrow. Well, maybe one leads to the other, and this is the way it's supposed to be. All right, Randy, the ultimatum deadline is hereby extended for one more agonizing 24-hour period. Now, before we go back in there, kiss me!"

"Merry Christmas, my love," whispered Randy, all too willing to abide.

The Carlisles greeted Randy as he returned to the reception room with Sarah. "Merry Christmas, Randy." said Carlisle. "I'm glad you could make it around that detour. Is everything in good repair?"

"Well, I wasn't too sure there for a moment, but the rough hath been made smooth, and your daughter has not jettisoned me--as yet!"

"The rest of your entourage have made themselves comfortable with a drink. What can I get you? We have egg nog or punch, or if you care to be frisky, a touch of wassail."

"Punch will be fine, sir And a Merry Christmas to you all," Randy said.

They all sat in the reception room, where a huge Christmas tree dominated the scene. Many candles were burning on the branches. Matt wondered how they could burn so freely without setting the tree afire. With the roaring fire in the hearth and the lighted tree the true spirit of Christmas prevailed. Barriers of time had been breached as love touched friends from different dimensions.

After a period in which silence echoed everyone's warm feelings, dinner was announced. They entered the dining room to the aroma of cooked goose, biscuits and fresh vegetables. Carlisle asked that they all hold hands and pray for blessing of the food, themselves and the project that involved them all--Titanic II.

Animated conversation and laughter filled the room.. The dinner, cooked to perfection, was more than they had anticipated. After dessert, they retired to the reception room where the many gifts lay under the tree. Carlisle himself passed out the gifts. As each opened his or her gifts, the others "ooh'd" and "ahh'd". The gift that created the most reaction was a porcelain doll in a Victorian outfit of green velour, lightly trimmed in gold, which Randy gave to Sarah.

When the gift sharing was done, Sarah announced that she had planned to have her father break her engagement to John Summergill. Since they were unable to attend the dinner, it would have to be done some other time. Even Emily was caught by surprise with this announcement. She hadn't been aware that Sarah had committed herself to anyone. "Where does Randy fit into this scheme of things?" she wondered to herself.

"It's been a wonderful Christmas," said Mrs. Carlisle, "now all we need to make it perfect is to sing some Christmas carols. Sarah, why don't you set yourself at the piano and warm us up with 'Tannenbaum'."

"I'll do so on one condition....that Matt teach us all 'Jingle Bells'."

"Oh, no!" moaned Emily, "that tune filled my dreams for days after the last time Matt sang it for us....and sang it for us....and sang it for us."

"Maybe my mother and father would like to learn it, Emily."

"Emily, if you'll join me, I'll sing it once, then you can all join in for another round," said Matt

"Sounds like you've been overruled, Emily," Mrs. Carlisle said, laughing.

Sarah then played "Tannenbaum" with great feeling. and everyone joined in. "Jingle Bells" followed along with several carols that had survived from one century to the next, and which everyone knew.

Randy, Matt and Emily left thanking the Carlisles for everything. After a discreet hug, Randy assured Sarah he would pick her up after work on Monday.

When the boys came to work on Monday, they were asked to come to Carlisle's office. Randy joined Reggie, who was already seated at Ms. Collins' desk. Matt went through his usual routine---giving Emily a kiss on the cheek.

She pulled away just enough and said, "Not here, Honey."

"Oh, I forgot!" He snapped his finger. "I'll try to remember next time, young lady."

"Matt!" she whispered loudly.

"What, Honey?"

"The office is beginning to talk about us."

"That's great!" Matt caught himself talking too loudly.

"Please help me adjust to this, O.K.?"

"I know, I feel the same way. I really do. We'll talk about it tonight."

She nodded and smiled. That made Matt's day. He squeezed her hand gently and walked briskly to their office, where he knew Randy would be waiting with a few words designed to poke fun at him.

"Every day, the same old stuff," Randy said with a smile, as Matt came in. "Mr. Carlisle said he would talk to you as soon as you all arrived. Why don't you go right on in," Ms. Collins suggested.

"Good morning, here's the unholy trio reporting in. Would you have words with us?" jested Matt.

"Yes, Mr. Miller, I certainly would. I met with Bruce Ismay earlier today. He was in a much better mood. He was not, as I had suggested, looking for your black hide, Reggie. As a matter of fact, he said to pass along his appreciation to the three of you for the excellent work you had done. He all but apologized for his anger, stating that he understood your young, strong desire to have the recommendations accepted.

"There was nothing in his conversation suggesting they would reverse their decision on the design changes or the additional lifeboats. He did, however, ask that you take it upon yourselves to develop training manuals for lowering lifeboats both for crewmen and passengers, and collision avoidance for bridge personnel. These to be in accordance with 'Knight's Modern Seamanship.' The manuals will be used by White Star's entire fleet. He also asked that you develop an outline for keeping the coal cool, designing a fail-proof system to install in all our ships, if necessary.

"Sounds like he has more confidence in our operational knowledge than he does in our business acumen. Mr. Carlisle, we said we'll do anything that will help improve the safety factor on Titanic II. This is certainly an effort in that direction," said Randy. Then, turning to Matt and Reggie, he asked, "How do you two feel about that?"

"Well, Randy, knowing what's going to happen, it seems a futile effort, but it may provide for further justification of our lifeboat objectives. And our training manual for the bridge just might contribute to a successful evasion of the iceberg. That would make our whole trip worthwhile," Matt observed.

"What's your opinion, Reggie?" Randy asked.

"I don't know, fellas, it seems like we're being pushed aside into a project that will keep us out of Mr. Ismay's way. It's like he's offering us a reason to keep working, but has no intention of making changes to either the ship or the lifeboat situation. I'll work with you on it, of course, because it's better than the gopher work, but I anticipate little impact on the White

Star Line emanating from our efforts."

"You may be right, Reggie," intervened Carlisle, "but it is associated with the problems we are working on, so I suggest we become very involved. I'll stay close to you, and will be here to set up meetings with Mr. Ismay as you need them. Incidentally, I don't think I can justify having all three of you on the project full time. Reggie, perhaps you can fill in at both posts, working as a 'gopher,' as you put it, and with Matt and Randy as needed. Do you all have any problem with that?"

"That's pretty much the way we've been working," said Matt.

"I suggest you begin with the manual for the bridge personnel. I have a friend at the Naval office in London who has developed a five week crash course on Lifeboat Utilization. Perhaps he can arrange for instructors to meet with us on site, so that all bridge personnel can be trained here. I'm fairly certain they provide instructional materials along with the course. That should save us a lot of time.

"My friend has told me that there have been significant changes to the regulations. They require 12 oarsmen, a commander and assistant in each boat. The Captain would subject all passengers and crew to a pre-departure safety drill in which they actually board the boats. "

"Sounds like someone else is doing some thinking on this subject. Praise God, the whole world needs it," commented Matt.

"Remember, now, I'm here for you anytime. Just let Ms. Collins know you wish to see me. Good luck, chaps," concluded Carlisle.

Chapter 17

Monday evening arrived and Randy with it. Sarah had been in a moderate funk since Randy had left on Christmas day and had been anxiously awaiting his arrival. This might be the most important day of her life. She knew she would be faced with a momentous decision, and was terrified that the choice might be one she couldn't live with. Randy also knew that what he said and how Sarah accepted it would determine how, or if, their love would continue or endure.

They took the horse and carriage and drove to their favorite park overlooking the harbor.

"I knew that sooner or later we would have to discuss where we are, where we are going, and maybe even who we are," stated Sarah. "There's been a mystery about you that is unfathomable. You heard even my mother mention that she detected something unresolved in you. I've mentioned it several times, as I saw you draw away from me every time I alluded to anything beyond tomorrow. Somehow this has to be resolved! I just hope its resolution is not going to break my heart."

"Maybe yes, maybe no. I guess it will depend on how much you really love me," he said expectantly. The atmosphere suddenly became quite different They were dead serious. She also noticed that he had become subdued and distant. She began to wonder if he was going to break it off. That, she could not possibly live with. On the other hand, if he asked her to marry him, how would she respond? The reality of the latter scared her because, if he did, what on earth would she say? "How absurd," she thought. "What else could I say, but 'yes -- forever'."

Seeing a bench they had sat on several times before, they walked to it and, before sitting down, fell into each other's arms as a testimony to their love and to temper the intense emotion they both felt.

As they sat down, Randy said determinedly, "I've got to get this off my chest!"

Sarah pulled back the loose hair from her eyes and held his hand as he began to explain. "I know telling you this will make me feel better, but I'm not sure about how you will receive it," said Randy.

"Try me, Randy," Sarah said somewhat impatiently. She was so beautiful in the lamplight. Her trusting eyes were fixed on his, waiting for one of life's most precious moments to unfold.

"First of all, my intentions have always been honorable. I like you very much....no, I mean, I love you very much. I wouldn't trade anything for the wonderful times we've had."

At this point, Sarah knew she was right; he was about to propose.

"Anyway," he continued, "If it had been under any other circumstances, you would have already been my wife." He looked down, took a deep breath and went on, "I just don't know how to tell you." He was so drained. He began to struggle for the right words.

Sarah slowly began to withdraw and softly asked, "What are you trying to say?"

Except for the increasing night sounds, all else was silent. After a few moments of deep thought, he went on with his agonizing chronicle.

"Sarah, honey, Matt and I belong to another time." She nodded, unsure of what Randy actually meant, and waiting to hear more.

"It's now 1910, right?" She nodded again. "We live in 2010!"

Her lips moved, but no sound was uttered as she mouthed "2010? You're being humorous, aren't you?" she finally said with a smirk Then, in desperation as she searched his eyes, "No!....you are not being humorous....you're serious! You're not teasing me, are you, Randy. I love you too much." She put her hand on his arm. "If for some strange reason, you believe you do live in 2010, we will work it out. We all have emotional problems at times....we get hung up on things for no explainable reason. You've been working so hard." She waved her hands across each other several times in gestures of frustration, then touched her finger tips to her forehead.

"I don't know why....I just don't believe you!" she said sharply. "This kind of thing is impossible. I don't understand why you would even want me to believe it!"

He was not surprised at her reaction. He knew she wouldn't grasp the significance of the problem, even before he began.

"We came because of the Titanic. She sank on her first voyage on April 15, 1912. That's sixteen months from now. We loved her so much that we came to change as many things as we could to prevent the disaster....the second time. I mean the first time. It is confusing even to me, Sarah."

"My word, it's getting worse!" she shouted, looking around to see if anyone was listening. "Now you're telling me you know the future! The gossip around the ship was right, then. Where is it all going to end?"

"Sarah, this is not a plot to make it possible for me to slip out of your life....it's the truth!.... If you would just think it through, instead of getting mad...."

"I am not mad! You're the one who's mad," she interrupted. Randy chuckled and squeezed her hand, "I didn't mean mad, as in crazy; I meant mad, as in angry." Almost hysterical, she stamped her feet and, sounding exhausted, said, "What am I going to do?"

"Honey," he grinned lovingly, "Everything I've told you is exactly the way I said. Remember when I told you about some changes that would be ordered by Ismay after he took a trip on the Olympic? When I told you what they would be, you thought they were just lucky guesses. Well, they are history where I come from."

"If what you say is true....I mean, assuming you are telling the truth....oh, Randy," she started to cry. "What happens to us?" She was getting more upset. "For heaven's sake, you knew this all the time! You led me on!" She struck him in the chest with both hands and bowed her head.

"Sarah, please! How did I know you would become the most important thing in my life?"

"I knew! Why didn't you know?" she interrupted. "You say you love me, and then you play games with our lives! How could you do this to me?" She arose from the bench and started to leave. Randy grabbed her by the hand. "No, Sarah, don't! Please let me explain."

"I don't want to hear it!" She was still crying. "You manipulate my emotions, then you make me fall in love with you. Now you are going to fly away somewhere else in time....I can't stand it!. I wish I could just disappear."

Randy had had enough. "Hey, no more....sit down!" He was glaring at her. She obeyed because she had never seen this side of him before. He became a dominant male, with fire in his eyes. She knew that whatever he said, he meant. Her respect for him made her receptive at that point. He held her hand firmly and spoke with conviction,

"You cannot go on thinking of just yourself in this. If we love each other, then we are both in love and, if something comes down, it hurts both of us. If you love me as much as you say you do, then help me to solve our dilemma." There was a moment of silence as she tried to sort things out. Her voice was trembling as she said,

"What you say to be true is so inconceivable to me, that I can't even respond to it. It contradicts what I've known and learned all my life. Never have spacemen been seen or heard from in this or any other century. How can I possibly accept that?"

"We are not spacemen. We are time-travelers!"

"'Spacemen,' 'time-travelers'....What difference does it make? We exist in different worlds."

"Sarah my love, the concept on which we based our travels from 2010 to 1910 is that everything exists in an eternal NOW. Time is like an illusion, but we are separated by that illusion. Taking advantage of the work of an eminent scientist, Matt and I are the first ever to break through to another dimension of time, existing parallel to our own. We were motivated by the terrible disaster that befell Titanic, and, even more so, by your haunting call to be saved That is why we have worked so hard to convince everyone that our recommended changes are essential to keep Titanic from sinking."

"Somehow I can't believe it is true, but because you say it is, I must accept it as part of you. But what happens when your work is done here? Do you just bow out of my life and return home? Is this to be chalked up as just another romantic interlude in your life, something impossible to take seriously? Oh, Randy!" She was almost ready to cry again.

"Sarah, that is a question that only you can provide the answer for."

"Well, Randy, one thing is for sure; I won't be able to make any decisions without a lot more thought and meditation, and a firm faith in what you have told me. To do that, I believe we should not see each other for the next several months."

"But, Sarah, do we have to take such drastic measures? Maybe we should try to work together to solve our problem."

"No, Randy! I love you too much to think clearly while I'm with you. I'm going to have to go it alone." Standing up once again, Sarah headed for the carriage feeling almost in a stupor from the things she'd been hearing.

They rode from the park in silence. At the point closest to the apartment, Randy slowly stepped from the carriage and, holding Sarah's hand, squeezed it gently. With bowed head, he turned and walked away. Sarah watched after him for a few moments, until the horse became impatient. Was she watching Randy walk out of her life, forever? What other choice was there?

Sarah had a hard time sleeping that night. She tossed and turned until it was late. It didn't really help to sit on the edge of the bed in the dark. The window in her room was open about a palm's width and the night sounds were growing more intense as Sarah thought through the events of the day. What could be happening with this young man from – who knows where?

"Who are you, Randall Kaplan?" she cried out in the shadows in a loud voice that frightened her for a moment. "Where is he from? What is his intent? Why did he involve me in this madness? Am I angry with him, or am I pleased? I think I'm going to go insane!"

There was a soft knocking at her door. She hesitated. The knocking continued. Moving slowly toward the door, she whispered, "Who is it?"

"It's Hanna, let me in." She whispered.

"Go back to bed, Sis'. It's after midnight," came the nervous reply.

"No! I want to know who you're talking to, Sarah. I heard voices."

"I was talking to myself. Now please go back to bed!" Sarah was becoming impatient with her fourteen-year-old sister.

"But, all I want is to find out what's bothering you. Isn't that what sisters are for?" Hanna had a way of wheedling her way into Sarah's confidence, but she was usually able to provide an outlet for her. And Sarah appeared to need one, desperately. As quietly as possible, Sarah turned the knob, opened the door, and let Hanna in.

"Hanna, sit down in that chair and be still!" Sarah closed the door quietly, then returned to her bed and sat down with her legs crossed in a half-lotus position. She spent a few moments getting her thoughts together, then began explaining her problem.

After revealing only the facts she felt pertinent, Sarah stopped as abruptly as she had begun. Hanna was the first to move. She squirmed about in the big chair, then spoke slowly with mature concern Sarah had not previously seen or heard before from her sister.

"What an awful situation!" Sarah sensed she may have discovered someone she could talk to when it was needed.

"I've never seen you like this before, Sarah. You really are upset, aren't you?"

"Yes, I am."

"But....I thought you could do anything....solve any problem, handle any crisis." Hanna was growing emotional, "What are you going to do?"

"I don't know, Hanna. I've suggested to Randy that we not see each other for the next few months, so we both could get things straight in our mind."

"What about Daddy and Mommy....what about me? If time travel is true and you go back to wherever....with him? "What about me?"

"Hanna Marie, please, will you relax and calm down?" Let's discuss this as two grownup young women. Remember, you pushed your way into my room and had to find out what was going on. Well, now you know." Sarah paused to let that last statement sink in.

"Now, are you a child or a young lady?" Her words brought about an immediate change. Hanna sat up straight, made motions indicating she was getting control of herself, and said firmly, "I am a woman."

"Fine; then you must understand. When a woman finds her man, God said she would leave her parents and cleave to him. What that means is...."

Hanna broke in, "I know what that means, but....what about her baby sister?"

"You are not my 'baby' sister. You are a woman. We are sisters, and that means we will do whatever is necessary to help each other." She put her arms around Hanna and whispered in her ear, "I will always love you no matter where I am."

"I know, I know," Hanna said reluctantly.

"Can you go back to bed now?"

"Yes, I suppose....at least I think so. Sarah, promise you will always pray for me."

"As you wish." They hugged once more, Hanna slipped through the dark doorway, turned and whispered, "Good night."

Sarah closed the door and returned to her bed. She sat for a few precious moments, then asked in a plaintive, childlike voice,

"What about me?"

Chapter 18

The next morning, as Matt and Randy were getting ready to go to work, Matt asked,

"Well, Bud, how did it go last night?"

"Not too smoothly," he replied, "I told her why we are here."

"Wow, I'll bet that went over like a herd of wild robots." He was a little surprised that Randy would tell her. "Do you think it was wise?"

"I had to," he responded with a far-away look.

"I understand," Matt said.

During the conversation, they were getting dressed for work. To keep his mind on what he was saying while he dressed, was more than Matt could handle. Randy could not believe his eyes. Matt had his trousers, shoes, socks and coat on, but no shirt.

"What color tie were you planning to wear today?" Going along with the fun. Matt said, "Probably chest hair. I can't believe I did that. I need a rest.," he groaned.

"Yeah, sure," said Randy, still thinking he had done it on purpose.

Checking himself out in the mirror, Randy headed out the door, saying, "Hurry up, Matt, or we'll be late."

That was the day that great strides were made in putting on paper what was needed to maneuver Titanic II out of the path of the iceberg. It had begun one evening when the trio assembled at the flat to develop an outline for the Collision Avoidance Manual.

The first part of the outline would necessarily describe and define the mechanical and technical properties of the ship. Some old but modified systems were in use, and other new ones had been added to the plans.

This section would deal first with the engines, then with the rudder. The propellers were described by a shipyard observer as being the size of windmills, the rudder as tall as an elm tree. Titanic II had three engines capable of moving the 46,000 ton vessel with over 50,000 horses at a speed of 21.5 knots or greater. Most of the amenities aboard were also run by this plant.

The power plant was arranged in 16 watertight compartments, divided by 15 transverse bulkheads. Titanic II had two 4-cylinder reciprocating engines that ran the two wing propellers with a maximum rpm of 60. Two cylinders from each of these exhausted into a low-pressure turbine engine that ran the center propeller, positioned directly forward of the rudder. The turbine engine was not reversible, It had a maximum rpm of 77. In addition to contributing to the ship's propulsion, it also provided a slipstream for greater rudder control and turning efficiency.

Knight's described the Captain's choice of maneuver as the most likely to cause a collision. When the engines were ordered. full astern, the center engine was stopped completely. The ship slowed to a point where the rudder was rendered almost useless, but the ship's forward movement was still enough to bring about the collision.

When the iceberg was recognized, Murdoch's order to reverse the port engine while maintaining continued forward motion of the Starboard engine, combined with his "Hard 'a starboard" order to the helmsman, would have brought the bow around more smartly to port, slowing the ship down considerably less and, most likely, completely clearing the path of the iceberg.

At that time, procedures called for the helmsman to use the stern as the ship's direction rather than the bow. This would mean that with the call, "hard 'a starboard," the helmsman would turn the stern to starboard (right) by turning the wheel counter-clockwise. The ship's bow would then move to port. (left). The diagrams subsequently submitted to investigators showed the iceberg to have been about five degrees off the starboard bow. Coming left was correct, but stopping the engines at the same time was disastrous.

Knight's recommended that, under these circumstances, the port engine be reversed while the starboard engine remain at full ahead. This would maximize the steering capability of the engines, the rudder and the center engine's slipstream. A rapid turn would move the ship out of the berg's path, preventing any damage. Of course, paying attention to the Californian's ice field warnings, or reducing the underway speed, would probably have precluded the need for any evasive maneuvering.

The third project, to come up with a technique or equipment to keep the coal cool, was tailor-made for Matt. He had an ability to design new concepts and equipment that was well known to Randy. Perhaps Ismay was keeping them out of the main stream, but their original objective--to save

Titanic--could be well-served by these projects.

Meeting frequently at home, and working either together or on separate projects, the trio was making significant progress on the two projects. Matt was secluded in a makeshift laboratory working on a 'cool coal' system. If he were successful, such an item would sell itself to the shipping industry. Randy had no doubt that Matt would develop a practical, inexpensive way to mist the coal with water on a scheduled basis.

For the next several months, time seemed to drag on. Matt had a tiff with Emily, and Sarah was carrying out her intention to solve their problem without involving herself in her love for Randy. Although she wasn't making much headway, she was still maintaining a tough front.

These conditions provided much time for their projects, but things were very quiet. One evening, Matt had arranged to meet with Emily to try to patch up whatever was bugging her.

Randy decided to go out for a walk, get some exercise and straighten out his priorities. It was a bit chilly, quite like the weather in New York where he'd been brought up. Thoughts were racing through his mind, all mixed up, nothing clear. What he was thinking was impossible, and he knew it. How could he ever explain it to Matt:? The heavy weight he felt crushing his chest was more than he could bear. This was a totally new emotion he was experiencing. There had always been girls in his life, but not one like this, and certainly none who generated such feelings.

"I can't believe I'm actually giving it consideration," he thought. "Stay here? I must be losing my mind!"

He walked down one street and up the other. It was about eight o'clock. Children were still playing outside. He watched some boys play a game he hadn't seen before. They were hitting a small rubber ball with a small stick and running to just one base.

Children always seemed to become very involved with what they were doing, particularly their play. They played with abandon and without care. "Why is it that adults can't do the same?" he wondered.

His mind began to race again. How could he even let such a thought cross his mind? He couldn't just write off his parents, or, less importantly, the many conveniences of the 21st century. And, how old would he be, or his parents be, assuming they were all still alive, when he arrived at 2010? But that would be impossible, and, as Professor DeVane said, his parents would have moved along beyond 2010, always 100 years apart from Randy. He continued to walk, lost in his thoughts, trying to figure out what to do about Sarah. Should he try to take her back? No, that would be unfair to both Sarah and her parents.

Randy realized the sun had gone down and found himself on a rather dark street, so he hurried along. The gloom of the night surrounded him like a cloak. Suddenly, a man stepped from the shadows and demanded, "Life, limb or your lovin' gold, Mate!" He might just as well have said, "Trick or treat!" because it so startled Randy, he began to unravel his tale of woe.

"My girlfriend is mad at me, my best buddy borrowed all my money, I'm out walking tonight contemplating suicide, and you want to take my life! Go ahead and shoot me!" He threw his arms up in total surrender.

"Sorry I bothered ya, guvna," came the robber's reply. As quickly as he had appeared, so did the night seem to swallow him. Randy was frozen in his steps, his heart pounding like a bass drum. Without moving his head, he looked around for any sign of the man. Fairly certain he had moved on to a more rewarding victim, Randy walked quickly to the nearest streetlight Here he stood, catching his breath and waiting for his heart to slow down, so he could walk to the flat.

Matt was already home and not in a very good mood.

"You're home early. What happened?" Randy inquired. Did you run out of money or something? I know -- you had another spat with Emily. Right?"

"Spat? You should have been there!" Matt said as he went to brush his teeth.

"That's the truth. I should have been there," Randy murmured. Then, in a louder voice, "What did she say?"

"She wants to get married!" Matt sputtered through his toothbrush.

"What did you say to that?"

"I said, 'I can't. No way'!"

"That's a fact," Randy said, taking off his boots. "Boy, you should have seen what happened to me tonight."

"Right on! I told her I didn't know where I'd be tomorrow!"

"I was walking down the street near O'Malley's pharmacy, and a robber jumped out at me, demanding cash."

"She said she didn't care where I went! She wants to leave town with me," Matt said through the foam.

"I just stood my ground and told him to go ahead and shoot! I mean to tell you, I was scared out of my tree!"

Matt came walking back into the parlor saying, "Do you suppose we could work it out to take the girls back with us?" Matt, was having a tough time with the laser and the cool coal project, as well as with Emily. Randy's confidence in his ability to produce operable prototypes for both projects had never diminished. What he was to do about Emily, no one really knew , but what transpired with Randy and Sarah was likely to affect the Matt/Emily outcome.

Randy had no idea how that question got into their conversation, but he did know that the answer was simple...."Have you lost your mind?"

"Why do you always answer my question with another question, Randy?"

"Why not?"

"I guess that answers my question," Matt said. He sat on the bed for a few minutes trying to make some sense out of the little talk he had just had with his best friend.

"Good night, Matt."

"Good night, Randy. Maybe in our next conversation both of us can be speaking on the same subject. Tomorrow, let's go through this one again. I think I missed something."

The hundreds of men working on Titanic II could take immense pride in building the world's largest moving object. Though each had his assigned tasks, his efforts joined with those of all other workers in meeting the specs outlined in the ship's plans.

One of the workers laboring that day around the stern area was

Reggie. He was asked to bring a very large, bulky box to the other side of the ship. Walking toward the stern, he was unable to see in front of him. Someone had placed a few small hull plates in front of a section of railing which had not been completely secured. It was intended that these plates would keep anyone from leaning or falling against the railing.

The box Reggie was carrying prevented him from seeing directly in front of him. He was walking very cautiously. As he approached the fantail, Randy and Matt saw him from where they were working on 'E' deck. Realizing he was approaching a dangerous area, they avoided any greeting and watched to see that he was not imperiled.

Suddenly, they saw Reggie trip over one of the plates. The box he was carrying flew into the air as Reggie fell against the loose railing. He tried to catch himself. He missed. His body began its fatal descent, his piercing shriek echoing throughout the yard.

Randy and Matt watched in horror, stunned, as they witnessed their beloved friend plunge five stories before their eyes. The scream ended abruptly. The mind-shattering incident was over in less than four seconds.

Randy reached his side first and quickly bent over the twisted form. He slowly turned Reggie over and took him in his arms. Realizing their black friend was dead, he began to groan aloud.

Matt knelt down next to them. He watched Randy swaying back and forth, cradling Reggie to his chest. "No! No! No!" Randy moaned. "Please, God, help him. Don't let him be dead!"

"Randy, he's already gone," Matt said, attempting to console Randy.

"I know! I know, but why?" he said, sobbing. They were both crying. They tried to hold back the tears, but their sobs could be heard between blasts of the disaster whistle. The crowd that quickly gathered stood in silence, appalled at the drama before them. Many were just curious. Others were astounded at the display of emotion these two white men displayed over the death of this African laborer. It was obvious they loved him very much.

"Please say something, Reggie," Randy pleaded, still not willing to accept the truth. After a minute or so he sadly said, "He is dead, isn't he, Matt?"

He wiped away some of Reggie's blood with his hand.

"Yes, he's gone." Matt touched him on the shoulder. Their conversation was so stirring that some of the bystanders could not hold back their tears.

Later, men in white prepared the body for transporting. Randy asked the men who came down from the area where Reggie was walking, exactly what had happened. "We don't really know. It looked like he was unable to see past the box, and tripped on the plates we'd put there to avoid just this kind of problem.

Two older and wiser men with aching hearts walked away from the scene. Another test was endured today; another memory stored away in their minds that they would never forget.

The day after Reggie's funeral, there was a drizzling rain from early morning until late evening. It seemed that even the elements mourned his passing. The overcast skies and faint sounds of thunder, made the afternoon in the cemetery very dismal. Yet, Olivia came quietly and undetected. She was dressed in black, like the day before at the funeral. Even her cape and umbrella were black, a silent protest against death. She fell slowly to her knees before the marker, then placed a white rose atop the newly formed mound.

The constantly falling rain had already eroded small crevices in the mud. The stark realization of her man's permanent absence from this life caused her to weep uncontrollably. It was an eerie sound -- half cry and half moan -- typically heard under such circumstances.

A small dog, trotting across the east corner of the peaceful cemetery, heard the sounds. He stopped, changed direction, and stood still. He stared at her, as if hypnotized. When the figure in black stood up, the frightened animal turned and bolted away.

Olivia wiped her eyes, blew her nose, then spoke in a tone just above a whisper. "Reggie." She moaned again, closing her red-rimmed eyes. She hoped against hope that she might see him, perhaps in her mind's eye. She felt faint and weakened by the intense emotion swelling up inside her. It was as if her chest would explode any minute. She managed to regain control and spoke again.

"Why did this have to happen? We had only ten months together. Oh, honey, I miss you so much. Where will I go? What will I do now? All the plans we had made...." She squeezed out the words, almost choking on the anger and pain she felt, and dropped back onto her knees. "God, don't you know how much I love Reggie?" She paused and glanced upward. "Forgive me, God, but I don't think I can go on. Please let me have him back."

Struggling with her composure, she bent over to kiss the rose with affection. She took a deep breath, closed her eyes and said lovingly, "Goodbye, Sweetheart." She stood up and walked up the path to the wrought iron gate leading to the street. She was still trying to suppress her tears.

Randy and Sarah were waiting for Olivia outside the cemetery wall. They respected her silence. She reached out to embrace them. Sarah clasped her fingers between Olivia's and whispered, "There, there, we're here now. It's going to be all right. You will have to cry it out. Please forgive me for rattling on so."

"I understand. What you say is true. Who, if not friends, can share each other's feelings?" She smiled at them both.

"Come on, Sarah," said Randy, "Let's take her home so she can relax without people around. I know that's what I would want."

Three friends walked together, sharing the burden of the tragedy that had befallen them. Everyone, at one time or other, is similarly burdened and pushed to the outer limits of his or her endurance.

As they made their way down the dimly lighted boulevard, an old man staggered by. "Have a sip of wine, kiddies," he drawled, holding out a near-empty bottle. "I got to get rid o' the rest, ya see, or me ole lady will kill me dead!" He stumbled and fell, rolled over and got back up. They could find little humor in the situation, but the old man giggled as he staggered off.

"That old duffer doesn't have a care in the world.," observed Randy.

"He will when he wakes up." Olivia shot back with a slight grin. "His wife."

"How true, how true," agreed Sarah.

Chapter 19

The days that passed began to ease the pain as the two young men buried themselves in their work to salve their feelings. "We've just got to forget about our loss of Reggie. There is nothing we can do about it. If we are able to prevent Titanic's accident, I'm sure Reggie will be credited with a significant contribution to it," Randy said.

Their work had been slowed by Reggie's death, but their spirits were buoyed by several unrelated events. First, The Collision Avoidance Manual was almost finished. Matt had drawn heavily upon Knight's Modern Seamanship, and had strongly emphasized that head-on collisions were less likely to sink a vessel than one in which the hull was torn below the waterline.

Second, Carlisle had carried out his promise to bring lifeboat training to the scene when the deck crew was hired. Manuals covering the course would be distributed to training personnel when they were printed, and made available to those completing the course.

Third, of considerable interest to the boys, was the arrival of David Banks, the man who provided the names for the monster ships. He was an understanding man. When it was explained to him why the 'II' had been added to Titanic's name, he was quick to comprehend the thinking behind it. Banks' support of the name would take a lot of pressure off the company.

. Fourth, the Olympic was just a few days from her maiden voyage. The word was that it would take place at the end of the month---May of 1911. Titanic II was coming along nicely, right on schedule as well The changes Ismay would initiate after Olympic's shakedown should not interfere with construction too seriously, nor delay their return to the 21st century.

Fifth, was the most encouraging to the boys. Somehow, perhaps through the strong influence of Lord Summergill and the lobbying of seamen's unions and other involved organizations, the ratio of lifeboats to total passenger/crew complement was changed by the Board of Trade. The change would apply to all ships operating under the British flag. This gave the boys hope that certain of their recommended changes may yet be adopted, despite Ismay's rejections.

The net effect for Titanic II would be to increase the required number of lifeboats from 16 to 26. While still not enough to take care of all personnel aboard, this was certainly a partial victory for the team.

"Let's count our blessings, Matt," said Randy. "Lord Summergill must have been involved. If so, there is no question he was influenced by our presentation. That means that our intervention will have saved 650 more people--double the number destined to survive the original disaster. Also we can estimate that proper manning and launching of the original 16 lifeboats could result in another 300 survivors. I thank God for letting us participate in this life-saving mission.

"It seems a strange decision, since this still leaves thirty four percent of the passengers and crew without a seat on Titanic II's lifeboats," observed Randy. "Politics is a matter of bargaining and compromise. Go for broke, but accept something less if the whole package is in peril. Hopefully, Lord Summergill went for the whole package, but lobbying by the industry may well have brought about the seeming compromise."

."It seems, Randy, that in each of our experiences, time is the essence of life itself." Matt said, staring into space. "What we do here and now affects all of eternity, and everyone."

"Matt, believe it or not, that was a profound statement."

"Serious?"

"Serious," Randy nodded.

"Well, the reason I bring it up," Matt explained "is that we have, in effect, extended the life span of over 900 people. Won't these survivors affect the lives of everyone they live with, work with, or just have contact with? If so, then on and on it goes 'til eternity with everything and everyone in their lives being changed in some way or other. Are we really going to change history by saving these people? I remember Captain Jim saying he didn't want to be anywhere near us when and if we did."

"I really believe we can do it. Those dark angels I keep seeing in my dreams persist in their discouragement of our efforts. Maybe it's all wrong to be doing this, but there are too many things impelling us to go on with it," Randy responded.

Olympic was scheduled for her maiden voyage from Southampton on Wednesday, April 19, 1911. To meet this goal, she would have to have her outfitting completed, and her shakedown cruise taken, at least one month prior. The shakedown was scheduled for Thursday, March 16th. This would be a very busy time for everyone on both ships, since Titanic II was to be launched on May 13th.

Great expectations and pride were developed among both the workers and residents of the Belfast area for their participation in the construction of White Star Line's three "monster" ships. Olympic was the first of these to be launched and, as the largest ship afloat in the world, she drew a large crowd at every major step in her construction. The shakedown cruise crowd was one of them.

Bruce Ismay, with Captain Smith at the helm, and several other executives from both White Star and Harland & Wolff were aboard to check all aspects of the ship's operation.

During the cruise, the starboard engine propeller cracked at a welded seam. The high-speed test apparently had been too much for the weld. Ismay brought the rest of the executives together to discuss the best way to handle this incident and not delay Olympic's maiden voyage date. They determined that it would be necessary to strip Titanic II of one of her props, since her needs were not as impending as Olympic's.

Other shortcomings that appeared during the cruise were not of major importance, and were put off until Olympic had returned from her maiden voyage. They would, of course, be added to the list of open projects on Titanic II, with some built-in delays possible. These delays would be less than the three weeks or more required for manufacture of a new prop.

Even Sarah had come out to see the show. Seeing Randy and Matt as they watched the departure, she approached them.

"Hello, Randy, hello, Matt. What a magnificent sight! I know it's not 'your' ship, but it certainly is a good facsimile, good enough to hold you 'til Titanic II slides down the ways and prepares for her maiden voyage.

Randy looked at her, his love for her emanating from his eyes. She was so beautiful. The loneliness of the past weeks came washing over him, and he melted in front of her.

Matt responded with a combination of awe and pride as tugboats nudged Olympic slowly away from her slip, where she had spent ten months being re-outfitted.

"Randy, would you have time to visit me tonight or during the next few evenings? I want to discuss our future, and the truth of your claim to be from some other time."

"Gathering his wits, he managed to say, "Have you changed your mind about what I told you?"

"No, not really. I'm still having trouble believing you. I wanted to give you another chance to change your story, so that we can face each other in truth and understanding."

Randy became disturbed over her continued disbelief. "Sarah, I've told you the truth, I'm not going to change it, and unless you change your attitude, there is no future for us, either in 1911 or 2011!"

"You are such a mule-head!"

"That may be, but I'm only available tonight if you assure me **you** won't be a 'mule-head'."

"I guess that makes sense... I won't be!" Sarah retorted.

"Am I watching a domestic quarrel here?" Matt interjected.

"Keep out of this, Matt!" Randy snapped. "Sarah, I'll be there about seven. This is too important to both of us to leave it the way it is."

Randy arrived at Sarah's at seven sharp. Her father answered the door. Randy was quite nervous until Carlisle said, "Well, young man, we are proud to have you visit us tonight. Make yourself at home, son. That's where you ought to be. 'Sparrow', your young man is here."

Randy couldn't help speculate on whether Sarah had told him. His ascending tone of acceptance seemed to suggest he was testing Randy and had not actually been told.

When Sarah entered the room, everything else faded. Once again, he had trouble breathing and stood without motion or speech in the presence of her loveliness. She saw it. Her father enjoyed the effect she had on Randy. It was time for a "three's-a-crowd" look. It wasn't actually necessary since Carlisle excused himself. "I'm sorry, but I must go. I have plenty of work to do, but I'll see you before you leave."

"Yes, sir," Randy was relieved to hear his footsteps resounding down the hall. Once again he turned to look at Sarah, hoping she would speak first.

"Daddy's a bear," reflected Sarah, trying to soften any harshness her father might have portrayed before she came in.

"That he is."

"Come, sit down," she said, pointing to a love seat. "We need to talk about some things."

"About what things?" He sat down beside her.

"You know....what we talked about today and before.

"Sarah, you asked me to come. You explain what you want."

"All right, I will!" She paused. "Because I love you, I trust you. So...., Randy Kaplan, I'm going to accept your tale about 2011."

"It's not a 'tale'!" He was stern.

"Honey, don't be so sensitive. I'm trying to believe you."

"Then why do you say it in such a condescending tone?"

"Oh, men! Why do you have to be so stubborn?" she asked, becoming increasingly perplexed with Randy. "Why can't you let your heart guide your words and deeds, as well as your mind? I had something to tell you, but now I'm frightened."

"Hey, go ahead....it's all right. I just need you to really believe me---I mean 100%."

"Sweetheart, please understand what I'm about to explain to you. Try to look at it from love's point of view. If you don't, I'll just die!"

"Not really. Come on, say it," he said impatiently.

"All right, Randy, here goes. I was so frantic after you told me about your time travel experience, I thought I would lose control of my senses. I had great difficulty telling myself it was true."

"You said you would accept it..."

"Please....let me finish," she interrupted, her anxiety increasing with every word. Randy nodded resignedly.

"I went to our Rabbi today. I was hoping to relieve some of the agony I was feeling, so I told him my problem."

"Did you tell him about me, and....?"

"Yes." she cut him off again. Randy, please listen and let me get this off my mind and heart."

"O.K., but it's starting to make me very nervous."

Ignoring Randy's last comment, she went on, "I explained how I felt. After all, he is a counselor." She paused. "I told him I was hopelessly in love with a very brilliant young man from another place. I don't know how long I talked. I mentioned how wonderful you are, and how you treat me. I told him that my feelings for you grow deeper each day. When you are near me, I want to get inside you, so your love will engulf me. I long to be swallowed up in your person. Wherever you go, I want to be there, not only in spirit, but body, soul and spirit."

Randy was completely enchanted. His eyes surveyed this gorgeous young woman. He had no idea she felt this way about him. No one had ever expressed these things to him before, either directly or indirectly. His thoughts and emotions were in conflict with one another. He was upset; warm in the glow of her love, but angry because she wouldn't believe him, excited over the prospects of a future together, but convinced of the impracticality of it. He was unable to think straight -- about their love, of the decision facing him regarding his return, of his not wanting to ever leave her. He was so confused, words refused to come.

She went on, "I revealed your secret. I tried to put it into words like you used that day you told me. I could tell he didn't believe me, until I assured him I planned to return with you. His look changed as soon as he realized I was serious. I confessed that I didn't want to live without you."

"Sarah!" Randy interrupted, worried about her compromise of the confidentiality of what he'd told her.

"Oh, I do love you so much. Please don't ever leave me."

"Oh boy, what a development. What did he advise?" he asked, trying to avoid further mixed emotions.

She smiled sweetly. "He told me to obey my heart, yet not ignore the price one must pay for such decisions." She was smiling and watching each change of his face. "I know our souls are intertwined. That will always be true. We cannot continue in this direction apart. No matter what era you enter, we must enter as one. Nothing will ever separate us in the present or the future. I am yours, forever!" Her eyes and cheeks were wet with tears --of joy and anxiety; of love and fear. Her whole world had stopped as she awaited Randy's reaction. Would they overcome the obstacles and resolve this unfathomable dilemma.

Randy knew the conversation was not going to change, so he leaned over and kissed her gently.

"Does that mean you still love me, Randy?" she asked innocently.

"I think so," was his tentative answer. He was surprised that the discussion took such a tortuous turn. He said, "I do love you dearly. But remember, I can't take you back with me." He wished he didn't have to say that -- actually, he wished he were somewhere else.

"Why not?" she asked in a shocked whisper as she backed away.

"Just because we can't take anything back---if we get back at all," he mumbled, staring at the floor.

"You mean, there's a possibility you won't be going back?"

"Well, yes, but....."

"Oh, Honey, don't you see? That would solve everything!" she interrupted. Then, for the first time that night, she became physically warm to him. She began to hug and touch her cheek to his.

"Sarah, please think in terms of my going back. O.K.? Staying here will not solve any problems." Now he was begging her to understand and she knew it. For her part, his dismissal of her expressed hope reflected his confusion and frustration. He seemed to be making light of her feelings and her efforts to convince him seemed to hit the same wall they had in past discussions. She couldn't determine whether this was due to his lesser love for her, or just the independent project-minded posture of a highly intelligent male. Whatever the cause, she was clearly very upset.

"But, Randy, if all you can think about is getting back to your 21st century, why did you come here in the first place? I know you've told me in general terms, but just what are you trying to accomplish with the big ships? It seems that as soon as you are finished, you will hurry back to 2011 or 2012, whenever it happens to be."

He took a moment to organize his thoughts, then tried to explain their mission more thoroughly.

"Our plans deal with only one ship, the Titanic. Matt and I were disappointed with the way she was treated the first time. It's the same old story....cutting corners to save money, and sending her out to sea unsafe. The ship herself was safer than most, but just the right combination of natural occurrences and human errors or oversights, brought her to an end."

"Wait, wait, just a minute! You're confusing me. You mean this is the second time they're building it?" He could see the doubt rushing back. He took a pen out of the well, then looked around for a piece of paper. She held up a piece of ledger sheet. "Will this do?"

"That's the ticket." He laughed. That's just fine."

"Is that an expression you use in the future?"

"Yes. Apparently you do believe me, since you picked up on that expression. You do believe, don't you?"

"I really want to. Don't be upset with me if I find it difficult."

"O.K.," he said, trying to assure her. "Anyway....if I draw a date line, it will be easier to understand." Then he labeled one end 1900, and the other 2100. "2010, or slightly earlier, is where Matt and I came from . We have been living here since then. Now I'm here with you, and it's 1911. He printed the numbers on the paper, smiled and pulled her close to him."

She put her hand on his arm and squeezed, whispering. "Thank you."

"My pleasure," he paused. "Now, our mission is almost finished. We changed as many things as we could to make her safer. You know about the recommendations we made concerning lifeboats and additional hull plates, which were disapproved for monetary, not safety, reasons. You see, when she sailed the first time, (he pointed to 1912 on the line) she sank right here." He saw the quick response in her eyes. "Fifteen-hundred passengers and crew went to the bottom with her, two and one half miles deep".

"That's just awful!" It evidently shocked her.

"Didn't I mention it before?"

"Yes, I think so, but truth seems so final, no matter what period of time. Of course, you don't want it to happen that way with Titanic II. I certainly don't....My father and other company executives could actually be aboard her maiden voyage."

"Right."

"Although I still don't want to accept it, I am beginning to understand. I guess I really didn't want to believe it. You know, that really makes sense. It really does. Now I'm torn between what I know would be best and what I really want. Oh, Randy, I want you to stay!" She was crying again.

"I know, Honey," he agreed. "When she's finished, however, Matt and I must figure out a way to get back."

"You're not sure you will be able to get back?" she asked excitedly.

"Well, we know how. It's just going to be difficult to work it out, that's all. We have to assemble the hardware from odds and ends we come across. We're working with several very inventive young men to come up with the most effective design for our laser. They're a lot of fun to work with, and they just eat up the information we can provide them with about future inventions and scientific breakthroughs. Even that may change history. 'A Look Into the Future,' by Randy and Matt."

His feeble effort to reduce the tension with humor was lost in the maelstrom of her emotions.

"Randy, this has been almost too much for me to absorb. I am totally exhausted." Her face was still wet, her eyes red and swollen.

Suddenly, her father knocked and asked if he could come in. As he walked into the room, he couldn't help but notice Sarah's face.

"'Sparrow', Honey, are you all right?"

"Yes, Daddy, I'm fine." She quickly recovered. "We're just ironing out some wrinkles in our plans."

"Bless your heart. If I can be of any assistance to you two, let me know," he replied, seeming to accurately perceive his daughter's frame of mind."

"I'm certain we will, sir." Randy assured him. " Thank you." .

Chapter 20

A few days later, Randy and Matt were hard at work in their temporary office. It was slow getting the final details of their job in order. They pulled files, checked the schedule board, and ran through the checklist in their notebooks.

"Here's one," Matt said, pointing to an entry. "The extra blankets in each lifeboat; remember?"

"Oh, yeah," he nodded, picking up another notebook. "We'll run the inspection this afternoon. Say, Matt, did you finish that portable laser yet?" Matt turned and looked at Randy. "What brought that on?"

"Just wondered."

"Are you getting anxious, or changing your mind altogether? I mean, about even going back?"

"Of course we're going back, numskull!" Randy asserted.

"You must really be under a lot of pressure. You're calling me names again," came the defense. "It's Sarah....I'd bet a silver dollar on that!" At that point Randy ran out of the office with Matt close at his heels.

"Where are you going?"

"To work... where you ought to be!" Randy said, raising his voice.

"Now you're yelling at me!"

"Enough! Things were getting out of control. Matt realized just how seriously they were, as he watched his angry friend storm down the steps. The conclusion was obvious to him.

"It's Sarah. It's got to be Sarah."

Matt took some men and went directly to the warehouse, where they picked up several crates. He instructed the foreman to take them to the boat deck.

"You can use the big dolly. They're easier to handle on the gangway. I'll meet you at the boats. O.K., Mr. 'Toole?"

"We'll be there, sir," O'Toole responded.

As Matt hurried to the gangway on his way to "A" deck, he saw Randy. He thought it best to let him have more time to simmer down. He would let him speak first. They met face-to-face on the stairway leading to the boat deck.

"Hi, Buddy," Matt could not resist saying something.

"Hi, yourself," he answered with a slight smile. "I'm sorry....."

"Hey, we're friends. Remember?" Matt knew his friend well. "We're both under a lot of pressure these days."

Two workmen squeezed past them on the stairway, prompting Randy and Matt to step up to the boat deck and clear the way.

"I just didn't count on falling in love," he said bluntly and sighed, "And what a doll!" He kissed his fingers by way of emphasizing his admiration and love for this girl.

"Come on, let's finish the blanket job. #377, if my memory serves me right. Then we can take a break."

They spent the rest of the day discussing alternatives. When they returned to their office at the end of the workday, they found stacks of reports to finish. Only after they were finished, would there be time for a hot meal.

Randy found a note from Sarah on his desk It had two hearts on the frontispiece.

"Hey, that's it. You're on your way to getting everything worked out," Matt said as he updated the log from his notebook.

Randy ignored him. He was too busy reading Sarah's note. Opening up his notebook, he began to stare off into space.

"Well, what did she say?"

Randy stood up, went over to the project scheduling board and drew a line through #377. He looked at Matt and said, "She's inviting us to a party at her house. Tomorrow night at seven."

"That's great!" exuded Matt. "We'll be there....won't we?" He was tired and a bit confused by what was going on between Randy and Sarah. Randy had become quite sensitive lately and he did not want to complicate things further. He'd been having enough of his own problems dealing with Emily.

"Well, I guess I'll have to go....so I can find out what she wants," he said, with doubt in his voice. Maybe Emily will be there, too."

The next day was a busy one. They had been assigned overall engineering design responsibility for the changes Ismay wanted aboard both Olympic and Titanic II. Each ship's work crews would install the modifications, but Matt and Randy would develop them. As Reggie had said, by assigning these changes to Randy and Matt, Ismay was trying very hard to keep them out of the main stream. That way he would not be compelled to justify decisions that were actually unjustifiable.

Although they would rather have stayed home and rested, Randy and Matt showed up at Sarah's party dressed so well that nobody recognized them.

They did not escape Mrs. Carlisle's attention. She motioned for the butler to take their coats and said,

"Randy. Matt. I'm so glad you could come. It seems a long time since the partys."

"I know, Mrs. Carlisle, your husband has been keeping us so busy, our social life has diminished to near-zero." His smile indicated that it wasn't really all that bad.

Sarah walked up to them, saying, "My, you boys do look handsome tonight--visions of sartorial splendor. Thank you for coming to meet my friends." To Randy, her approach appeared somewhat stilted and distant, as she introduced them to her many friends. As the party went on, he became more conscious of her remoteness. Left to himself, he was finding little solace in the dancing, the conversation or the refreshments. He felt depressed and lonely.

Noting that Sarah and Emily had gone to another room, he motioned to Matt to meet him in the entryway.

"Matt, I can't handle this. Sarah seems to be punishing me for my unwillingness to commit to staying with her or bringing her home with us? From what I can determine watching you and Emily, you're having the same problem. I don't think I need to stand here and take it, so I'm heading home. If the girls or Mrs. Carlisle ask where I've gone, just tell them I wasn't feeling well....Whatever! This has got to stop! I feel like a yo-yo, and there's too much else at stake for me to be this distracted and frustrated."

"You mean you're going to leave without telling them?"

"Yes, I am! I'm not about to get into another long-winded 'what-are-we-going-to-do?' conversation with Sarah. If Mr. C. wonders what's happening to his precious 'Sparrow,' I'm sure he'll ask at the office. See you back at the flat."

With that, he walked to the large guest closet where he found his coat. Throwing it over his shoulder, he walked to the front door and, without turning around, walked out -- perhaps for the last time.

The next morning, as they were getting ready for work, Matt told Randy what had transpired after he had left Carlisles'.

"It took about twenty minutes for Sarah to realize you'd left. She sought me out to find out where you were. I told her you weren't feeling well, and had gone home. She was stunned, and said, 'You mean he just left?...without telling me? I can't believe it!'

"Then I said, 'Actually, what he wasn't feeling well about was the way you were ignoring him. He knew, as I did too, that he couldn't command all your attention, since you were hosting the party. But he felt your coolness was intended. I felt the same about how Emily was dealing with me, but Emily and I are always at each other. Randy took it very hard. Maybe that's because he loves you so much."

"Her eyes began to fill up, and she said, 'Oh, no! What have I done? Oh, Matt, please tell him I'm sorry. I didn't mean to hurt him. I just wanted him to take our problem seriously, and assure me that we'd always be together. But now it looks like I've lost him for sure'."

"And how did you respond to that?" Randy asked.

"Well, about then, Emily walked up and asked where you were. I just turned and left the two of them to reach their own conclusions about what had been done, and what to do about it. I think Emily got a clear message from me."

"Randy replied, "Maybe if we let them sweat it out for a while, they'll begin to understand what's ahead of us and how difficult it is to make any commitments when we don't know what the future holds."

"You may be right, Randy. We certainly have enough to keep us busy for the next year....maybe too much. If we're talking about real love, it should survive a busy year. When Titanic II is ready to leave next April, we'll know then what has to be done. Do you think we can all keep it on the back burner for that long, Old Buddy?"

"We'll sure find out, won't we, '**Ole Buddy**'?"

Neither of the boys heard from either of the girls or from the Carlisles about what happened with Randy at the party. Matt made a point of avoiding Emily at work, and Randy, cooped up in either their temporary office or at the flat, was unavailable. They were surprised at how much work they were getting done without the affairs of the heart interfering. There was little time to waste, since it was less than a month before Titanic II was to be launched.

On one weekday morning in mid-May, Randy awoke just prior to sunrise. He ate and dressed quietly to allow Matt to sleep. Matt had been looking exhausted, having worked many overtime hours on several modifications. Randy, eager to avoid Matt's early morning mood, slipped quietly out the door.

As Randy got on the primitive bike he'd bought to ride to work, he peddled into a magnificent sunrise. The multi-colored sky was like a giant canvas above the city. He began to think about home. Somewhere in time there was another sunrise where his Mom and Dad were leaving for work. They would kiss each other and drive away in separate cars, headed in different directions. His mother's real estate office was on the south edge of town, while his father, Chief Financial Officer for an aircraft assembly plant, drove further east on Long Island.

His genuine feeling of homesickness heightened the pressures of Randy's job. Since he was no longer seeing Sarah, and was a dimension of time away from his parents and all he held dear, the absence of expressed love in his life was taking its toll.

Chapter 21
The Launching

Meanwhile the whole world waited for news about the first of the mighty "monster" ships. With Olympic about to set out on her maiden voyage and Titanic II ready for launching, media focus was intense. Previous promotion had developed great interest in all quarters of the travel industry and general public.

White Star Line had intended to build at least the first two "monsters" as twins. The many changes Ismay insisted be incorporated after Olympic's shakedown cruise, however, made Titanic II a very different ship. They could no longer be called twins.

White Star would change the planned schedule to complete these modifications, if necessary. They would be giving the traveling public what Ismay assumed they wanted, so he was not concerned if it delayed the maiden voyage.

The plan called for Titanic II to slide down the runway into Belfast Lough on May 31, 1911, receive her fitting-out at the basin, and leave Belfast on April 3, 1912 for Southampton. At Southampton she would pick up her first passengers, top off food, coal and other consumables, sail to Le Havre, France, then back to Queenstown, Ireland for its last passengers.

From there, it would be across the North Atlantic where, as the crowning touch, she would sail into New York harbor amidst the entire fanfare the city normally accorded such events. At least that was the thinking among the executives at Harland & Wolff and White Star.

In their worst nightmare they could not have imagined the disaster that was to befall Titanic. Nor could they conceive of the potential impact on her destiny of two young engineers from another time.

When Matt arrived at work that day, somewhat later than usual, he asked Randy why he had let him sleep what with all the wrap-up work that needed doing. "Matt, you've been running on empty for several days. We can't afford to have you in the infirmary at such an inopportune time. End of conversation."

"Yeah, you're probably right. I feel 100% better after a night of sleep. I appreciate that. Don't let it happen too often, though. What's next on our check list?"

Randy replied, "We have to inspect some changes that were made in the aft wheelhouse." The long trip from the slip floor to the stern area gave them ample time to observe many portions of the fine work being done. Their eyes, like TV cameras, scanned the ten million-dollar spectacle. They could not help themselves. Titanic II had already cast her spell.

"Matt, we are actually walking around inside a dream that's coming true." Randy gave rein to his excitement.

"Of course," Matt answered, "She's magnificent, that's a fact. How much does she weigh?"

"Why do you want to know that?"

"Well, when they shove her in the water, I want to see all this steel float!"

"Matt, I....oh, boy...." Randy used his watch calculator to come up with the answer for Matt. "When she's finished, she will gross out at about 46,500 tons."

"Holy smoke! How can the water hold all that up?" Matt laughed.

"Of course, only about 30,000 tons before she is fitted out. Don't think about it! You know as well as I do that bigger ships than this have been launched before our time....I mean, during our day....no, I mean, in our time. No, I mean, in the future....from now.... anyway...." There were times when Randy became easily confused. This was an easier time than most. "Enough, Einstein. You have expressed the time-space continuum with great finesse."

Two weeks later, May 31st dawned cool and crisp. Today was the day everyone had been working so hard for---Titanic II's launching. A large crowd was expected, but no one was prepared for the nearly 25,000 people who filled every level square foot of docks, stringers, bridges---anything that was horizontal, dry and not part of the ship.

Colored streamers hung from every piling, railing or wire. A hefty northeast breeze coming off the Irish Sea and up the Lough kept the streamers standing straight out. A scaffold had been strategically placed for a small band. . Hundreds of small power and sailboats hovered as close as safety would permit.

Dignitaries, including the Mayor of Belfast, foreign visitors, the press and company executives, including Randy and Matt, had special passes for seats in a grandstand just off the ship's bow. The christening would have been held within that area, and would have been performed by the Mayor, his wife and the Archbishop of Belfast. However, white Star did not christen any of their ships.

Yard workers scurried about checking the last minute details, such as having twenty-two tons of soap and tallow smeared on the runway. Every square inch of the runway already held three tons of the ship's weight.

Matt was so nervous he began to mumble. "30,000 tons...eight stories high...She'll float....I hope."

"Matt, will you cool it!"

"Aye, aye, Sir," he returned with a grin and a snappy salute.

"I've got our passes to the grandstand. We'd better hurry!" Said Randy.

Having made their way through the special visitors' gate and found seats, Matt asked, 'Who's going to stay on board during the launch?"

"A skeleton crew to run whatever needs to be run, and probably Tom Andrews representing both companies."

Randy looked directly above him to the forecastle. "It's eight stories high, Matt. Look up there. Is that an imposing sight, or what?" They were reminded of just how monstrous this ship was. It seemed almost impossible that man could create anything so large.

The band was playing a number of inspiring military marches. Suddenly, a loud horn took command with a single long blast that could be heard for miles. The band stopped playing and the large crowd slowly fell silent. It was five minutes before noon, the scheduled launch, before all the work done would be put to the test.

The Mayor of Belfast began to speak of the pride so many in the city felt in having built the largest ship the world had ever known. He described his own pride in both the local people who had worked on it, and residents who so completely supported it. Finally he thanked the executives of Harland & Wolff and White Star Line for using the facilities available in Belfast.

The Mayor then introduced the Archbishop of Belfast. Who said loudly, "Please pray with me. We ask you, Lord, to bless this vessel, to keep it safe from storms on the high seas. Lord; be with those who ride her so they may bring peace and love to our brothers and sisters in other lands. We thank you for allowing us to render such an achievement, and we bless her to your service. Amen!"

With that, every horn in the shipyard and from all the boats in the Lough announced the launch. The enormous crowd cheered. The triggers releasing and propelling her down the runway were barely audible as they were discharged.

But the launch had begun. Movement was slow at first, but then, with increasing speed, she slid toward the water. It was a nearly noiseless launch, the greased skids providing little resistance. Finally, Titanic II sliced her way stern first into the water with a great splash.

Randy could not contain the monumental ecstasy of the moment. Tears came to his eyes. He had never experienced these feelings before and was totally enchanted by the awesome scene. He prayed silently that the changes that had been made would save her from disaster.

As she steadied herself in the channel, Randy glanced at Matt. There he stood, holding on to the grandstand railing with all his strength. His eyes were shut as tight as he could get them.

"I give up! Of all the 'dips' in this world, I had to pick one for my best friend. We travel one hundred years in time, three thousand miles in space to impact this vessel....a vessel we have risked our lives to save....and you close your eyes to avoid seeing it launched. Man, you are weird."

"I have an aversion to sea water. I've never trusted it, and I never will. Call it cowardice if you will, but that's where I'm at."

"Sounds like a case for the shrink, Friend. Should I have you committed?"

"Do they have rooms for two, Friend?"

Mumbling under his breath, Randy slowly turned to watch history in the making---again.

Four waiting tugboats had captured the ship and were pushing her to the basin, where she would spend nine to twelve months fitting out. After the tugs had docked her and her lines were secured, a gangway was laid for guests who wished to see the unfinished interior of the ship. Although Randy and Matt had been aboard daily, they crossed the gangway to see what she was like afloat.

As they were leaving, Matt noticed J. P. Morgan speaking animatedly with several gentlemen. He seemed truly impressed by what had been wrought here. Matt nudged Randy with his elbow. Surprised by J. P.'s presence, Randy was speechless. Recalling all the time they'd spent together with him, one would think Randy would have no problem approaching him. They had become convinced, however, that he was less interested in the details of the ship's construction and safety, and more in the international recognition forthcoming from her. They doubted seriously that he would take up the cudgel for them in their disaster avoidance battle.

J. P. happened to walk toward them with his entourage and, with a somewhat remote expression of recognition, smiled broadly at them. After walking past them, he suddenly turned and, in a loud voice, said,

"Randy! Matt! How have you been? Gentlemen, I would like you to meet two fine young men. I had the opportunity to travel with them for a few days. They are brilliant young engineers who taught me a thing or two. They came from the States to help put Titanic together. From the looks of things, they did their job to a fare-the-well. "Matt and Randy, these gentlemen are board members from British corporations in which I have some interests."

Never one to stand shyly by and miss an opportunity to needle, Matt said in a light-hearted manner, quite audible to those around J. P.,

"Yes, sir. We are most proud of her. And, our pride will increase substantially if she makes it to New York without ricocheting off icebergs in the North Atlantic."

Blanching visibly, J. P. quickly surveyed the expressions of his business partners. To a man, they registered shock and consternation at Matt's comment. J. P. then recalled the warnings the boys had left with him. With a strong voice and sardonic smile he said,

"Gentlemen, it is evident to me that these young men are not used to being disappointed by the vicissitudes of modern corporate management. If I recall correctly, they proposed modifications of considerable cost to render our unsinkable ship even more unsinkable. They were, as you 'Brits' might say, 'carrying coals to Newcastle'." One of his associates, well aware of his meaning, joined him in laughter at his humorous putdown.

"As for the two of you, I suggest you avoid any such doomsday discourses that might offset White Star's marketing efforts. Our ship's bright future will put all such conjecture to rest." With that, he turned back to his associates and continued his discussion as if he had never been interrupted.

"Well, Matt," Randy confirmed, "that should just about do it! I can't imagine his not going to Ismay and Carlisle' and expressing himself over your outspokenness. I realize that if he intended to do anything about what we told him, he would have done so by now. Also, with his strong interest in art, he has managed to avoid any involvement in the ship's construction. So, you might ask, 'If not before, why now'?"

"Yes, Randy, I just might ask that. I might also ask, was that a devastating putdown or what?"

"It sure was. Matt, you were playing in the big leagues with a little league bat. That gentleman did not get where he is; owning half the known world, without being as sharp as they come. You never had a chance. The positive thing about the confrontation is that you came off learning something....don't mess with the big boys."

With that, they walked off the ship, amused by their exchange and much less concerned for their jobs now that she was afloat.

Chapter 22
The fitting-out

Although the next three months went by quickly, with everybody working a lot of overtime, the challenge was gone. Busy as they may have been, they found thoughts of home were assuming an increasingly prominent place in the background. Their love lives were in shambles, the "Sword of Damocles" hung over their precious ship. What was left that could attract them more than HOME?

Randy had not seen Sarah. Emily kept her nose in her work whenever Matt walked through the office. The boys kept busy completing all their inspections, overseeing the installation of Ismay's modifications, helping other departments complete their work. What they weren't involved in, they watched. Installation of the four huge stacks, removal and replacement of the starboard prop fascinated them to the point where they began to fall behind in their own work.

Her fitting-out was moving along as planned. The operation involved the placing of all finished touches on the hull in preparation for presentation to the public. Everything that could be, was hand crafted to create the greatest luxury liner of all time. Almost 2,500 passengers would soon board her and be impressed beyond their fondest dreams.

The first-class section included restaurants, dining rooms, lounges, a smoking room, café, reading room, gymnasium, handball courts, squash court, a 30' x 14' swimming pool, baths and much, much more. Individual staterooms and suites would match accommodations of the world's most exclusive hotels. Ornate walls and ceilings, luxurious carpet, tile and marble were used in every conceivable way, to cater to the tastes of the rich and famous. Status was the call of the new century, and it was sought at every opportunity.

One of the central attractions of the great ship was the elaborate Grand Staircase that took one from "A" deck to the boat deck. Of course, if one preferred not to walk, three elevators were available. At this staircase the ladies in their designer gowns could be gazed upon by the most prominent men of the time. What a thrill it would be to descend those steps dressed like a queen -- no insignificant adventure, indeed!

What was the story of the exquisitely carved clock mounted at the staircase's first landing? It was a unique plaque---"HONOR and GLORY crowning TIME"---a fitting touch of class for a legend in its own time. The artistic piece was expressly ordered by Mr. Ismay to demonstrate his approval of the addition of II to Titanic. His dialogue with Randy had convinced him to make the change.

Randy explained all this to Matt as they were passing through the first class section. He couldn't believe Matt's response, "You know, as I see it, it's reversed. Because we did what we did, it should read, 'TIME has crowned HONOR and GLORY'."

"Matt. You are truly amazing!" Randy announced, shaking his head.

Matt surely was that. Beneath his apparent devil-may-care approach to life, churned a deeply emotional and intuitive character. In mentioning the plaque's rather subtle message and thinking deeply enough about it to discern an alternative meaning, he surprised Randy. Even he could not see through to the depths of Matt's spirituality.

"The plaque's original message reminds me of an article I read many moons ago," commented Matt. "It drew a time-line which clearly demonstrated how, over the centuries, the hand of God had intervened in man's history and his efforts to pull away from his Creator. In each case an 'ark' was involved. Certain of these convergences may be allegorical, but they accurately reflect the minds and hearts of the populace at the time.

"The first, and most well-known, of course, was Noah's. The people had left God, sinned against him and each other while chasing after worldly idols. Following several warnings, God's answer was a global cataclysm, the ultimate chastisement for all mankind except Noah. Him he instructed to build an ark to withstand the torrents, take his family and a pair of each of the species of animals, and after the flood waters had receded, re-populate the earth with grateful and loving sons and daughters in law.

"Now we are about to journey on the most recent and splendiferous 'ark' ever built----Titanic II. Thinking he could do it on his own, while setting God aside, mankind has come up with an unimaginable worldly masterpiece. It reflects perfectly man's ever-increasing devotion to the idols of status, creature comfort and personal gain, his misplaced confidence in his own abilities, and his disregard of the power of God's concern for the lives of his creation. The ship's builders went so far as to gloat over the statement that 'not even God could sink this ship!' As a result, even normal precautions were not taken in the dangerous pack ice of the North Atlantic.

"When told the ship was mortally wounded, many refused to believe, returned to their staterooms or other activities, and died. Lifeboats could have saved them all, had there been enough of them, and had the skeptics believed. But, much like others who turned from God to pursue self-fulfillment, they missed the (life) boat. No matter how many times He warns mankind, rescues him or chastises him, he just doesn't get it! Just imagine challenging such power. "We managed to escape destruction through the 20th century, but a century in God's time is but a fleeting moment in eternity. Hang on! Is Titanic's sinking merely a warning of greater disasters to come?" was Matt's concluding question.

"Perhaps we are as arrogant as those we criticize, to think we can play in God's sandbox and change history," observed Randy.

One morning, Carlisle asked them to meet with him. His purpose--to determine the boys' future employment plans. He asked that they meet in the early afternoon. Two P. M. was most suitable to all.

"Have a seat, chaps. It's good to see you. J. P. Morgan and other owners of White Star are extremely pleased with what they see in the 'monster ships.' They truly believe that Olympic, Titanic II and their downline sister ship, will open up a New World of travel. Still aimed at the moneyed class, the very existence of more ships will expand the company's horizons, making room for other classes. With that in mind, they are considering building more ships, challenging Cunard and spanning the globe with White Star!

"Which brings me to my purpose in talking to you. Would you be interested in continuing to work for Harland & Wolff and White Star in producing new, bigger and faster ships? You certainly have made a great contribution to their efforts so far."

"Mr. Carlisle, that's the finest thing we've heard since we arrived last year," said Randy, "As you well know, engineers' work done in the background, is seldom publicly recognized for its contribution. Thank you very much. It's good to hear."

Matt jumped and eased himself into the discussion.

"Thank you, Mr. 'C' we really appreciate it. There is, however, one big obstacle to our doing that. We are planning to go home some time before Titanic II sails. We miss our parents, our school and friends. It's been almost a year since we've seen them."

"I can understand that. How will you get there?" came the natural reply.

"Maybe we'll try to crew the return trip as we did coming over. If we do, the most practical time to leave would be before winter sets in. You know what the North Atlantic is like during winter," Randy explained. "That way, too, we can be home for Hanukkah and Christmas." Matt further assured Carlisle that the previous Christmas time had been wonderful. "There really isn't anything like being with family during the holidays."

"I can't help but agree with that and it was great to have you with us last Christmas and Hanukkah."

"Despite his ranting about your presentation, you can be sure Mr. Ismay will be very disappointed to hear you won't be around much longer. As a matter of fact, he's been dropping hints for some time now that I should approach you."

"Well, despite the resistance we've met, there are some solid gains in making Titanic II less prone to damage. We have learned a great deal, and have enjoyed working with you," said Randy.

"Thank you. That should do it, gentlemen. Randy, please stay for a few more minutes. I'd like to find out where you and Sarah stand."

"Mr. 'C,' if you would not object or feel awkward discussing Sarah and me in Matt's presence, I would appreciate it if he could stay. He's in the same boat with Emily. Maybe we can come to some conclusions that would apply to both relationships. I know 'Sparrow' is very precious to you, but Matt and I have been very close to each other and share most everything in our lives."

"I have no problem with that. If you wish, Matt, please stay."

"Right, sir."

"Sarah has been so hurt over your leaving the party that night without a word, but she has resisted any impulse to contact you. She has prevailed upon me to ask you what is happening and why. Can you give me something to tell her?"

"Well, Mr. Carlisle, let it be known that I have loved Sarah since before I actually met her. I love her still, if not more. But I was having great difficulty controlling my emotions, which Sarah was using up and down like a Yo-Yo...."

"Yo-Yo?" Carlisle interrupted.

"Oh, of course, you wouldn't know what a 'Yo-Yo' is. It's a wooden American toy or maybe I should say Filipino toy that looks like a ball cut in half, its ends flattened and a dowel connecting the two halves at their center, a fraction of an inch apart. A two-and-a-half to three-foot string, tied to the dowel and wrapped around it, is tied to one's middle finger.

"One then releases the Yo-Yo, letting it fall, and maneuvers it vertically to roll up and down the string." He made the motions. "Those highly skilled can make it do wonders. It has come to be used analogously to describe any ups and downs one may experience in life....emotions, blood pressure, finances, etc.," Randy explained. "Spoken like a true engineer, old Buddy," Matt jibed.

"Oh my, yes, Matt." Carlisle smiled, enjoying their banter. "They are really something, these two," he thought.

"Matt, you certainly are a big help! Thanks for nothing. To get back to the subject at hand, I love Sarah more than ever, and because I do I can't take her changing approaches with me. The night of the party she almost completely ignored me. I realize she had hostess duties to perform, but she went well beyond what was necessary. She apparently was trying to impress me with how frustrated she was over my unwillingness to make a commitment. I had told her it was impossible for me to take her back with me. She refused to believe my reasons, so we had reached an impasse. I had also told her I couldn't stay here. My walking out of the party was my way of saying there was no reason to continue our relationship."

"Why can't you take her back with you?" asked Carlisle. "I don't want you to think I want to lose her. But, if being with you somewhere else is what she believes will make her happy, then I can accept losing her."

"And never see her again, Mr. 'C'?" interjected Matt.

"Well, now, I hadn't realized that was involved. Are you saying that where you're going is a place I can't visit, or vice versa?"

"Yes, sir, that's exactly what we're saying!" Matt assured him.

"Where do you live, in a cloistered monastery on a mountaintop somewhere?"

"No, sir, we live in Glen Cove, a pleasant town on the north shore of Long Island. We attend Webster Institute there, while living with our parents."

"I don't understand. What are you trying to tell me?"

"Frankly, Mr.'C', we are very surprised that Sarah hasn't told you. Perhaps it is because she doesn't believe us at all."

"What doesn't she believe?"

"You recall that many aspects of our presentation were prophetic in nature," Randy explained. "Where we live, it has all happened....it's history! We came here from 2010 through use of a theory of Albert Einstein's. Einstein is only 31 years old now, but by the time of his death in 1955, he will have developed theories, which will make him one of the most revered scientists in history. He theorized that time travel was feasible using Spectrumology, as some have called it, in which a set of color bands is released and rearranged in order, according to their wavelengths. Calculations indicated that, if all systems are set properly, everything within a thirty-foot radius could cross over into another band or parallel dimension of time.

"We have been interested in the fate of Titanic in its collision with the iceberg. Our reason for traveling in time was, as we have indicated to you, to shore up weak spots in the ship's construction, and prevent its foundering. Unfortunately, the Board did not believe or accept most of our recommendations."

"Well, I certainly can appreciate why Sarah disbelieved you! That's a hard nut to swallow. Further, I'm certain she didn't understand a word of your scientific jargon describing your time travel."

"We didn't drag her through that. We merely told her we were from the future and why we had come. Incidentally, one of the reasons we came was the magnetic attraction of her vision in Randy's dreams. She would stand at the bow of the ship and plead, 'Save us'! She was the first woman we saw when we arrived in Belfast. The rest is current history."

"I have resisted consideration of the truth of your claims, simply because it was too much for even this technically-oriented brain to conceive. I've made no judgments, and, you will recall, supported your presentation. But I'm sure you realize how difficult it is for anyone to believe."

"Of course, sir, but it is that disbelief that has come between Sarah and me and Matt and Emily. The problem is that either we stay here and give up our families and lives, or the girls do, and return with us to 2012. It's as simple as that. That's not an easy thing to ask," said Randy.

"Well... what is bothering me is not only Sarah's depression, but Hanna's as well. She is most solicitous of Sarah's well being, and seems to be sharing a similar despondency. She would even be willing to give up her sister, if it would make her happy. So, whatever can be done to resolve this dilemma will certainly help the family's equanimity."

"I suggest, sir," Randy said, "that you discuss it with her, assuring her that I will always love her. Then, let her make up her mind. I just don't want her to do anything drastic."

"She has mentioned wanting to get away, perhaps crossing on the maiden voyage of Titanic II. That scares me in view of your comments."

"It scares us too. But we have some time to work on things. You should try to talk her out of it, though, to be on the safe side," Randy urged.

"How easily you slide into your roles as prophets. Here I sit, not knowing whether anything you've said is true, but discussing it with you as if it were. I know nothing of the scientific accomplishments you mention. I am confused, uncertain and have not really accepted it all. It is so far from the reality I know. Have others done what you claim to have done? If not, will more do so in the future? Will there be a day when Sarah, you chaps, Elizabeth and I will be able to move about through different dimensions visiting each other? My God, what am I saying? This is too much! There's no point in talking about this any further until I get my head straight. You'll be here for several months. Maybe we'll come up with some answers for 'Sparrow' and Emily. Thanks for making the time for me. Incidentally, if you finally decide to stay until April and return to the States on Titanic II, we would like to invite you for Christmas dinner. No matter what your relationship with Sarah may be, Elizabeth and I would be pleased to have you both there." They thanked him for his kind offer, and left.

Chapter 23

Back at their flat, Randy and Matt discussed what they should do about going home. They agreed that they would prefer being home for Christmas, but Randy could not imagine leaving his true love alone on the doomed ship. He would have to assure either that the disaster was averted, or, if not, that Sarah survived it. Of course, averting it was the highest priority of their young lives.

They were fairly confident that they could prevent it, even without sonar, radar or other magic tricks they had up their sleeves. They believed that the Collision Avoidance Manual plus a greater detection capability by the lookouts would assure the collision was avoided. If the ship went down despite their efforts, they felt that the "women and children first" approach plus the addition of ten more lifeboats required by the Board of Trade, would assure them that the chances of Sarah's being saved would be excellent.

A few weeks later, Carlisle left a message with his secretary to set up another meeting with Randy and Matt. She contacted them at their office and set it up for the following morning.

"Randy, Matt, welcome. I wanted to pass along some information that confuses me, it is likely to please you but upset Mr. Ismay. Today I received a message from Istanbul. Would you like to read it?"

"Oh, yes, sir!" they said in chorus. Passing it to them he watched with a smile as they read:

AM 9/22 Oceanic Capt. EJ Smith, collided empty Izmir-
Istanbul packet heavy fog. Severe damage packet, minor
Bow damage ship. No injuries. XS speed for conditions

McHugh 9/21/11

Looking up from the message, they both smiled sheepishly.

"Well, there's another 'swallow' for Ismay's summer." said Carlisle. I've left word with him that this message is in. I don't expect this to change things, but you did tell him it would happen, so we'll let him know."

"Your explanation at the last meeting makes this easier to understand. It still leaves me in a quandary. Am I to completely believe you? If not, what possible explanation is there for your foreknowledge?"

"Now, Mr. 'C,' we know where you are. If you profess to Mr. Ismay or the others that you have accepted what we say about time-travel, they will find a 'funny farm' for you somewhere. Excuse me---that is a late 20th century expression for a psychiatric institution---a mental hospital. Just let Mr. Ismay interpret it himself, reaching his own conclusions. Perhaps this is one situation where the less said the better," Randy concluded.

When he got home, Carlisle gathered his two daughters and his wife together.

"Girls, I wanted to let you know about my talk with Randy. Sarah, he and Matt told me how you didn't believe them and how you were running his emotions up and down like a 'Yo-Yo'. That's why, when you were ignoring him at the party, he left. He said that he had told you about his time travel and was, frankly, surprised that you had not told me. "

"I wasn't sure you would believe him, and I didn't want to try to explain something I had no knowledge about. Also, I was afraid that if you mentioned it to anybody, the boys might get into some kind of trouble. Oh, I'll explain about the 'Yo-Yo' later. Sarah responded.

"Well, the boys have shown their knowledge of the future to all the men on the Board of Designers at their presentation. Of all the members of the Board, Ismay was the most unwilling to accept what they said.

"Twice the boys had disclosed future accidents Captain Smith would have---one in Naples and one in the Sea of Marmara. They described the accidents to a fault and I have not as yet shared the second one with Mr. Ismay, nor do I intend to discuss it further with him.

"So, my dear 'Sparrow', what is it that will make you happy? To be with him as he travels through time with Matt---if that's really what the boys have done and will do? I believe Hanna has told you, and your mother and I will tell you, that it is your happiness we seek, even if it means losing you. Assuming it is what you want, you must understand that it is forever, not just a sojourn to the States."

"Is it really that drastic, Alex?" asked Mrs. Carlisle. If they are pioneers in time travel, won't others be following with new and different approaches? Won't it become increasingly common? Won't that change 'forever' to something less?"

"It may happen, perhaps in our lifetime, Elizabeth! Perhaps never." Carlisle answered his wife.

"Daddy, do you think that if Sarah is willing to go with him, he would take her?" asked Hanna "We all seem to be in agreement with her going--can't we just tell him that and solve the problem?"

"Advice from the young tends to be simplistic, free of restraints and filled with optimism," thought Carlisle. He responded to Hanna by warning,

"There is one problem. Matt has not as yet produced the equipment they need. They may not be able to go back themselves."

"Well then, Daddy, that would solve the whole thing....they'd have to stay here and be together with us," Hanna responded with delight.

"That may be, Sarah interjected. But, they are anxious to go back. The future is more comfortable, science is prolonging life, and there is less drudgery and more recreation. There's also his family, friends, school, etc.".

"Well, 'Sparrow', that may be so as well, but you need to tell him what you are willing to do, and assure him you will no longer play with his emotions," Carlisle advised.

Having heard this, Hanna began to cheer, convinced it was as simple as that. Mr. & Mrs. Carlisle joined in enthusiastically. Sarah was very moved and suggested they pray together about it. "We need all the help we can get!" she said. With that she intoned a moving prayer asking that the family always be together spiritually, despite the physical distancing that may occur. They concluded by reciting the Lord's Prayer. The family had never been this close.

"Thank you, everybody. I love you. I think I know what to do now," Sarah said confidently.

All areas of Titanic II's construction were on schedule. The April 3, 1912 date for her to leave Belfast for Southampton looked achievable, with some room to spare. But, one day in November, Lord Summergill visited Bruce Ismay, Alex Carlisle and Tom Andrews to tell them of a problem involving the additional lifeboats. He explained that the Board of Trade's across-the-board increase in required lifeboats had placed an impossible burden on the few lifeboat manufacturers in Britain. Contacts through J. P. Morgan to fabricators in the States had failed to solve the shortfall.

"The purpose of my visit is to determine if your mid-April, target for Titanic II is still reasonable at this point, or could you use the time that delaying her maiden voyage would provide?"

"No, sir! All areas of the project are meeting scheduled goals. We are unreceptive to any delay. Major portions of the project, such as replacing her starboard screw, have been taken care of, and we are actually picking up some time," Ismay responded sternly.

"All right, then, Bruce. We will place a hold on our requirement that you add ten lifeboats to your ship. This with the understanding that the hold will be dropped as soon as your complement becomes available," said Summergill. "Our decision to exempt Titanic II was based, to a great extent, on the reputed claim of her 'unsinkability.' I hope our faith in that claim is not misplaced."

"I'm certain it will prove not to be," Ismay stated confidently.

"Thank you, Bruce. I needed that assurance. I can release a number of lifeboats coming off the line to other ships affected by our edict. Good day, gentlemen."

After Lord Summergill had left, Ismay, with a twinkle in his eye, said, "Well, now, there's a break. I'm sure Randy and Matt will be upset, but this will be a blessing for our maiden voyage. We can deal with the additional boats when they're ready and, in the meantime, have an uncluttered promenade deck."

"Let's hope that is a reasonable exchange. It might be regretted," Carlisle muttered.

"Oh, come on, Alex, are you still living in the future with the boys?"

With that, Carlisle stood up from his seat, brought out the message from McHugh in Istanbul. Without a word, he dropped it on Ismay's desk and left the room.

(1) James Melville Autobiography, I., 163 (1583).

Chapter 24

Several nights later, Hanna wandered into Sarah's bedroom to find her writing in her daily journal. "Come in and talk to me, little sister. Thank you for your encouragement and optimism the other day. I know mom and Dad felt a lot better about what I'm going through. Thank you."

"Have you decided what to do?" Hanna inquired.

"I think so. Let me have your reaction. I know that Randy loves me and would do anything to be with me. His practical engineer's mind tells him to be cautious. He can't drive down the center of the road, either he commits totally or he backs off totally. That's one of the things I love about him. So I will continue to stay away from him, except for Christmas day. I'll wrap something that comes from my heart....I don't know what yet, but I'll come up with something that shows my love, and maybe provides a tension-breaking laugh."

"I hope, for your sake, it works," Hanna stated, "You'll need a good laugh before that day is over." She paused, "Be sure to pray for me, OK?

"OK."

As busy as the boys were, they were surprised to see December roll around so quickly. Only three months, or less, until Titanic II pulls out of the basin and completes her shakedown cruise. Since most of the changes made to her were a consequence of Olympics shakedown, Ismay should find little else to add or change.

"We're coming close to being with the girls again at Carlisles'. How are you handling that?" asked Matt

"I think I'm ready to make a commitment. Even if I weren't, we have to save her. That's how this whole thing got started in the first place....my seeing her in my dreams pleading with me to, 'Save us!' Right? But will she be mine on the other side?

"If she's within thirty feet of you when the 'boom' goes off, why not?" affirmed Matt. "If you bring someone into the 21st century, her amazement alone should assure she'll stay at least that close to you. What choices does she really have? She won't know anyone but us, unless she finds a living relative on the 'Buddy List." That world out there can get mighty lonely. As adaptable as she is, she would still be facing severe culture shock."

"I suppose you're right. Matt. Probably the best thing to do is just let it go, and trust that whatever happens is supposed to happen. I could drive myself nuts trying to control and focus this whole thing....saving Sarah, saving the ship, saving the 1522 who didn't make it the first time. We'll just have to do what we can."

"You got it, 'Friend'!"

This conversation seemed to calm Randy down, while increasing his productivity. He realized he couldn't deal with future events, only with the present. Plan for the future -- yes! Develop equipment and procedures to deal with possible glitches in the plan -- yes! But, be prepared for tomorrow, not immersed or drowning in it. As Randy thought about Sarah and Christmas day, he began to realize the seriousness of the commitment he had determined to make. His "yes" would involve considerably more than just this lifetime, or just these people. He would assume total responsibility for Sarah in an unfamiliar world....husband, father, brother, lover, friend....he would be the only person other than Matt (and maybe Emily) she would know.

In addition to his other roles, Randy would have to be Sarah's tour guide, instructor, counselor, interpreter....etc. Some things would obviously be familiar, but the cultural and technological changes between 1912 and 2012 were enormous. Few past centuries, if any, had encountered as dramatic an upheaval of the status quo. Randy would have to ease Sarah into it with loving patience and understanding.

"Matt, are you planning to give Emily a gift for the holiday?" Randy asked.

"I can't imagine the girls not having something to give us. That would be unfeminine," responded Matt.

"I think I'll hit the jewelry and antique shops to find a necklace, Only a diamond ring would communicate a greater commitment. I know Sarah would consider that somewhat premature. So, a necklace it will be, if I can find one good enough for her."

That afternoon, Randy left the office early to find Sarah's gift. He had previously found that jewelry stores carried high-priced, somewhat unimaginative or unoriginal pieces. His search, therefore, was restricted to antique and pawnshops.

On a quiet, narrow back street, Randy came across a small shop with a worn sign hanging from one hook, threatening to break loose in the brisk afternoon breeze. On it was but the name of the proprietor....William W. Willoughby. Randy's entry was welcomed with a squeaking door and a cacophany of bells, which devolved into competing Irish tunes. The proprietor entered as the last tune moaned to a halt.

"How may I help you, sir?" he inquired.

"I'm looking for a one-of-a-kind necklace which I intend as a gift for my soon-to-be fiancée. I have not bothered with jewelry shops, as such, only shops that are likely to have something very different....as different as will be our engagement and marriage," Randy said, effusively.

"Well, sir, we don't deal in jewelry as such. If an estate sale happens to include a valuable piece, we will attempt to sell it, but will most likely discount it to estate buyers. We have, however, just received miscellany from a large estate sale that, I believe, contains a few odd pieces of jewelry. If you will follow me to the rear of the shop, we may find something suitable."

The small storeroom in the rear of the shop was overflowing with furniture. At times, they had to climb over pieces to get to the new shipment. Randy smiled, as he saw nothing but complete confusion. "He could certainly use a computer program to organize this mess," he thought.

Whatever he may have thought of this man's inventory control, Randy became ecstatic when the proprietor brought out a magnificent piece from a bureau drawer. From a filigreed, long gold chain hung a large emerald, rectangular in shape, in a delicate gold setting with four small ruby baguettes dangling beneath.

It was immediately obvious to the proprietor that he had a sale. Only the price he could extract was in doubt. After a limited negotiation, Randy exuded, "I'll take it!" With the purchasing power of his money, it seemed almost dishonest to have obtained a piece of such beauty for so little.

Returning to the flat, Randy found Matt catching up on the sleep he'd lost working overtime. Everything was in good shape aboard ship and, although there were several projects to be finished, the pressure was off. This gave Matt more time to complete the time-travel equipment, (laser). It had to be done soon, since they may be surprised by some last-minute oversights demanding of their time.

Matt stirred as Randy entered, which gave Randy the opportunity to bring him all the way back to consciousness.

Blinking his eyes to awaken, Matt said, "Did you find what you were looking for?"

"I sure did, my friend. Take a look at this."

Matt sat up to inspect the necklace.

"Wow! That's beautiful! You've got good taste, ole buddy....as much as I hate to admit it. Sarah should turn to jelly when she sees that. Nothing will impact our lady friends more than an expensive piece."

"Well, it wasn't that expensive. You know, with the exchange rate and all" Randy responded. "Now what about you, Matt? What are the plans for you and Emily? Do you expect her to come with us back to 2012?"

"I really don't know how that's going to turn out. If she wants to go, I'll probably take her, but I'm not sure either of us is in it for the long run. And, if we're not, she'd best stay behind."

"I can certainly agree with that," Randy said, "There's too much to be given up. It will require total commitment to justify it. Do you intend to bring it to a conclusion on Christmas day?

"I think so, Randy. There's no sense in prolonging the agony. We have fun together, and we can continue to do so until T-2 ships out, but only on a friend-to-friend basis. I might pick up a small Christmas gift for her, but nothing of significant value or meaning."

Christmas morning was overcast with an occasional drizzle--cold but not enough for snow. Randy had always felt there was something special about snow, especially in the downtown area. It covered the blight, quieted the rattling garbage cans, the off-key caroling and the loud talk of exiting bar patrons. He wanted this to be the perfect Christmas, and he prayed for snow. Don't all the kids pray for snow? How else could they use their new sleds?

Randy and Matt were getting dressed to leave for dinner at the Carlisles'. The past year had gently matured them; Randy was no longer the youngster on his first date who generated Matt's chiding. He was in control of his life as well as that of his beloved. We're talking about different fellows here, brimming with self-confidence and ready to meet the challenge of another big step through time.

Mr. Carlisle had told them he would arrange for the carriage to pick them up at their flat, so they would not have to walk through the rain. As it turned out, they truly appreciated his offer.

Emily was already at Carlisles' when the boys arrived. The butler took their coats and preceded them into the sitting room. There, on either side of the large Christmas tree sat the two girls, both beautiful in their red Christmas outfits. The boys were overcome by the sight, more so as the girls smiled a warm welcome. It was all that Randy could do to keep from hugging her on the spot. But this event was programmed by the girls. It would be inappropriate to display feelings before the script called for it. Certainly the girls would lead off at the right time. The boys' self-control was further evidence of their maturation.

"Hello, girls. Merry Christmas and Happy Hanukkah," Randy offered, softly.

"Welcome, and a Merry Christmas to both of you," Sarah said for both of the girls. "It has been a long time.".

"Yea, verily," Matt responded with humor to allay existing tension.

"I say, Amen to that!" Randy said, completing the biblical exchange.

"You're both looking great," four said simultaneously, then laughed out loud together. To Randy, it seemed a repeat of their first night in Belfast when they bumped into Sarah and her escort. Looking into Randy's eyes, she could detect the intensity of his feelings, as he recalled their first meeting.

Unable to restrain her emotion, Sarah ran to him and threw her arms around him, "Oh, Randy, I've missed you so. I love you so much!"

He melted in her arms despite their audience, vigorously returned her hug, and kissed her. "It's been terrible, Sarah! I don't ever want to go through it again."

"You won't, Randy, I promise. Take me with you."

Hearing the girls' squeals and the boys' deep voices, Hanna and her parents entered the room. "What's going on in here?" Hanna asked, "It sounds like a wedding or something."

"That's pretty close, Hanna. Maybe not now, but it can't be too far off," replied Sarah. "Am I right, Randy?"

"Absolutely," Randy answered cautiously.

"Well, now, 'Sparrow', it sounds like a dramatic beginning to our Christmas celebration," observed Carlisle. "Is there something you want to tell us?"

"Oh, yes, Father! Although we haven't worked out any details, or even discussed what we should do, we seem to have made a strong commitment to each other. It didn't happen the way I'd planned, but in a more loving and sudden way. When we let it go, our love returned to us, stronger and more substantial than ever." her eyes toward Randy.

"Does this mean we'll have a wedding in the family soon, children?" asked Mrs. Carlisle.

"It might be a good bet," commented Randy. "We just don't know where or when. You can understand that, I think. Lots will depend on how Titanic II behaves in the North Atlantic. If she makes it to New York, we'll be with her. If she runs into an iceberg before getting there, we may have to take other action, and wind up somewhere else. In any event, we'll be together."

"Father, I have to admit to fears of the unknown. They don't do much for my peace of mind, but I'm willing to take them on. Any other choice would keep us apart, in time and in space."

"Well, 'Sparrow', I've told you before, there is nothing I want for you more than your happiness. I am convinced that you and Randy can find it together, no matter where you are. Your mother and I hope against hope that you will wind up where we can visit you. Thinking we may never see you again is difficult to deal with."

Chapter 25

"Why don't we go into dinner and toast the lucky couple," suggested Mrs. Carlisle. "I hope you boys liked the duck last year, because it's what we have every Christmas."

As they were seated, the butler poured each, including Hanna, a glass of an excellent French white wine. This practice was only for special occasions.

"Here's to the loving couple," Carlisle began. "May they always find happiness and new challenges in an exciting and productive life. Keep them safe, Lord, and bless this meal for us. Amen."

"Amen," they all echoed, then clinked their crystal glasses together and began to sip. Inhaling deeply with her glass beneath her nose, young Hanna then exclaimed, "Ooh, this Chardonnay has an exhilarating bouquet. It's dry yet not bitter; boisterous while not overbearing, a perfect accompaniment to our duckling."

Through everyone's laughter, Mrs. Carlisle's voice was heard asking, "Now just where did you learn that, young lady?"

"I've become a label reader, and listened carefully to your friends. If you will recall, Mother, you also have several magazines in the library which include advertisements and articles on wines of the world. One need only read them, without tasting."

"Well, missy," said her father, "I hope we won't have to smell your breath after you've been in the library."

"Excuse me, Mr. 'C', I believe Hanna's just trying to jerk your chain." Matt interjected.

"'Jerk my chain'?" Repeated Carlisle, "Whatever does that mean?"

"Oh, forgive me," Matt replied, "that's just a 21st century expression meaning she's trying to get a rise out of you. She seems to have succeeded." Laughter from everyone at the table, including her parents and sister, assured Hanna that she had not overstepped her bounds. At that, the butler announced dinner was served. Once again, the meal was delicious, and everyone ate too much. "Shall we retire to the entry room and see what's been left under the tree for us?" Mrs. Carlisle suggested. Everyone agreed.

Beyond the family gifts, which were distributed by Sarah this year, there were just four others for the two young couples. Sarah passed them to

Randy, Matt and Emily, keeping her own. After the family gifts had been opened, Sarah suggested that Matt and Emily open theirs, then she and Randy theirs.

Matt opened his first. It was a finely tooled leather wallet with an image of Titanic II burned into the front panel. In one of the large pockets inside, Matt found a facsimile of a White Star Line ticket from Belfast to Southampton to New York, dated April 10, 1912. In another pocket was a note from Emily telling Matt that she would not be accompanying him to New York. In yet another pocket was a sealed envelope with two hearts on it and "Strictly Personal" printed across its face. Matt slipped that into his pocket.

The contents of Emily's gift suggested rather clearly to Matt that her decision was to remain permanently in Belfast with her family. He assumed her personal note would reveal the factors behind her decision. He felt mixed emotions, since he truly loved Emily and her fun-loving nature, and was consequently disappointed with the outcome. On the other hand, he felt relieved that he did not have to make the decision himself, and was now free to face whatever life had in store for him.

Emily then opened her gift from Matt. It was a beautiful antique silver jewelry box. Fine silver leaves decorated the top, surrounded two silver doves passing a twig between them. The box was lined with red velvet. Attached to the lining of the lid was a white envelope with the United States flag embossed on it. In it was Matt's note, on which he had written:

"I had hoped to fill this box with pieces that would speak of my love. In anticipation of your decision, however, I had the U. S. flag inserted with the hope that you would be reminded of me each time you opened the box. Also, that the doves would serve to remind you of the love we shared so briefly.

Emily did not know whether to laugh or to cry. Her relationship with Matt had been like that. Most of the time they laughed together, but there were times when tears were called for. She would really miss him, as she knew he would her. They would always be good friends, but not more than friends. They looked intently at each other, stood up and gently hugged. This "farewell" scene touched everyone. Though sad, it was air clearing. The couples had become such an article that the Carlisle family felt involved in every part of their relationships.

It came Randy's turn. His gift was wrapped in a manner normally associated with clothing. When he opened it, the first thing he saw was a large white Webster Marine Institute emblem, on a light-blue background. The emblem was circular, with the school name embroidered between two outer concentric circles. The inner circle surrounded the picture of a steam pump. The founding date of the school, 1893, was embroidered at the base of the emblem.

Randy was astounded at how accurate this replica of their school emblem was. He pulled out the paper that had been covering the emblem and found it had been embroidered on a beautifully knitted, light-blue pullover sweater.

"This is unbelievable, Sarah. Where did you ever find the emblem? It's absolutely perfect. And the sweater is the most well-made and attractive pullover I've ever seen."

"Randy, I embroidered the entire emblem on the sweater using the picture you had of Roxanne in her cheerleader's outfit. The emblem was quite clear on that photograph. Further, you've mentioned your school colors, so there you have it. I'll have to admit that Mother was more than a little help in the knitting and embroidering."

"There must be a hidden meaning to the sweater. Let me guess. Does this mean Sarah that you want to be involved with Webster and/or its students? Would I be jumping to conclusions if I interpret this to mean you want to come back with me? Wait, don't answer me. Open your gift and see what it tells you."

With that, Sarah unwrapped the necklace. Its rare beauty overwhelmed her. "Oh, Randy, it's beautiful. Where did you ever find it? Emeralds are my favorite stone, and this one is set off with such dazzling rubies. I love it!"

"This must mean that you are ready for a committed relationship. It tells me you are willing to invest everything in us together. Am I right, Randy?" "Looks like I'll be marrying a very bright young lady. Yes, you are right!" At this point, everyone was laughing and cheering and wishing them well.

"Now, wait a moment," cautioned Randy, "We still have to complete our responsibilities on Titanic II. Matt has to finish the time apparatus. We have to be assured of the integrity of the ship. There's a lot that has to happen before we can think about Mr. & Mrs. Randy Kaplan. For now, just pray for us."

"Well stated, my man, Carlisle said. "It sounds like your head is sitting squarely on your shoulders. That's what prompts me to give my approval to your marriage. I know this may mean we'll be losing 'Sparrow', but as long as she is happy, we will be happy. If you accept her, you also accept the responsibility to help her be happy. Go with our blessings and with that admonition."

The loving couple, armed with these blessings, looked forward with great anticipation to their cruise together on Titanic II. Sarah had considered the real possibility of the ship experiencing difficulty. Between her love for Randy and her faith in the improvements that he and Matt had been able to install, she pushed aside her fears.

During the four months preceding Titanic II's maiden voyage, they spent as much time together as Randy's work schedule would allow. They planned for their life in the future. Randy was able to inform her in detail of the scientific, industrial, technological and biological advances that had been made in the century between them. They hoped that through such detail, she would be able to adjust to the New World she was entering.

There were occasional get-togethers with Sarah's parents. During these, the Carlisles expressed their wish that the wedding could take place in Belfast. They understood why the couple wished to get past both the Titanic II and the completion of the time-travel hardware before joining hands forever. They wished, however, it was otherwise. Sarah's parents had confidence in her as well as in Randy, so did not concern themselves with the morality aspect of an unmarried couple traveling together.

Meanwhile Matt and Emily were enjoying each other openly and without the tension of further commitment.

Chapter 26
The departure

At least one pre-departure project on their list was completed each day. The bridge personnel received their training in maneuvers designed to evade icebergs, and went through a seminar describing North Atlantic/Arctic Ocean ice---how it looked, what to expect. Captain Smith had assigned all bridge personnel to the training, but did not, himself, attend. He believed that his 36 years of experience precluded the need for such a basic seminar. As time would tell, however, it would become evident that his knowledge, though broad, was not adequate to meet the ship's needs. The point most emphasized was the need for vigilance on the part of lookouts. One year, 1,350 icebergs had drifted south of the shipping lanes Titanic II was to travel. Many were dark in color and difficult to detect on even a moonlit night.

Twenty-four lifeboats had been installed. Randy and Matt continued to place pressure on Ismay to add the additional twelve required by the Board of Trade. They actually wanted these twelve plus another twelve to take care of everyone aboard in the event abandoning ship was called for.

The final "No!" from Ismay came following his meeting with Carlisle, Andrews and J. P. Morgan. Although J. P. was not supportive of the proposal, he was civil and chose not to mention the dialogue he'd had with the boys the day of the launching.

Deck-crew training in lifeboat utilization was accomplished when the last lifeboat was hung. Practice sessions would be held several times prior to departure. This should provide them with sufficient expertise to handle passengers during their pre-departure exercise. Many more might survive the disaster that was to befall them.

During the time immediately preceding Titanic II's departure for Southampton, Randy and Sarah tried to spend as much time together as possible. They realized that either one or the other, or both might not make it to New York or beyond in either 1912 or 2012. Matt and Emily were undergoing a somewhat similar trial. Their relationship was unquestionably more whimsical, and not as deep as Emily needed to endure the sacrifice involved. Matt, himself was not certain of his own true feelings.

Ismay finally published a schedule for Titanic II's departure.

March 27th: Shakedown cruise. This would provide four days to correct minor items. Departure would be delayed for any large items.

April 1st: Last day of work on the ship.

April 2nd: Loading supplies and testing equipment and systems.

April 3rd: Departure. 9 A.M.

Ismay informed all White Star and H. & W. upper management, the Mayor, the Archbishop, Rabbi Stein and several industrial and financial world leaders, of a party aboard on the evening of the 2nd. Matt and Randy, Emily and the Carlisles were among those invited.

As he left the office to prepare for the party, Ismay ran into Carlisle. "Alex, I understand that your daughter Sarah will be coming with us on Titanic II's trip to New York under the aegis of Randy and Matt. Is that so?"

"Yes, Bruce, it is, " replied Carlisle.

"Alex, with all the warnings Randy and Matt have put forth, aren't you concerned for her safety?" This was put to Carlisle to trap him in an inconsistent or contradictory response regarding the ship's fate.

"Bruce, as much as I believe what the boys say about the disaster-to-come, I believe just as strongly that they will be able to save at least Sarah and themselves, if not everyone, through use of their control of time. Another factor that makes me believe Sarah will survive, is the tradition of filling lifeboats with women and children first when abandoning ship. Whether all three will survive, or get together again, is not guaranteed, but a hope nevertheless."

"What confuses me, Alex, is that, as a father, you can entertain thoughts of an imminent disaster involving your daughter, yet as the ship's designer, still go about your business as if nothing existed out there. Can you compartmentalize the various roles you play to such an extent that they operate totally separate from each other?"

"Again, Bruce, it is a matter of faith. First, in a benevolent God, second, in Randy and Matt's abilities and knowledge. As father, I have spent many hours with Sarah, discussing the pros and cons of her decision. Because it is her happiness I am concerned with, it becomes easier. On the other hand, as designer I have made every effort, within what has been allowed me, to reduce the hazards that should have been totally eliminated. I am satisfied that I have done both jobs well."

"Alex, that degree of faith is more than I think I will ever acquire. I envy the serenity it obviously brings you."

"As I've mentioned before, Bruce, one can always change."

The next morning, Tuesday, April 2nd, was unseasonably brisk and cool. The trees were still bare and everyone was dressed for warmth. The distinct odor of thousands of stoves and fireplaces filled the air. Smoke lifted heavenward like a slowly unraveling rope, rising to where it blended into the gray overcast sky. The wind buffeted Randy and Matt as they walked the nearly deserted streets. It seemed that only those who had to work ventured out into the elements.

It was a very important day for the yard crew. Titanic II would leave for Southampton tomorrow. The only things to be done now were last minute chores. The company was so proud of their work. It was in the air. The publicity people had created excitement, as well as intrigue, about "the best of the twins." Harland and Wolff and White Star were on a roll and pride was rampant.

J. P. had invited Benjamin Guggenheim(1), John Jacob Astor(2), Isidor Straus(3) and his wife, and other industrialists and financiers, to attend the party, then ride with the ship from Belfast to Southampton, believing they would be sufficiently impressed to spread the word about the ship in key places. He had also arranged for them to sail from Southampton to New York at his expense, if they desired. Each had business to attend to in Southampton and its environs, and would sojourn the balance of the time before departure on the 10th. Previously J. P. had advised his guests that due to business demands, he would not be with them beyond Southampton. To assure their comfort in Southampton, however, he arranged for them to use their staterooms as home base during the layover. The balance of the passengers would embark at Southampton, LeHavre, France and Queenstown, Ireland. Then on to New York!

When evening came, the two young men dressed to attend Ismay's bon voyage party. They, and the girls, had planned to use the party as a going-away for Emily, or, more accurately, a going-away for them. With the A.M. departure of Titanic II, it was not likely that they would have time to wish her well then. During and after the party, however, they would be able to say their good-byes individually and together. The Carlisles, with Hanna in tow, arrived at the party with Sarah and Emily. Greeted by Randy and Matt, they drifted together through the many guests, spending a few moments with the Mayor, the Archbishop, Rabbi Stein and others.

While they were together at the party, Sarah and Randy displayed discretion, and made no attempt to show their love for each other. This was a big-time international event and they felt they should treat it as such. The voyage itself would provide a more desirable climate for the nurturing of their love for one another.

Meanwhile, the Grand Staircase and the opulence of the entire first class area overwhelmed Hanna. She had seen the Staircase with carpenters swarming about it, but this was the first time she had seen it completed. She became transfixed and somehow driven toward it. In a fog, she entered one of the three elevators to reach the boat deck and top of the staircase.

When Matt and Emily were ready to leave and spend time together alone, Randy and Sarah joined them on the boat deck with beverage in hand. The three toasted Emily, expressing their regret at her not coming with them to New York and/or 2012. Then, as her tears flowed freely, they wished her well and hugged her.

"We will miss you, Emily. You've been a true friend. God bless you.

After the good-byes, they took an elevator back down to the lounge, where they noticed some commotion in the direction of the staircase. Looking up, they saw Hanna at the top, completely alone and posing as would a fashion model. Suddenly, someone began to clap, which brought Hanna back to awareness, but too late---the stage was set. She had no choice but to continue on.

The few people on the staircase quickly stepped off to watch as Hanna began her gracious descent. Her age was evidenced in the unfilled size 6 dress she wore. The exaggeration of her body motions reminded Randy of Roxanne and her cheerleading. The applause mounted, so that by the time she reached the bottom, everyone was clapping and cheering, including the

Archbishop. Spying her parents, she blushed deeply and ran to them amidst the ruckus.

"Hanna, maybe you'd better let us smell your breath this time. Have you been at the Chardonnay again?" asked her father, amused but embarrassed for her sake.

"High spot of the evening, daddy?"

"That took some spunk, young lady."

"Many more will follow, my girl, but you will always be the first." were some of the remarks from passers-by. Everyone laughed and congratulated her. Sarah was amazed and said, "Hey, little sister, that was some act. Maybe we should enlist you in a thespian school."

After the guests had settled down, Matt left with Emily and headed for a quiet interlude at a nearby sidewalk cafe. With a full view of Titanic II, they sat quietly holding hands assuring each other of how much they had enjoyed the relationship. A few tender kisses spoke of love, but they both knew it was over. Tomorrow Matt would be on his way home, in whatever year, and she would return to her normal droll routine.

The next morning the boys packed their meager belongings, thanked their landlady for her great kindness, and left for the dock.

"Did you remember the laser and prism, oh wondrous one?"

"Yes, of course. Did you remember the pocket computer?"

"Oh! I knew I'd forgotten something," Matt confessed.

"If you had, it would be the last time you'd ever forget anything."

Arriving about two hours before the scheduled 10 A.M. departure, they found the stateroom they would occupy, then wrapped up the last few details of their projects. An hour before departure, Sarah arrived with her family. They saw to it that she was properly ensconced in her stateroom, and that everything was in order for the sailing.

Chapter 27

They all met on the dock the next morning to exchange farewells.

"Mom, Dad, Hanna, you've been wonderful about this whole thing. I wish there some way to do this without leaving. But, when my man says, 'Come....! I come. I love you all. I know Randy'll come up with some way to get us together again. I'd write to you, but I'm not sure to which century I should have you write."

"Now, there's one you'll never top," exclaimed Mrs. Carlisle.

"Randy, you take good care of my girl, you hear?"

"Aye, aye, sir."

With that, they all hugged each other, wiped away the tears, and headed into their separate futures.

At precisely 9:55A.M, with a few hundred onlookers, including the Carlisles, the ship's horn sounded its departure. Hawsers were released and tugs began to turn Titanic II into the channel leading to the mouth of Belfast Lough. Having cleared the dock and been released by the tugs, her speed was brought up to 12 knots. After clearing Belfast Lough into the Irish Sea, she soon reached her cruising speed of 20 knots.

J. P. had seen to it that his guests were served nothing but the best for luncheon and dinner. Much of the midday was spent sampling the many international treats after the luncheon. Matt left Sarah and Randy on their own, and spent a few hours on the bridge. The bridge crew was more than eager to share their enthusiasm over the ship, its beauty and technical advancements.

Randy and Sarah toured the first-class area. Sarah was, once again; amazed at the money that was spent on the embellishments, particularly the Grand Staircase and its clock. Randy mentioned that Matt had responded to the message on the plaque ("GLORY and HONOR crowning TIME.") by saying that, in view of what they had done, it should read---'TIME has crowned HONOR and GLORY'. Sarah was surprised to hear that Matt could dig so deeply into something that was not technical. Seeing and discussing the plaque prompted her to ask questions that had been bothering her for some time.

"Randy, I'm finding it difficult to sit here quietly, knowing that within the next fortnight, all of these famous people might be dead. I know it, but there's nothing I can do about it."

"Sarah, you can drive yourself crazy trying to determine what is and what is not, your responsibility, or even your concern. If the Lord wants them home on that day, they'll be there no matter what anyone does. Matt and I have been going through this since we found there might be a way to travel back and fix it. I've always wondered if it is within our power to change history."

"Then what you're saying is that you and I may wind up unavailable to each other....for reasons of time separation or because we are destined to go at that time and nothing's going to stop it. That sounds very threatening. I believe man's decisions make the difference in his destiny and if you are willing to take the chance, I certainly am. No matter what happens, you know I'll always love you.

"There's one other question that has been gnawing at me. How can you talk about Titanic and Titanic II in the same breath? Isn't it the same ship? Your influencing Ismay to add the II to the name doesn't change a thing does it? It's still one ship, one destiny, one ocean bottom."

"Not exactly, Sarah." Randy paused. "The time-travel we have been involved in is between parallel dimensions. Our ship heads for what we may believe to be her destiny. Unknown to us, however, others are working on her equivalent in a parallel dimension They are headed for the same destiny. There is only one ship and one destiny....One Titanic. Using Titanic II allows us to put a handle on the difference; much like your watch helps us, chronometrically, to organize our time in accordance with solar orbit and earth rotation. Actually, the objective was a marketing ploy of a somewhat more complex nature. I'm not sure I can explain it in more detail."

"My, oh my, Randy, that really clears it up for me," Sarah said facetiously. "It makes it clear as mud. To think that I'm basing my willingness to go with you on something I don't understand at all! I must be crazy!"

"Sarah, my love, being crazy helps. If you're crazy, you don't develop ulcers worrying about anything," Randy joked.

The weather remained somewhat inclement until late afternoon, when the clouds parted in time for a beautiful sunset Randy and Sarah had planned to be on the boat deck when the sun set. They made it in the nick of time, and were rewarded with a golden sky enveloping everything. As the sunset progressed, high puffs of clouds brightened into brilliant pink, then faded with the light from bright to deep oranges and reds with no visual obstruction. They were able to see the entire sunset, horizon to horizon, much like a full rainbow.

"I've always been fascinated by the horizon when the sun is sinking behind it," Sarah explained. There seems to be a gap between the sun and its reflection on the water."

Randy agreed. "Add a fully-rigged sailboat silhouetted against the sun and you have my favorite picture."

"Randy, I would imagine that heaven is like this. Being with your love and watching the magnificent beauty of God's handiwork."

They walked forward to the forecastle, stood behind the White Star pennant flying straight in the strong wind. All the blight, the misery and man's inhumanity to man, were shrouded by the light of nature's greatest artwork.

"Randy," Sarah began, "I feel like I'm going to explode, I am so happy and filled with love."

"I know, love, I know," Randy responded. "We are very fortunate to have each other and feel the way we do."

The ship arrived at Southampton that evening shortly after 9 P. M. So much had transpired during the trip that it seemed as though three or four days had gone by. By the time she was completely docked, it was close to midnight. A brief get-together in the lounge allowed them to make some comments on how great a ship it was. Everyone going on from Southampton was looking forward to it with great anticipation.

Some of the guest passengers had arranged business meetings in Southampton. All the guests were told that they could remain aboard or use their stateroom until the ship got underway on the 10th. J. P. himself disembarked immediately, leaving his guests to fill in the days until then.

Randy, Matt and Sarah visited several historic sites, including King

John's Palace, built in the 13th century. Sarah very much enjoyed ancient edifices, but Matt and Randy, with American history not extant much before the 17th century, had a somewhat different perspective. They experienced a similar disparity when viewing the many works of old masters at the Southampton Art Museum.

A few days later J. P. came aboard briefly. Seeing Randy and Sarah together, he felt compelled to suggest that she had put her life in the hands of a genius, but one involved in things he shouldn't change.

"Randy, I hope that you and Matt will forgive me for lashing out at you the day of the launching. I, myself, was unaffected by your comment concerning Titanic II playing the part of a billiard ball among the icebergs. It was essential, however, for me to counteract the obvious negative reactions of the gentlemen who were with me, and who invest in my ventures. They can be the source of good or bad press. Someone had to be the goat. Unfortunately it was you and Matt. Please relay my apologies to him and assure him I am most grateful for the contributions you have both made to our ships."

"Thank you, J. P.," responded Randy. I told him he was playing with a little league bat in the major leagues. He rather enjoyed the whole scene."

"I'm certain he did," concluded J. P."

Chapter 28
The maiden voyage

Southampton was, and is, one of the busiest passenger ship hubs in the world. At times ships sit in line in the harbor awaiting dock space. With such traffic volume, every possible facility is available. Very well organized harbor administration delays very few ships for lack of supplies, or additional crew.

Titanic II arrived at 9 P.M. that evening, and was finally docked some time shortly after midnight. Randy and Sarah watched from the bow as she entered the port, was met by two tugs, and wrestled into her slip. The next day, while further loading of supplies and coal was being done, the guests went ashore to pursue their business or their sightseeing.

Isidor Straus and his wife had returned early from their tour of Southampton. Isidor had been here before, but Mrs. Straus had excitedly told everyone at the party that her loving husband was to take her around town to see history, art and royal gardens, and, if time allowed, some of the non-tourist spots. She returned exhausted, but raving about her visit. The love between the Strauses, despite their marriage of forty-plus years, still glowed. It was wonderful to behold.

Ben Guggenheim and John Jacob Astor dined together at a well-known watering hole downtown. They returned early, hoping to catch up on sleep lost at the party. Sitting about the lounge and the boat deck suited them fine for at least the first few days.

Several people bragged on the dinner that had been served late at night after the ship‘s arrival. Everyone figured that J. P. had made special arrangements for it, but they soon realized it was normal fare for J. P's personal chef.

At 9A.M., on the 10th, all hands were checked back in. Only J. P. was missing from the group who had sailed from Belfast. Following the sound of its loud, deep horn, the magnificent ship was being pushed to center channel. This was history in the making, and none of the passengers were going to miss it.

At times, the immigrants in steerage violated the space of the higher class accommodations. The waiters and other service people proffered gentle reminders. As Randy and Sarah walked by three immigrant boys, one yelled out in broken English, "My father is to meet us at the Statue of Liberty. He went to the United States a year ago to find work. We have really missed him." His voice was heard by anyone on the boat deck.

Once underway, the ship headed across the Channel for the port of Le Havre, France. Here they took on more than one hundred passengers. A quick turn and they were headed for Queensland, Ireland for their last passengers.

Before leaving Queensland, the Deck Division conducted a hands-on lifeboat drill with the passengers---first for those in forward quarters, then for those aft. It went quite well for their first effort. Only once was a line let go, causing a boat to drop suddenly, and a rather large woman to suffer a few well-placed bruises. The divided drills prompted questions about why there were only half as many lifeboat seats as there were passengers and crew. Of course, everyone blamed it on Her Majesty's Board of Trade. Although Bruce Ismay and Tom Andrews observed the exercise and were generally pleased with it, they did not jump in to discuss the Board of Trade or any other aspect of the ship's outfitting or construction. Tom Andrews was without his wife since she was six months pregnant. Bruce Ismay did not usually take his wife along---he was reluctant to share his sense of accomplishment and responsibility when a new ship was put into service.

Titanic II soon reached its insertion point of the great circle route that provided the shortest route between Queenstown and New York. At this time of year, however, Captains still had to take into account the ice fields and icebergs floating south across the shipping lanes from the Arctic. The gulfstream normally melted the smaller ones, but now and then, a monster would threaten shipping as late as April. It was an unpredictable month. The great circle route chosen by Captain Smith would increase the threat of ice, since it would require his sailing north of the longer, more southerly straight-line course. Given the competition between White Star and Cunard with its faster ships, it would become fairly obvious Captain Smith had been instructed to beat Cunard's time. Thus he

chose the shorter more dangerous route.

The weather throughout the first few days was ideal. During the warmer part of the day, the pool was well used. The 1st and 2nd class gentlemen, of course, competed in the billiards room---large, dark Cuban cigars hanging from their lips. The recreation director managed to provide enough games for the 1st and 2nd class children. Most of the passengers walked the decks, enjoyed each other's company and the gourmet meals served either in the dining room, on deck, or in their staterooms.

Matt spent a good deal of time checking out the systems he and Randy had installed. He also continued his work on the time-travel hardware. It wasn't as easy as he thought, and time was running short.

Meanwhile, Randy and Sarah promenaded frequently, engrossed in their conversation. They were introduced to Ben Guggenheim and John Jacob Astor.

Randy and Matt spoke with as many people as possible, alerting them to the fact that much ice still existed in the North Atlantic. They were obscure in their detail, and approached the subject with reserve and in an off-handed manner. Their objective was to prompt them to be better prepared for the possibility of tangling with a berg, by increasing their awareness.

Sarah and Randy happened to be seated at luncheon next to the Strauses on the second day out. Mrs. Straus was a very shy woman, and, only after his encouragement, did she welcome social interaction. She did, however, take a liking to Sarah, and when told Sarah's father was one of the designers of the ship, expressed her admiration and became friendlier. She spoke knowledgeably of many subjects, and shared recipes and other womanly items freely.

While Sarah occupied Mrs. Straus, Randy engaged her husband in conversation. Since Randy was of Jewish background, he felt at ease speaking of Jews in the past, and in the immediate future. There was little reason to hold back on talk of the future, now that it had all but arrived. Randy informed Straus that a Communist revolution would depose the Czar and commence a reign of terror in Russia, beginning in 1917, the same year that World War I would begin. Straus found that hard to believe, and wondered upon what Randy based his facts. Randy avoided that part of the discussion.

"Mr. Straus, it sometimes is hard for me to understand the role of

God's 'chosen ones' in the pre-Christian world. Our history is rife with slavery, uprooting and loss of home territory. Pressed into slavery in Egypt---Moses led us out of it, to the Promised Land. Living under similar conditions in Persia---they were repatriated by King Cyrus. They were oppressed by the conquering Romans during Jesus' time.

"The worst of all will come in 1935, lasting until 1944. Adolph Hitler, a paranoiac Austrian, will gain control of Germany, and declare his intention to find a 'final solution to the Jewish problem'!" His solution will be to build gas chambers and kill 6,000,000 Jews from all over Europe. The killing stops when the war Hitler will have begun, is ended. I can't tell you what happened in the town of Otterberg, but you can be assured that nowhere in the country was it safe to be non-German especially Jewish."

"Did you say, '6,000,000 Jews'?"

"Yes, sir, but our people will be rescued from near-oblivion by the newly established United Nations who, in 1948, will create a homeland called Israel, at about the same location as earlier. Jews from all over the world will immigrate, tripling the area's population within 10 years."

"How did the surrounding Arab states accept this?" asked Strauss.

"They didn't," replied Randy. "Syria, Jordan and Egypt joined an attempt to drive them out of the mideast altogether. In the 'Six Day War', the Israelis, with the help of French jet fighters, will win over the Arabs..

"All this for a 'chosen people'! Is that what you're getting at?" asked Straus. "It almost sounds like, 'with friends like these, who needs enemies'?

"Mr. Kaplan," perhaps heaven is reserved only for those who suffer but endure; those who maintain their faith and obey the Lord though their lot be pure misery."

"You may be right, sir. I've heard my Christian friends say, 'there can be no resurrection without the crucifixion'. Suffering is, apparently, an essential adjunct to the human condition."

"Randy, it seems to be the nature of people continuously persecuted and left without the security of their own homeland and government, to strive tirelessly for individual, family and community excellence."

"I've seen that in the U. S., in the legal, medical, entertainment and other lucrative industries. At the end of the twentieth century we find these industries even more heavily populated by Jewish individuals over-achieving in response to persistent national oppression."

"You are right, my son. You have been presenting an excellent study in sociological phenomena. I surmise that political, ethnic or religious pressures placed upon a people over the centuries could easily form their behavior as a nation or race.

"Randy, I have enjoyed speaking with you, but I'd best get back to my loving wife I look forward to running into you again before we arrive. Perhaps we can discuss another of the mysteries of the world.... if I can find you on this huge vessel."

The ship was due to enter New York harbor mid-morning of the 16th. It was expected that the fireboats, tugs, private boats and many thousands of people would be on hand to welcome her. The great welcome was not to be, if history were to be fulfilled once again.

Matt had not quite finished his work on the time-travel equipment. He needed the answer to where they would generate a second source of light, strong enough to match that from the laser itself. During daylight, the sun was the primary source, but not at 11 P.M. Randy and Matt asked Sarah to leave them alone in the stateroom while they attempted to answer that extremely important question.

"Matt, our laser operates at 50% efficiency at any power setting," said Randy. "Our first test showed that we had enough power for time transport of the two of us. I've been thinking that if we used mirrors to reflect one portion of a split beam to each side of the prism, we may provide sufficient power to complete the deal."

"Where are you going to get the equipment necessary in these times and on this ocean?" inquired Matt.

"Well, Matt, all we really need is a small mirror or mirror tile, or, better yet, a convex reflective surface. We know there are hand and wall mirrors throughout the 1st class section, and in staterooms. There may also be a magnifying shaving mirror, or two, available somewhere.

"Here's how it might work. First, turn the highly reflective internal mirrors of the laser to allow their focusing on a series of external mirrors. Second, adjust the external mirrors so as to reflect one-half the laser beam to each side of our prism. Third, adjust the power so that in the CW (Continuous Wave) mode we are doubling our previous power. We should be able to do this without losing more than 10% of the full spectrum (IR to UV) at either end. If the iceberg we're to hit is clean enough (minimal silt and plankton), we might be able to use its vertical surface as a reflecting device"

"Randy, that just might do it. Too bad we can't have a dry run. But the best you can do in preparation is to align the internal and external mirrors, set up the power source, and wait for the fatal moment. If we plan to use the berg itself as a reflective agent, we'll have a very small window of time to initiate it," Matt pointed out.

"Matt, I think things are under control. We will set ourselves up to go just as the ship's prow contacts the berg."

Randy returned to the boys' stateroom, where he found Sarah resting. "We've done it, Sarah! We've come up with a way of using the time machine without benefit of sunlight. Hallelujah!!"

"You see, Randy, my faith has not been misplaced. I knew the two of you could do it. So, now, if the ship hits the iceberg despite the training the bridge crew's had, we have a way out."

"Yes, we do. But our timing of the laser and prism must be very precise. And, remember you must remain within 30 feet of Matt and me when the gong goes off. "

"The 'gong goes off'?"

"Oh, pardon me, what I mean is 'when the switch is thrown'."

"Kiss me, Randy!"

"That'll be a nice thing to come home to every day....I love you, Sarah."

"Yes, Time Traveler, yes!" she responded as she hugged him tightly.

Each night the ship's orchestra played on 'A' deck. Randy and Sarah joined in the dancing for a short time after dinner. They were so engrossed in each other; passengers sitting about could not help but be impressed. They looked deeply into each other's eyes, and danced as though their feet were not touching the floor. Sighs of envy could be heard from the older passengers, as they recalled their own days of romance and passion.

When Randy and Sarah left the dance floor each night, they walked up the Grand Staircase to stroll on the boat deck, inhale the salt air, and bask in whatever light the moon provided. The pure Victorians would have been indignant rather than envious if they had known the couple were neither married nor chaperoned. Fortunately, they would not learn of it, so were not deprived of their vicarious enjoyment.

If one were to describe the most idyllic scene for a loving couple to share, it would doubtless include an ocean liner cutting the waves in near silence. A slight rolling motion from passing waves creating a hypnotic state, relaxed and carefree. The moon reflecting on the water from the "A" deck, issuing soft, late night music of the ship's orchestra.

"Sarah, do you suppose there is some way to capture this scene, and hold on to it for a lifetime together? Wouldn't you think that two guys who can move around in time, could do something about that?

"No, Randy, you may be able to move around, but I'm not sure you can change the surroundings---they're there forever.

"Well, I'd sure like to give it a try, and this would be the scene I would want to work on."

"Randy, accept what's offered. We are very fortunate to have even this much time to be with each other."

"All this for 'special people!"

Chapter 29

Although Randy and Matt slept in the same stateroom, they did not see too much of each other during the voyage. The reason -- Sarah. Once they had made preparations for the return to the future, there was little else to consume Randy's time besides Sarah.

"Why, hello, Mr. Kaplan,"Matt chided. "Are you still aboard, or have you jumped to the sharks for fear of the upcoming disaster? What I'm really seeing before me is the ghost of 'Ship Saver'?"

"All right, wise guy,"Randy replied. "The only reason you haven't seen me is that this is such a huge ship."

"Oh, baloney! You can't kid me. You wouldn't know what to do with yourself if she weren't aboard with us. Maybe I should have kidnapped Emily, if only for company, then sent her back on the next boat."

Their conversation did not increase the time they were together, so Matt sought out Captain Smith, Mate Murdoch, Chief Engineer Bell and other department and division heads, individually, to discuss the peril of ice in the North Atlantic. He found that, to a man, they had experienced icebergs, had never been touched by one, considered April a low-risk month, and were convinced the ship was 'unsinkable' in any event.

Trying to alert each of them, subtly, to the real possibility of contact, he projected their course to New York, and said,

"We will pass 95 miles south of Grand Banks, Newfoundland. In this area, any number of various size icebergs could be floating, some of them enormous. They will have broken off from Greenland's land ice, floated through Baffin Bay into the North Atlantic, where the Atlantic gyre sweeps some southeastward, almost paralleling our projected course."

"Well, Mr. Kaplan, it hardly seems likely we would run into ice that could cause us trouble in mid-April. They'd all be melted by then. Right, sir?"

"Wrong, 'Mac.' replied Randy. "The bigger ones, up to 300 feet above the water's surface, don't melt much before they are picked up and sent back north again to re-freeze."

"Then how long do they 'live'?"asked Chief Engineer Bell. "It would seem impossible for them to make it through the summer before returning above the Arctic Circle."

"Mr. Bell, they can survive for up to three years. They have been sighted as far south as Bermuda. The problem is that from April through the warm months, bridge personnel and lookouts become blase'. Their vigilance is compromised and Whammo!"

"Well, now, guvna', Captain Smith runs a tight ship. Whatever comes up, we can handle it. Besides, as one of our deck crew said, 'God himself couldn't sink this ship'!"

"I don't think so, Bell, I truly don't think so." concluded Randy.

Friday, the 12th of April, the weather continued perfect.. The only thing not at its best was the waning moon. Having reached its third quarter, it was now headed for the dim crescent of the New Moon---least desirable of its phases for crossing iceberg territory.

Sarah and Randy spent a good deal of quiet time with each other on the12th and 13th. They both acknowledged that it was a strange feeling to know that within the next two days, one of the greatest ship disasters in the history of the world would take place. To make it worse, the ship was brand new, had unlimited amounts of money lavished on her and, as passengers, some of the most famous names in the world.

"Randy, I've come to know Mrs. Straus quite well. I'm still finding it difficult to live with the notion that she will probably die with her husband. I don't consider it my responsibility to tell her, and there's actually nothing anyone can do about it. Am I being overly sympathetic to someone who is to die anyway, whether or not we're involved?. Since we may die with them."

"Sarah, there are 2,200 or more passengers and crew aboard; Mrs. Straus is only one of them. I don't think you are in a position to decide who you help, who you try to save, or who you don't."

"I know you are right, Randy, but we've become such good friends. There's a kindred spirit between us I can't define."

"This was one of the things we pointed out to the Board at our presentation--no Captain, or anyone, wants to play God and say who boards the lifeboats and who stays to die. Ergo--more lifeboats! One seat for each posterior."

Chapter 30

Everything aboard was operating smoothly. The Captain was holding 21.5 knots, well above what would be considered a safe speed for the conditions. An American vessel, the Californian, to avoid the hazard, had steamed toward the southern end of the ice field, and had begun to send out messages concerning the danger. Seven messages had been received by Titanic II, but Captain Smith disregarded them. This seasoned veteran wasn't about to stand still for taking direction or reacting to caution from an American ship captain!

The young trio, faced with what could easily be their own disaster, are invited to a party thrown by the White Star Line on Saturday, the 13th---routine with any of their ships underway over the weekend. Several toasts are proposed by Ismay and Andrews, and the ship's orchestra has been reserved for the night.

Matt and Randy are approached by Ismay and Andrews. "So far, so good, boys. Things seem to be going well, Looks like we may make it despite your dire projections, said Ismay. Anyway, why else would you be aboard?

Matt responded calmly by saying. "It might be deceiving, Mr. Ismay. We won't be running into the main part of the ice field until tomorrow. To apply an old Norwegian proverb, 'Don't sell the skin 'til the bear's been shot.'

"We have talked to Captain Smith and others on the bridge, warning them to continue their vigilance. We're not sure they're as receptive as they should be. The field we'll be penetrating tomorrow, carries with it more and larger bergs than are usually seen in mid-April." Andrews' face began to show tension as he realized the boys were still holding to their warning that tomorrow would be the day of disaster.

It was approaching 11 P.M., Randy suggested they retire. Tomorrow would be a long day---the beginning of the disaster was not until almost midnight. Matt had no problem with that suggestion; he'd been working very hard these past few days.

"It'll take more than a collision with an iceberg to keep me awake tonight" said Matt. They wished all a good night, and headed for the boys' stateroom.

"Sarah, just stay with us for a few moments, then I'll walk you back to your room, " said Randy.

Entering their room, Randy suggested a few moments of silent prayer for those who might die tomorrow, and for their own safety.

Facing the actual disaster was becoming increasingly difficult for Sarah. She hugged Randy and said, "Randy, don't lose me. I can't live without you."

"Fear not!" Randy said in a firm, somewhat jocular tone. "I will make you a part of me; then you will never be lost." They then sat in silent prayer, basking in the warmth of its generated love.

"Fear only derives from lack of faith," Randy said, picking up where he had left off. "Speaking of fear reminds me that one thing we have not discussed is Bruce Ismay's behavior during the sinking. The newspapers severely castigated him for having survived in a lifeboat while so many were left to die. They compared him to the Captain of the ship, as well he might be. His influence on the number who died was considerably greater than that of the Captain. At any rate, tradition has it that the Captain should go down with the ship.

"One of the papers went so far as to print a poem one of their reporters had written, obviously pointed at Ismay:

'To hold your place in the ghastly face of death,
On the sea of night,
Is a seaman's job,
But to flee with the mob,
Is the owner's noble right.'

"This seems an excellent commentary on the choices we have under fire --fight or flight. Unfortunately, tradition dictates that flight is not an option for owner or captain. What should one do in this case? Flee with the mob? Would any of us pass this critical test? Perhaps, if our efforts to save the ship are successful, Mr. Ismay will escape his moment of public shame."

On this speculation, they called it a day. "Sleep well, friends, tomorrow will be a long day," intoned Matt. Randy walked Sarah to her room, kissed her and said, "I love you, Sarah---forever!"

Sarah hugged him as in a last hug, hoping never to be without him. "Wherever you are, I will be. Wherever you go, I will go. Years, distance, even death, cannot separate us, I would fear for tomorrow, but our love is greater than fear.......Good night, my love."

Chapter 31

The fateful day had arrived. Clear and cool, with light breezes, the passengers took advantage of the day and filled the decks from bow to stern walking, sitting or staring from the rail, mesmerized by the sound and sight of the ship's wake. Few were encumbered by knowledge of what was to transpire that day.

Randy and Matt worked through most of the early morning assuring themselves that all was in readiness for the event. Sarah sought out Mrs. Straus who was sunning herself on the boat-deck.

"Good morning, Mrs. Straus. The Lord certainly has provided a fine day for us."

"Yes, my dear, he surely has. Come sit with me."

"Thank you. How are you this morning?"

"Oh, as well as I might expect at my age, when one does not move around quite as easily."

"I wanted to talk to you about how someone your age looks at things," Sarah began, "You recall I mentioned that Titanic was to run into difficulty during this voyage. Today is the day. Later tonight we hope it will be able to avoid the collision on its own due to our prior warnings and preparation. Either of these will change history, since originally she sank after striking the iceberg, and 1,522 people died. So, you can see how momentous tonight's events will be."

"Sarah, at you age, you become more and more the fatalist. As each day dawns, you are more aware of the brevity of life and the imminence of death. The events that lead up to the transition are more to be welcomed than feared. You claim the blessings and disregard the pain, suffering or anxiety that may accompany an event."

Sarah responded, "Randy told me of a song written in the 1940's which said, 'accentuate the positive, eliminate the negative, don't mess with Mr. In-Between.' It is too bad we gain such wisdom only after spending most of our lives in anxiety and worry. In addition to the three R's, maybe our children, and their children, should regularly be taught how to accept what they are dealt in life.

"I wanted to tell you I'll be praying for you and Mr. Straus that you be kept safe during the emergency we will be running into tonight."

"Thank you, dear. You have been a wonderful shipmate. Will I see you at lunch?"

"Yes, ma'am."

Randy and Matt did everything necessary to get the time-travel equipment ready if needed. If greater vigilance caused the ship to avoid the iceberg, then, praise God, it would not be needed. Everything else was packed and ready to go, no matter what happened.

Sarah knew she would have to leave most of her clothing if time-travel was used. Although there were many stylish and expensive garments that could not come with her, she looked to a new life with her love---a worthwhile sacrifice in any case. "Besides," she muttered to herself, "1910 styles are not likely to fit in with those of the future."

It was just about nightfall when Ismay and Andrews, now seeing the amount of ice along the route, were beginning to take the boys more seriously and spending more time near the bridge. More than once they reminded a lookout or helmsman to keep a sharp eye out. They felt quite insecure as they looked forward into the darkness ahead.

"This is ominous, Bruce," said Andrews, "On other maiden voyages, I don't recall ever feeling as insecure as I do right now. We seem to be sailing quietly and rapidly into a dark void, an enormous peril. Perhaps we should take the boys' advice and slow the ship down in these unpredictable waters. We need not feel compelled to arrive precisely on time at the risk of self-destruction."

"That's true, but Smith is our senior captain and should be sufficiently familiar with these waters. I have given him permission to maintain this speed. We selected him for this trip; perhaps we should rest easy with it"

"It's bloody cold out tonight, Mate. and it's likely to go down even further before sunup," said Fleet. "This humidity doesn't help any. It's no good for spottin' the bergs, either." They were in the crows nest as lookouts.

"Ya can say that again, Mate," said Lee. Each berg carries its own fog around with it. Ya needs an eagle's eye to see them." He and Lee were in the crow's nest on the 4 P.M. to Midnight shift. Earlier in the shift, Randy had left them a pair of binoculars to increase their chances of seeing the iceberg in time. Lee had reached for them, and while attempting to hang them from his neck, his cold hands let them slip. One bounce on the boat deck and they were in the water.

At exactly 11:38 P.M., Fleet suddenly sees an enormous iceberg lurking in the mist directly in the ship's path. With panic in his voice, he grabs the bellpull and yanked it three times to indicate object dead ahead. Then he yells through the phone to the bridge, "Large iceberg dead ahead, less than one-and-a-half miles!" He and Lee brace themselves for a collision.

Murdoch, 2nd mate on the bridge watch, immediately issues orders to the Engine Room and the helmsman.

Arriving on the bridge, the Captain is informed of the orders given. Murdoch had responded correctly to the challenge he faced. Captain Smith, on the other hand, without benefit of the training provided his bridge personnel, countermands the order with ALL ENGINES FULL ASTERN and dooms the ship. This begins the scenario of conflicting orders, rendering the ship incapable of avoiding the oncoming iceberg. Collision is inevitable, sinking a real possibility.

Thus far, the details of the original collision were following Randy and Matt's presentation to the Board of Designers to a tee. The subsequent report of the Senate committee chaired by Sen. William A. Smith,(1) suggested that confusion in orders to the helm and the engine room may have contributed to the accident as much as the ship's excessive speed. Several writings of interest were published which supported this conclusion. None of these accounts, however, was witness to the breakthrough in time-travel achieved by two young engineering students from the future.

With Matt and Sarah, and their possessions, nearby, Randy had begun counting down from 30 seconds, which he calculated to be the time left until impact with the iceberg. 29, 28, 27, 26, 25--- "This feels like NASA sending the shuttle into space," observed Matt. 24, 23, 22, 21, 20---"Sarah, are you O.K.?" asked Randy. 19, 18, 17, 16, 15---"So far. Are we going into space?" Sarah asked. 14, 13, 12, 11---"No, love, we should wind up pretty close to here." 10, 9, 8, 7, 6, 5, 4, 3, 2, 1.-----------"She's not going to clear the berg!"

Randy immediately set off the time machine, causing the now familiar implosion and sending a shudder through the ship. Sarah put her hands over her ears to avoid the tremendous noise created by the implosion. Randy and Matt watched their wall clock's hands begin to move counterclockwise, then the entire stateroom rotate. In her panic, Sarah screamed as on the first drop of a roller-coaster, but with greater fear and intensity

The three time-travelers found themselves propelled through a vast void, spinning, out of control, thunderous sounds, lightning flashes in every color of the rainbow. As quickly as it began, it was over, and they found themselves, one at a time, deposited rather ignominiously on the 'A' deck, immediately forward of their stateroom.

A young couple, walking arm in arm, were almost sat upon as Sarah was dropped on the deck.

"Where in the devil did you all come from?" was a logical question. Matt, quick to see the humor in the situation, responded,

"Oh, we thought we'd just drop in for a nightcap. Where's the lounge on this crate, mate?"

"Let's get out of here!" suggested the man to his companion.

"Our rig didn't do the job!" Randy said, "we're still on Titanic II.

"But the iceberg's gone!" replied Matt Did we bring the ship around the berg?"

"We must have," declared Randy. "How else account for no iceberg?" Meanwhile, on the bridge, Murdoch realizes that the Captain's order to the engine room is still FULL ASTERN. "Captain, may I order 'ALL ENGINES STOP?' We are beginning to go in reverse."

"Yes. Mr. Murdoch. Please do." Captain Smith responded.

"What happened to the iceberg?" he asked. "It's gone!" At that, answer all hands on the bridge looked to confirm the disappearance.

Fleet and Lee had watched the iceberg begin to slide down the starboard side, when it suddenly disappeared!

"Where did the bloody berg go?" asked Lee. "How can a piece of ice sixty feet above the water and God knows how far below, just vanish? It certainly didn't melt! Good Lord, Fleet, what else is gonna happen tonight?"

When the iceberg disappeared and Titanic was backing away from the impact site, a smaller ship of more modern design, obviously home base for some form of marine expedition, suddenly appeared just off the starboard bow.

"Look, there, Lee, that wasn't there a minute ago. One of us would have seen it! What's goin' on 'ere? We'd better notify the bridge."

"Small supply ship ahead. Running lights show she's moored for the night," Fleet reported. Murdoch reached for his binoculars, focused them on the ship's stern and read;

B O L L A R D   M A R I NE
Boston

Aboard the Bollard ship, Richard Bollard, owner of this well-known marine salvage company, was awakened by the night watch, and was astounded to see this enormous ship, lighted from stem to stern, and only a few hundred yards away.

"Where'd she come from? Who is she? There hasn't been a ship this close to our salvage operation in months! Try to raise them on the radio," he asked John Michaels, his assistant Michaels was a Marine Biologist who accompanied Bollard on every dive.

"This is Richard Bollard, owner Bollard Marine. We are here salvaging Titanic. Who are you?"

No answer was forthcoming. Bollard then suggested they try morse code. This time, the response was, "This is Titanic II, departure Southampton, April 10, 1912. Arrival New York April 16, if no further delay. E. J. Smith, Captain."

"We are in year 2012. Your ship sank on this spot 100 years ago. Is this some kind of joke? Or are you promoting a cruise line?" Bollard's radio operator asked in morse code.

Back on Titanic's bridge, Captain Smith, stone-faced and chewing vigorously on his ever-present cigar, ordered Murdoch to "get those two young American engineers up here on the double. I've heard they've been fooling around with time-travel, or whatever they call it. They've probably gone and brought us into the next century! Also, have Mooney check the forward starboard hold to assess amount of damage, if any, and have the damage control crew shore it up."

Without waiting any longer for a response, Bollard sent a message requesting permission to approach and board Titanic II. His request was immediately granted. He and Michaels dropped the dinghy and made a circle about the newly arrived ship. As they rounded the stern, they noted the name emblazoned on it:.

T I T A N I C

Liverpool

"Do you see that, John? There's no 'II' there. This has to be the real McCoy. But how did it get here, and why did they tell us she was Titanic II? Where has she been for a century? What have we been working on for three years?"

They headed for the ship's starboard gangway, which had been lowered to receive them.. Stepping on deck, they were greeted by Ismay, Andrews, Captain Smith, several well-known financiers and a host of curious passengers.

"Gentlemen," Bollard said, "May I suggest we retire to the privacy of a conference area. What we have to discuss may not be for your passengers or crew." Ismay and Andrews agreed with his suggestion. "E. J., we can use your underway cabin conference room," said Ismay.

"Right, Bruce. Gentlemen, please follow me," said Captain Smith. Passing the bridge, Smith instructed Murdoch to have Randy and Matt join them in his cabin and for Mooney to report to him on the extent of the damage. As the group took seats, Captain Smith stated he had no idea what had happened, nor why the iceberg had disappeared. "Two young American engineers aboard, I understand, have been experimenting with time travel. I've asked them to join us." At that point Randy and Matt, with Sarah in tow, entered the room.

"Mr. Kaplan, you know everyone here except Richard Bollard, marine salvage operator, and his assistant, John Michaels, a marine biologist," said Smith.

"Yes, we have been working the wreck of Titanic for three years aboard the ship you see up ahead, uncovering and removing artifacts/"

"You've been doing WHAT?" bellowed Ismay. Before anyone could respond, Mooney knocked and entered.

"Captain, you wanted a report on the damage done to the bow. It appears that the berg has not even touched the plates when it disappeared. All that it managed to do was scare us all into a panic. We should have struck it, but we didn't and I don't know why."

"Thank you, Mooney,"replied the captain. "Now, getting back to our subject, I...."

"Wait a minute! Now, just wait a minute!" Ismay interrupted "Am I to understand that you have been salvaging this ship for the last three years?"

"Yes, sir," said Bollard, "It took from 1912 until 1985 to find the wreckage, and between the French and us, enough artifacts were recovered by 1987 to hold an exhibit in Paris. We acquired rights to the wreck in 2008 and have been working it ever since."

"Then, what these two have been telling me about Titanic's sinking is a fact?

"That many people lost their lives because I refused to listen? But how can we be going past this point in time again? What is this all about?"
The captain picked up where he had been interrupted, saying,

"Yes, Bruce. Perhaps the boys can explain their mission and where we're at in the life of our ship, its passengers and crew. Would you explain it, please, Mr. Kaplan?"

"Yes, sir. Matt and I had traveled back in time from the year 2010 to 1910 in Belfast, using theories propounded by Albert Einstein. Our objective was to save the ship from experiencing the disaster we could have faced tonight, by persuading management to make certain modifications and additions to Titanic's design . "We worked with Alexander Carlisle, master shipbuilder, for the two years we were in Belfast. Please meet Sarah Carlisle, his daughter.

She has decided to return to the 21st century with us, with the hope that she and I might be married. Captain Smith, perhaps you could perform the ceremony for us before we arrive in New York. It's a bit late for invitations," Randy said with a broad smile, "but we have here a captive audience of 2,200 or more." A slight nod of his head and almost imperceptible smile implied Captain Smith would be happy to do it.

"Well, now that the important matters are taken care of, can we get back to the business at hand?" asked Ismay,.

"Is Mr. Bollard aware we are a 1912 ship, brand new except for crew that has been shaken beyond belief?" asked Randy.

"Yes, Mr. Kaplan, he is fully aware of it and absolutely dumbfounded, as are we all, at seeing the ship in its near-virgin condition 100 years later.. He also advised us that the number 'II' was no longer on the stern. Would you care to explain that, and your role in this fantasy." asked Captain Smith.

Matt jumped in, saying, "Randy, here, is an engineering genius. Although still in school, he has developed a viable means of time-travel which even Albert Einstein had not done, despite his theses on the subject. For those of you from 1912, Einstein is to become the most renowned scientist in history in the 1930's and beyond.

"Randy has had a passion to return to the early 20th century and, through design or influence, save Titanic from sinking on April 14/15, 1912. It appears he has done just that."

"Matt, I appreciate the kudos, but there are a few questions we don't have the answers to. We set our time-machine off at the moment of the supposed impact with the iceberg. Our purpose was to bring Sarah and the two of us safely back to 2012. It was not our intention to bring the ship, and everyone on it, back with us. We had no idea how much power we would generate using reflected laser beam only. Our previous experience was with sunlight and laser combined. We actually were concerned that there might not be enough power for the three of us, much less the entire ship!

"As assistant engineers with Harland & Wolff, we had gone as far as we could to effect changes that would either prevent the accident or minimize the loss of life resulting from it. As it turned out, however, our major recommendations were not accepted. The reasons for their rejection is not our concern at this juncture. History will be the judge of the decisions that were made.

"We then settled for minor changes such as bridge training for collision evasion, lifeboat handling for the deck crew, etc. Judging by the timing of the implosion that transported the ship tonight, moving it into the 21st century may have saved her and her passengers. But, we have no idea if the transition is permanent or, if not, how long it might last. The time-warp may be strong enough to hold things together until we reach New York, but it could revert at any time. Also, we have been warned in dreams and otherwise, by what appear to be dark angels, that we should not mess around with time....history cannot be changed.

"Concerning the number 'II' on the stern. That was appended to the ship's name as a marketing ploy. It was intended to take the focus off this ship and put it on an apparently successful imaginary predecessor. This was to stem the tide of bad publicity accruing to the steamship industry due to several major accidents with great loss of life.

"Being pioneers in this time business, I'm afraid neither of us can explain scientifically how the 'II' disappeared from the stern. It has always been the first Titanic that we were working on. Mr. Ismay and Andrews, here, can certainly attest to that. Apparently we have merged Titanic and Titanic II, the same ship, from parallel dimensions of time.

Chapter 32

Tom Andrews interrupted Randy to acknowledge that the boys had warned them of the many dangers inherent in the ship's design. "If she and her passengers had not been brought forward to the future, hundreds would no doubt have died. We have these two young men to thank for that."

Randy and Matt found it interesting to hear Andrews admit to the warnings they'd been given. Ismay, on the other hand, was silent throughout, reacting as he had previously with an evident lack of courage.

"Thank you for your support, Mr. Andrews. Another question that needs answering regards the wreckage remaining on the ocean floor and the artifacts that have been removed from it. It seems illogical for us to be sitting on the complete ship, while her wreckage lies below. The ship and its artifacts would most likely have reassimilated at the instant Titanic and Titanic 'II' joined in a single dimension of time. Concurrently, we must have lost the 'II' on the stern.

"Mr. Bollard, it would help us to know what's still down there, if anything. Could you make a dive first thing in the morning to assure us of which way this is going? You may be surprised at what you find, or don't find," Randy concluded.

"Also, Mr. Bollard," Ismay jumped in, "after you have determined what's going on below and informed us, would you kindly call New York, advising of the situation here, and when we will arrive in New York harbor. We were scheduled for approximately 6 P.M. on the 16th.

"E. J., do you think it's possible to make it by then? We've been slowed down with what we're doing now; Mr. Bollard will take time to search the bottom; the ice field is still a menace, and we will doubtless be deluged with press. Perhaps we should give them 9 A.M., Wednesday the 18th as an approximation."

"You're right, Bruce. That sounds good," replied Smith.

"One more thing;" Randy requested. "Our parents don't know where we've been for the last two years. Please have someone call them and tell them when we will arrive. Here are the phone numbers. Thank you. New York has never waited 100 years for a new ship to arrive. It should be quite a show. We wouldn't want our parents to miss it."

Bollard then said, "We haven't had a chance to conduct a search tonight, of course, but with first light you can be assured we'll be down there in our deep-water submersible. In anticipation of early rising, I suggest we all turn in. We'll figure this all out, somehow." At that, he wished everyone a good, if short, night's sleep and, with his associate, returned to his ship.

True to his word, Bollard had his crew ready to go at first light. He morse-coded a message to Captain Smith that they would return to the surface in an hour. He and Michaels then boarded the sub and were let down. When they reached the two mile depth, they turned on the powerful searchlights in anticipation of viewing the familiar site of the Titanic wreckage. At the two and a quarter mile depth, there was still no sign of it. Finally, when they reached the ocean floor, they were still unable to catch it in the light.

"Maybe we drifted a bit during the night. Start a circular search pattern with all searchlights on. It's got to be somewhere!"

"I don't know, Boss," said John Michaels, "If what they say has any truth at all to it, we're looking for a ship that doesn't exist down here.

"But, where would it go? You don't just disappear 900 feet of steel ship one day, after working with it almost every day for three years!"

"That may be, Dick, but we're dealing with something here that nobody understands. Even the kids who developed the time-machine couldn't tell us what's going on," Michaels responded. "I may be all wet on this, but there has to be some rational explanation for what's happening.

"Could be that when the two parallel time dimensions were enjoined, the physical attributes of each -- one the wreckage of the past, the other the pristine aggregate of the original vessel---were brought together in their common future without the blemish of its past. This is probably also true of every artifact we've removed from the wreckage. Speaking of artifacts, I kept a small ashtray with the White Star logo from our last haul. It should be in my floppy disk file box."

"There's nothing here, John. My God, do you realize what this means? Museums, exhibits, individuals will all find empty cases of Titanic artifacts. Every police organization in the world will have someone contacting them about vanished artifacts---Interpol, FBI, Scotland Yard, down to your village police.

"We'd better take the first step, notify the world about what's going on here and, at the same time, prepare New York for Titanic's arrival. Won't that be a show-and-a-half! I hope the FBI won't cart us off before we get to see it." Despite the seriousness of the whole show, Michaels could not help but laugh at his boss's expressed hope.

"John, when we get up, you contact our office, the New York Times, the major networks, the Mayor, Governor, even the White House. I'll contact CNN from Titanic in case I need some backup from the Captain or the other people involved. CNN is best equipped to handle a significant international incident. This will be the biggest happening since Apollo astronauts walked on the moon. If we all can travel in time, someone out there will be setting up travel agencies to handle it, while museums will close for lack of interest.---'See The Real Thing!' Uncle Sam will set up a new 'NASA' to explore it."

"I'll also have the crew prepare the helipad for the chopper visits we'll be getting," said Michaels. "CNN will probably be first on the scene, but, with room for only one to land, we'll need some traffic control. I'll take that."

"Right, John. Thanks. But, before we do, let's look at that security film footage. There may be some answers there."

Starting up the VCR and TV, they sat back, expecting to see the usual footage -- the broken hull, rusting and deteriorated, an occasional large deep-water fish -- but, suddenly at 11:38 P.M., the camera began to pick up some most unusual activity. Amid the wreckage, a porcelain doll's head looks hauntingly into the camera....

The artifacts on the ocean floor began to disappear one by one. The entire wreckage disappears along with them."

"Wow! That's awesome!" emoted Michaels. This is so far out it's impossible! Spineberg couldn't dream up anything this wild."

"It's bigger than anything we can handle. This scares me, and very little ever does." contributed Bollard. "I'll go back to Titanic, report our findings and give them help with whatever they need. Hand me that cellular phone. Set us up on a satellite channel. I'll call CNN with it, and we can keep in touch ship-to-ship."

"One other thing, Dick. I think it would be nice to let the boys call their parents themselves, rather than having one of us do it."

"Good thought, John. Tell surface we're finished down here."

Speaking through the intercom, Michael's said, "Bring us up. We're done down here -- really done!

The most significant reaction to the news came from CNN's Rolf Blittner. "Will you repeat that, please! 'Titanic, the ship that went down in 1912, is less than two days out of New York?' Of course. Right! Who is this? And, which funny farm are you calling from....Bellevue?"

"This is Dick Bollard, Bollard Marine out of Boston, salvaging Titanic wreckage for the last three years. Believe me, if anyone knows what's happening here, it's me." Get the word around. We have a helipad, that can receive one chopper at a time. Get someone out here to photo and interview, asap. Both ships are located at site of original disaster---49o 56' 49" West---41o 43' 57" North. Captain anxious to get going. Will try to delay him through today."

"You're serious, aren't you?"

"Never more! Your first photos will tell you how serious I am."

"We're on it. Thanks. This is Rolf Blittner."

Bollard rejoined the group in Captain Smith's cabin.

"What have you to tell us, Bollard?' asked Tom Andrews. "Judging by your wide eyes, it looks like you've found something."

"I'll say! We found nothing! He commenced to tell them of the security camera's recordings and Rolf Blittner's reaction at CNN. "It is a little much to expect anyone to believe this whole bit. I've seen and heard it first-hand, and I'm still not sure I believe it. If I weren't a God-fearing man, this would surely make me one."

"Is there anything else to discuss at this point?" asked Captain Smith.

"This afternoon at 3 P.M., I will conduct a memorial service for those that would have died on this ship. At 9 A.M. tomorrow we will have a beautiful wedding, after which we will get under way. My word the Titanic has been born again!"

"Yes, sir. That is so true and the wedding will be fine, said Randy. "My best man will, of course, be my fellow time-traveler Matt Miller, here. How about you, Sarah?"

"I have become very close with Mrs. Straus, and would like her to stand up for me," said Sarah.

"Great!" replied Captain Smith. Then that's what we'll do. I am certain that most of our time will be taken up with the press, who should start arriving within the next few hours. Mr. Bollard tells me he will provide his....what did you call it?....'helipad' for landing our visitors, and his dinghy for transport between the ships. Now all we need to know is, 'What is a helipad?"

"Oh, excuse me, Captain, I'd forgotten that you've never heard of or seen a helicopter. Helipads, which are usually mounted on the stern of receiving ships, as is ours, are for landing helicopters. If you'll look to my stern, you'll see the pad. I'm certain you'll see a helicopter land on it any time now.

(1) Senator William Alden Smith, Chairman of the Senate committee investigating Titanic and steamship safety, while poring over papers from his billfold, is struck by a curious coincidence.

He extracted a piece of yellowed newsprint he had clipped in 1912. It was a poem about a shipwreck:

"Then she, the stricken hull,
The doomed, the beautiful,
Proudly to a fate abased,
Her brow, Titanic."

Chapter 33

It wasn't three hours before a helicopter could be seen on the horizon, the whirring and thumping propellers stirring up a plume of spray behind it. It couldn't have been flying more than 30 feet off the water. From a considerable distance, one could see the huge letters 'CNN' on the side of the fuselage.

"Now this should prove very interesting. CNN has the capacity to broadcast directly from the site of an event, using satellite communications. When the switch is turned on back in New York, the whole world will immediately see and hear what's going on here.

"And when the reporters hear there'll be a memorial service today and a wedding in the morning, their human interest neurons will go bonkers.. Captain, you should find these next few days very exciting.." added Bollard. "I'd best get back to my ship to make ready for the troops." After he had left, Randy confided in the rest -- Ismay, Andrews and Smith.

"Captain, I think you need to be prepared for the real possibility of the ship sinking, returning to the watery grave it's occupied for the past 100 years."

"I am devastated by the possibility of us meeting the fate you and others from this century have told us about. Nobody would listen to you....least of all, me. If there were only some way to make it up to the world. My remorse has overcome my fear," said Captain Smith in a most genuine tone.

"It might be a mistake to inform the passengers of these details," said Randy, "What you might do is to hold a lifeboat drill after the memorial service. This will allow the passengers to at least have handled the gear. If you have two drills, we may avoid bringing attention to the fact that we have only half enough lifeboats. It will also provide the opportunity to insist the deck crew members make sure all boats are full. Some left the original sinking with as few as twelve aboard, with seats for sixty-four.

"Excellent idea, Randy. I'll schedule it after the memorial." With that, those in the meeting room went to the stern to watch the activity on Bollard Marine. The young trio followed them, noting the reactions of passengers to the scene. Few of them could know it might all be gone in an instant.

The CNN helicopter was hanging motionless just aft of Bollard's helipad, waiting for the pad to be cleared and tie-downs at the ready. Her props continued to stir up a circular wake and attendant spray.

Hundreds of passengers, hearing the racket, were running toward the stern to watch. They may have heard of the Wright Brothers' brief flight in 1903, but they certainly were not prepared for an aircraft capable of flying 200 mph, or suspended motionless in the air like a hummingbird.

As the chopper sat down on the pad and shut down her engines, two young reporters stepped out. followed by two photographers with cameras, microphones and other TV equipment. They, and their studio personnel, considered this a spectacular event.

Presented with 2,200 potential interviews, many of them famous, a scientific breakthrough, the threat of the ship's return to the grave, they were ecstatic. When told there would also be a wedding, a memorial service and a lifeboat drill, they said. "We've died and gone to that great Media Center in the sky."

They were greeted by Bollard and Michaels on the pad.

"Hi! I'm Ray Fletcher and this is Jim Moesley. CNN sent us to find out what we can about Titanic's strange reappearance. Not too many back in New York believe anything like this has happened, or could happen. They would have sent more than just us if they believed it.. But, obviously, here she is, brand spankin' new." They kept shaking their heads. "Can we interview the people most involved? We'll also want to take pictures of most of the ship, particularly the Grand Staircase and its famous clock."

"There are no restricted areas. We've arranged for you to use Captain Smith's conference room. We can also arrange for on-site interviews and pictures. Our dinghy will take you to the ship where Captain Smith will assign someone to each of you.

"We'll have to ask your pilot to leave and come back for you, or wait until we get to New York. We are expecting a lot more action on that pad before long," said Bollard. "We'll arrange for a place for you four to bed down."

"Thanks Mr. Bollard. We appreciate your help. C'mon, fellas. Have we got all the equipment? OK, let's go!"

Randy, Matt and Sarah withdrew from the hubbub, headed for their rooms to catch up on a lost night's sleep. Sarah intended to contact Mrs. Straus concerning the wedding, after a few hours rest.

But, then came a knock at the door. It was Mooney, sent by the Captain to advise the trio to be immediately available for the CNN reporters in the Captain's conference room.

"Well, Sarah, I can understand where they're at. We're at the bottom of this whole thing, but if we don't get some sleep, we're going to nod off during the wedding."

"Nod off? "

"Sorry---mod lingo for 'fall asleep'," responded Randy.

"Mod lingo?"

"That's modern language for 'modern language,' Matt interjected,

"Maybe I should come along on your honeymoon as Sarah's translator, right?"

"Hey, my man....Chill out!"

"Chill out!?"

The interviews with the reporters did not bother Randy and Matt, but Sarah was apprehensive. Before being pressed with questions she might have difficulty answering, Randy stepped in and said, "Go easy. She's not used to this fast-paced world. 100 years is a big cultural gap."

"I understand," said Fletcher. Then, with Sarah's beautiful face filling the monitor screen, Fletcher said,

"We are here aboard the renowned British vessel RMS Titanic. Launched in 1911 as the largest and most splendid ship ever built, she left Southampton, England on April 10, 1912. Four days later she lost a battle with an enormous iceberg---the 'unsinkable' masterpiece of mankind's ingenuity sank to the bottom with the loss of over 1,500 lives. Somehow, she has risen from the depths of a century of time and two and one half miles of ocean, through the genius of two American college students. Taking Albert Einstein at his word, they have penetrated the many dimensions of time, to bring forth this apparent near miracle. Please meet Randy Kaplan and Matt Miller, under grads at Webster Marine Insitute in Glen Cove, New York. Randy, would you tell us about your return to the last century, culminating in this amazing event?"

"Certainly, Mr. Fletcher." Randy then went on to tell how he and Matt were moved to this project, how they had traveled back to 1910, spent two years working as Assistant Engineers, hoping to change major flaws which had ultimately brought about her destruction; how he had met Sarah, the girl he had seen in a nightly dream, calling, "Save us!" How they had fallen in love, dealt with the problems of different dimensions of time, and now were to be married in the morning. "Please meet my fiancee, Sarah Carlisle."

As Sarah's striking face filled the screen, Fletcher said, "Sarah Carlisle is, or should I say, 'was' the daughter of Alexander Carlisle, master ship designer for the British Navy and Harland & Wolff, Titanic's builders. Sarah, are you now older than your parents, or just displaced in time?"

She laughed and said, "Mr. Fletcher, I can't really say. I don't feel over 100 , but, then, I don't know how one feels when one is over 100 in 2012. The whole thing is a big mystery to me. But, it's brought Randy and me together, and that's all I care about. As you probably know by now, Captain Smith is marrying us in the morning."

"Yes, we've heard. We will be there with our TV cameras."

"TV? Oh, yes, Randy told me about that wonderful invention. May we see the pictures you will be taking with all that equipment?"

"Certainly, Sarah. This monitor will be available for anyone. We can set it up in the Grand Ballroom for everyone to see."

"Thank you, Mr. Fletcher."

"Sarah, some highly placed people are saying that we know so little about 'time-travel and 'time-warps,' that great danger exists in attempting it. Also that trying to change history is a spiritual no-no. How do you feel about your husband-to-be tampering with the past and future?"

"Mr. Fletcher, it was his tampering, as you put it, that brought us together. If, from tomorrow on, we have only one day together as husband and wife, our faith will help us savor that day forever, through all dimensions of time. Who knows what the future holds in what Randy refers to as 'chronometric technology?'

"Sarah, did you find it difficult leaving your family in Belfast?"

"Yes, it was very difficult, but you know what Matthew 19:5 and Genesis 2:24, in the Bible say, 'This is why a man (or woman) must leave father and mother and cling to his wife (husband), and the two shall become one flesh.' I miss my mother and father and sister Hannah badly, but if it's biblical, it can't be wrong. The most difficult part is that I may never see them again. My faith in Randy's and Matt's abilities makes it easier. I believe that at some time in the future, we will all be together in one dimension. Could that dimension be the one we are promised.... 'Heaven'?"

"That's a very brave statement, young lady," commented Fletcher. Then, turning to Matt, he asked,

"Matt, how do you feel about the dangers inherent in this segment of science?...I mean traveling through dimensions of time"

"Mr. Fletcher, being a close friend of Randy's, one gets used to danger. But, it is most exciting, and that's what life's all about -- taking risks and making advances in a worthwhile field. One thing about this field is, as pioneers we have little backup and few places to go for advice. Space exploration is equally risky, but thousands of people are involved in that field, both friend and foe. Some day that may also be true of time-travel."

Fletcher then continued to interview Randy, Matt and Sarah. He concerned himself with what prompted them to go back in time, the technical details of time-travel, its relationship with Einstein's theories, the Titanic's future in the future. Matt and Randy had an opportunity to promote Webster Institute, more specifically Professor DeVane, as the motivation for their research.

After more than an hour, the interview now concluded, Fletcher said, "Sarah, we can't do this for you, but Randy and Matt, we have your parents on cellular phone setup. Your conversation will be broadcast to the world. We hope you don't mind, but a nation awaits the return of its 'prodigal sons' from the past."

Randy whispered on the side to Matt. "You know, Matt, it's amazing how this world can catapult people who've never been heard of into instant fame or notoriety." Matt nodded his agreement.

"Mr. and Mrs. Kaplan and Mr. and Mrs. Miller, we have your sons here to tell you they have returned from the past. Here they are!"

In chorus, they both said, "Hi, Mom and Dad." Then Randy took over to apologize for their disappearance and explain why they had no opportunity to communicate. "Will you forgive us for bowing out without letting you know?"

An emotional Mrs. Kaplan, in tears over the great news, said, "Oh, my baby. We thought you were gone forever. I can't believe I'm hearing your voice."

Somewhat embarrassed by his mother's emotion, Randy said, "It really is us, and I've brought back the girl I will marry....TOMORROW! This is my fiancee, Sarah Carlisle, from Belfast. Captain Smith will perform the service aboard Titanic at 9 A.M. Matt will, of course, be best man. If CNN can arrange it, we sure would like to have you here. Dad, how are you doing?"

"Great. son," said Mr. Kaplan. It'll be so good to have you back in your room. Except for the addition of a number of sympathy cards, nothing has been touched....Oh, wait"....then, with a chuckle in his voice, he said, "....your mother made your bed the day you left."

"Thanks, Mom, you're the most. I knew I forgot something. I could really use that bed now. Things around here have been hectic....heavy chopper traffic, not much sleep last night."' replied Randy.

Mr. Kaplan then said,

"One blessing from all this....we've become good friends with Matt's parents. It has helped all of us through the rough spots these two years."

"We're both glad to hear that," said Randy.

With that, Matt said, "Hi, folks. Gee, it will be wonderful getting back home....Forgive me for running out without leaving a note, but my good ole buddy, Randy, suggested I meet him at the lab the morning we left. I wasn't sure what was happening, but knowing him as I do, it promised to be exciting. I'm sorry we were gone as long as we were, but when Randy says, 'C'mon, Matt,' I never know whether he's talking about down the block, around the world or through the centuries."

"Oh, Matt, I don't care how long you were gone. All I know is our prayers have been answered and it's wonderful to have you back with us. We hope to see you tomorrow. We love you, son."

"Thanks for letting us film your conversation," said Fletcher. I'm sure there are many parents out there who can identify with the Kaplans and

Millers....a son or daughter who has disappeared, and never been heard from. There are many more heart-rending and heart-warming stories among the 2,200 passengers and crew of this famous ship. We hope we can bring some of them to you in the next few days. This is Ray Fletcher, CNN, live from the deck of the original Titanic, and still having trouble believing it."

Off camera, Fletcher then assured them they would have their parents here for the wedding. Sarah excused herself, saying,"

"Thank you so much, Mr. Fletcher. I'd best get down to see Mrs. Straus about her role as maid-of-honor. Randy, I'll be back shortly."

Isidor Straus had joined his wife sitting on deck when Sarah returned.

"Good morning, Mr. Straus. It certainly is a beautiful day. I hope it stays like this for our wedding tomorrow."

"Oh, is someone getting married?" he asked with an impish grin.

"Why, you know, Isidor," said Mrs. Straus.

"Of course, and I wish you the best."

"Thank you, sir....Mrs. Straus, would you be willing to stand up for me as maid-of-honor. I would be very proud if you did."

"I would like very much to help you celebrate. I may have to ask Isidor to stand me up; the old legs aren't what they used to be."

"I'm sure we can make some provision for that, Mrs. Straus. Thank you for joining us. Captain Smith says he will perform the service at 9 A.M. tomorrow. We will hold the wedding on the foredeck, then walk down the Grand Staircase together. The reception will be held in the Grand Ballroom."

"Oh, that should be beautiful. I can hardly wait!" exclaimed Mrs. Straus. "It has been so long since I've been in a wedding, but then you don't find too many people my age getting married.

"What will you be wearing, Sarah? Knowing what you did about the ship, you certainly didn't bring a wedding gown along. If we had more time, we could arrange to have one sent out from Macy's department store. There's one on a manakin in the bridal department that would fit you just fine."

"Oh, I'll be all right, Mrs. Straus," replied Sarah, "I have a brand new dark green velour dress with a gold-embroidered jacket, short in the front, long in the back, and a modest white dickey. With it I will wear a large white picture hat with matching dark green trim."

"Sounds refreshing, Sarah. I will try to match your choice of green."

Mr. Straus joined in the exchange, by saying, "If the wind gets too strong tomorrow, we may have to send one of those new-fangled helicopters to retrieve you. Don't tie your hat on too tightly."

Captain Smith had assured them he could provide champagne, hors d'oeuvre and patisserie, along with people to serve. He also contributed the ship's orchestra for both the wedding and the reception, and had suggested they inform the leader of the songs they'd like. Sarah, of course, was interested in having them play some of her old favorite British tunes, since nearly half the passengers and all the crew were from the Isles. Randy deferred to her wishes, asking only that his great-grandparents' favorite song, "You Belong to Me," be included. Since the song did not appear until decades later, he would have to teach it to the orchestra.

"Randy, what are you planning to wear? Your space suit? Oh, no....I remember now....J. P. Morgan gave you a very sharp naval outfit, which is as formal as you'd want and, certainly, appropriately contemporary. Is that what you'll wear?

"To be honest with you, Matt, I'd forgotten about that, but it's an excellent idea....you have the same outfit, we'll go together handsomely."

"Randy, who is going give the bride away? I think we've taken care of. everything else."

"I would like my father to do it, if they get them here on time. I don't think he'd object to being part of a Christian service. He's mellowed quite a bit over the years. I've discussed it with Sarah and she was enthused over having one father substitute for the other."

When three o'clock came, the deck was completely filled with passengers waiting for the memorial service. Their curiosity was piqued when they heard it was for those who died on Titanic.

"Isn't this her 'maiden voyage'?"

"Didn't I see 'Titanic II' on the stern?"

“Yes. but it’s not there now!”

“Was there a Titanic I? If so, did it sink?”

Some found it most unsettling; others seemed to care less. Still others could not comprehend what was happening. But there was no way that the word about time-travel wasn’t going to spread, what with several reporters on board almost around the clock.

Grabbing a bull-horn so as to be heard by the large gathering, Captain Smith introduced Brother Joseph Clint, Minister-at-large, to render the memorial service. A heavy-set man with silver-white hair and a booming voice, he stood on a platform and said,

”As you are aware, my good friends, strange things have been going on here. We all know what day it is, but we’re not sure of the year. The whirly-birds coming and going tell us it isn’t the time we thought it was.

“We had a near bout with an iceberg on the 14th/15th that could have done us in, but we managed to glide through without any damage. Praise God! The adventure, however, is not yet over.” He paused, took a long look at the ocean, as if listening for a message, then smiled at the passengers and crew.

“Yes, my friends, we have a ways to go before we find that peace-filled port. We concern ourselves with our physical being, but let us go beyond the physical nature and share a glimpse of the spiritual. What a glorious truth exists beyond the grave. This earthly life is not all there is. God, in his Word, assures us many times of much, much more to come. He offers us personal hope and pure love. I would simply pray, Father, give us strength to live this life well, obeying your will always. Bless those who came before, and those who will come after us in eternity. In the name of the Christ, our Lord and Saviour....Amen.”

A solemn and hushed ‘congregation’ wrestled with their thoughts and feelings as Captain Smith dropped the wreath over the side. The orchestra began playing as Brother Clint said,

“Brothers and sisters, please join in singing ‘Nearer My God to Thee.’ Thank you and bless you.”

Chapter 34

"Prepare for Lifeboat Drill!" barked Murdoch.. "Crew, man your stations. All passengers quartered on the Port (left) side of the ship, put on your life jackets and proceed to the nearest lifeboat on either side. Crew will assist you in proper handling of life jacket and entry into boat. Move quickly but in orderly fashion. All passengers on the Starboard (right) side, will don life jackets and stand by for the second drill. Our evening meal will be held until both drills are performed satisfactorily. Proceed now, please."

Amid the murmurings, several reasons for not doing this were voiced by the passengers. Possible postponement of the evening meal seemed to head the list.

With the drill in progress, one full boat suddenly dropped by its bow, threatening to dump its sixty-four occupants into the frigid water far below. Panic ensued! Not only among the occupants, but the crew handlers as well.

"Hold that hand brake! You! Get in there and help him crank that boat back to level! Quickly now, or your next job will start with a long dive!" Then, to the passengers, the crew chief yelled, "Calm down! Stay seated! Stop screaming! We'll have you back on deck in a minute." Responding, somehow, through the screeching of the hysterical passengers, one crewman held the hand brake while the other turned the hand crank. Gear tooth by gear tooth they managed to bring the heavy load back to level. Other passengers and crew joined to help the terrified occupants exit the boat. Smelling salts were made available for the more faint of heart.

Between assisting women with their life jackets and into their boats, the crewmen learned a great deal about crowd- and self-control. Aside from the quick drill with the new lifeboats and their lowering mechanism while in Southampton, this was the first hands-on experience for many of them. Why would they have bothered? Wasn't Titanic "unsinkable?

At the end of each lifeboat drill, Captain Smith announced the ship would be underway the next morning immediately following the 9 A.M. wedding. The reception would be held in the Grand Ballroom while sailing to New York. Bollard's ship would accompany Titanic all the way.

The trio was exhausted from the constant goings-on. After a slow walk around the boat deck later that evening, Randy and Sarah headed for their rooms. "Sarah, you have given up everything for me. More than it is possible for anyone to give---family, friends, home, culture---everything! If giving is loving, then I am most loved. I thank you and I thank the Lord; he has been so good to us. He must always be part of our life together. Come here and let me hug and kiss you for the last time....as fiancee."

"Oh, Randy, I would have given more if there were more, because I love you so. Then they hugged and kissed as though their world was about to end.

"Good night, my beautiful."

"Sleep well, Randy dear."

The wedding day dawned clear and cool, with little wind to mess the ladies' hair. As he stretched himself awake, Randy envisioned himself as the loving husband of this beautiful girl of his dreams. She had visited him again in a dream that was somewhat different from the usual. Instead of saying "Save us!" her voice resounded across the waters, "Take heed, my love. Love still labors behind the veil."

Randy could not avoid a haunting sense of danger. After all, they were now starting their third day since the change of centuries, in a warp that was not intended for more than the three of them. At any time now, it may weaken to the point where everything reverts to 1912. He prayed at length that the occasion of such return not be before their wedding.

Sarah awoke with the same nagging feeling of fear. Her image of herself as Randy's wife was so strong, however, that she was able to shake it off. Her plan was to have breakfast brought to her stateroom, get dressed for the wedding without seeing Randy. Though not overly superstitious, she thought there was good reason for the husband not to see the bride before the service.

Matt, having slept like the proverbial log, was ready to handle any eventuality. Randy was already moving about the room, preparing for an early breakfast while not seeing Sarah. They had discussed this and she had been adamant.

"Hey, 'Lucky', ready for the big step?" taunted Matt. "You are, indeed, fortunate to have lassoed such a prize."

"Agreed, 'Punk.' Somebody is looking out for me."

They both threw on casual clothes and went to breakfast. On the way they met Ismay and Andrews, both of whom seemed out of sorts.

"What are the possibilities of our ship being called back to the iceberg? Should we be taking extraordinary steps to prepare for it?" asked Andrews in a timorous voice.

In a light-hearted manner, Matt assured them it had to happen some time. It wasn't a matter of 'if, it was, rather, 'when.' We just hope we can make it through the wedding and on into New York."

"Well, Matt, maybe you and Randy can take this lightly, but you are at your assigned point on the time-line. We're not, and we are afraid we are going to lose all this if the warp weakens. Is there anything you or we can do about it?"

"No, there's little more we can do now. You know, fellows," Randy said as gently as he could, "it strikes me that you are the only shipbuilders in history to have been given a second chance to save your ship and its many lives. But you rejected it and went on pridefully toward the original end. Now you are convinced you could have saved the day, had you but capitalized on the suggested changes."

"Yes, I suppose you are right, Randy,' said Ismay.

Randy put things in perspective when he said, "American poet John Greenleaf Whittier summed up where you're at, when he wrote,

> 'For of all sad words of tongue or pen,
> the saddest are these: "It might have been'!"

"Right on, Randy!" Matt concurred. "Gentlemen, we forgive you for ignoring our proposals. As another great American poet, Matt Miller once said,

> 'Dawn shines forth yet another day,
> Let us enjoy it while we may.'

"Would you care to join us for breakfast?" concluded Matt. "Mr. Straus will be joining us after dropping his wife off with Sarah".

"Sounds great, Matt. After you, Bruce," replied Andrews..

"Nice job, man, Randy whispered to Matt. "We may get everyone on the same wavelength before long."

Mrs. Straus had offered to help Sarah with her dress and her hair. It was as if her mother had arrived, Sarah felt that close to her. She was now convinced that love transcended the centuries through one existential, all-encompassing and life-giving spirit.

"You will be an exquisite bride, my dear. Your happiness shows through very clearly," said Mrs. Straus. A Victorian princess for a watching world."

"Thank you, Mrs. Straus. I want to appear at my best for my lover."

"Have no fear, you will overwhelm him and the world."

A large crowd had gathered around the foredeck in anticipation of the wedding service. Everything was in readiness. At 8:45, however, the CNN chopper had not yet arrived with the Kaplans and Millers.

Randy and Matt, splendid in their naval outfits, stood at the helipad waiting for their arrival. Randy hoped they would not have to use their backup plan. But then, before it could be seen, the characteristic sound of a helicopter came to them on the west wind. Within minutes it had arrived at the helipad and set down gently.

After the engines had stopped rotating, Dick Bollard opened the door and the two couples exited as TV cameras whirred. The boys ran to them and, almost in tears, hugged them. The Bible's prodigal son was welcomed with no greater love and enthusiasm than was observed here.

"Come with us," Randy stated. "We are about to start. Dad, I hope you don't mind, but Sarah and I would like to have you give her away, since her own father will not be here."

"Randy, how could I refuse?" stated Mr. Kaplan. Then, jokingly he added, "With any luck at all, my rabbi won't be watching."

Arriving at the foredeck, the group was confronted by a battery of TV cameras and reporters. CBS's anchor man spoke out first, saying, "An extraordinary event is taking place here today....a wedding of two people from different centuries and different walks of life. That would appear to be the ultimate in oneness. Were all our world's events to be equally devoid of relational division and rigidity, how more peaceful would we find it. You are making a great contribution toward that end."

An ABC-TV anchor then said, "This is the most impressive wedding since that of Prince Charles and Diana."

Matt then escorted his mother and Mrs. Kaplan to their front row seats and took Mr. Kaplan to Sarah's stateroom, where he introduced him to Sarah and Mrs. Straus.

"Well, guys, we're on." With that, Matt took Mrs. Straus' arm while Mr. Kaplan took Sarah's. As they approached the red-carpeted walkway, Captain Smith took his place at the other end while Randy stood to his side. After turning Mrs. Straus over to her husband, Matt took his place with Randy.

Captain Smith's signal to the orchestra began the familiar notes of "Here Comes the Bride." Mrs. Straus, supported by her husband, began her slow walk down the aisle. Then, from behind the crowd, Sarah, looking like an angel and smiling widely, processed with Mr. Kaplan. An audible expression of appreciation ran through the crowd. TV cameramen filmed her from every possible angle.

"This beautiful bride brings to us all the principles and class of the Victorian age, from which she hails," was one accompanying comment broadcast to the world.

Upon reaching Captain Smith and the boys, Mr. Kaplan kissed Sarah on the cheek and turned her over to Randy.

"Brothers and Sisters, we are gathered together here today," began Captain Smith, "to share in this happy occasion, the joining of the lives of these beautiful young people in marriage. You are invited to witness this ceremony and add it to your memories of the auspicious maiden voyage of this magnificent ship.

"Marriage is an honorable state, and has here been duly considered.

Who is giving this woman away?"

Mr. Kaplan stood and said, "I do, sir, for her parents."

"Thank you. Will you two now please join your right hands . Randy Kaplan, do you take Sarah Carlisle as your wedded wife....to cleave to her, and her only, until death?"

"I do," he answered proudly.

"Sarah Carlisle, do you take Randall Kaplan as your wedded husband....to cleave to him, and him only, until death?" Her lips quivered as she answered in a soft voice, "I do....I really do."

"Then, under the authority of Maritime Law, and as Captain of this ship, I pronounce you man and wife." He nodded to Randy, "You may now kiss your bride."

The delighted groom took her tenderly in his arms and kissed her firmly. His mother, having done so during the entire service, continued to cry. Handkerchiefs were everywhere to be seen. Captain Smith asked the couple to stand facing the audience. "Ladies and Gentlemen, I would like to present to you, 'Mr. and Mrs. Randall Kaplan.' Immediate applause filled the air, and everyone stood and cheered. The orchestra then played "You Belong to Me."

With the orchestra in the background, Captain Smith invited all present to the Grand Ballroom, where a reception would be held. After most of those present had migrated to the ballroom, the TV cameramen took their place at the foot of the Grand Staircase, anticipating the newlyweds and their wedding party.

Before the wedding party could leave the deck, however, Randy was accosted by an aggressive reporter from the Chicago Tribune, who introduced himself as Stu Browerson. "I am really impressed by this ship and the strange circumstances surrounding her sudden appearance in our century. What I want to ask you is, just what is actually going on here?"

"I can only tell you what I said during the interview with CNN. There will be another news conference upon our arrival in New York. I just can't explain the whole thing yet."

"Is that all the story I am going to get from you? You just want me to wait and not be curious.?

"Hey," he smiled, "be curious as you want. I promise you all the answers at that news conference."

"Not good enough! The world has a right to know the truth now."

"There are those famous words," Randy chided. "You think they are the golden key to open every door. You media people use that line as often as the televangelists use, 'The Lord needs your money.'

"Let me tell you something. I agree that the world needs the truth. But I also believe it is presumptuous for any reporter to think he is the only one qualified to say when and by whom it's going to be broadcast to the world."

"You're not going to help me, are you?"

"You guessed it, friend. This conversation is over!" Randy turned and walked away, rejoining his anxious bride.

The bride and groom appeared at the top of the staircase arm-in-arm with the wedding party. The rest of the party stood aside. Slowly, taking one step at a time, Sarah and Randy began their descent. Seldom had such beauty been framed in such a setting. It was a cameraman's paradise. More applause greeted them as they reached the bottom. Matt then led the four couples---the Kaplans senior and junior, Millers and Strauses---to a reception line. Here they greeted many of those attending. Sarah's warm smile captivated everyone, man and woman. alike. Sincerity, empathy and love emanated from her, even with strangers. A woman with no guile, she opened her heart and soul to all. Randy was so proud of her, he could barely handle it.

After several minutes, the reception line was closed and the couples took their seats. Captain Smith had gotten Titanic underway. It was not evident to most aboard, since the ship had been slowly steaming in tight circles around Bollar Marine for two days as it was. Only Bollar's craft would have an anchor tether long enough to reach the ocean bottom....two-and-one-half miles below.

To announce their departure, Captain Smith blew three long blasts on the ship's horn. Taken by surprise, several passengers directly under the horn almost left their shoes. Those in the Grand Ballroom were fascinated by it, and impressed with the strength its message implied. How could anything so large and so strong, experience a major disaster? Rumor of the possibility she might was circulating among the passengers and crew. Captain Smith's memorial service did little to discourage such rumors.

Preparation for the departure of both vessels had been accomplished quietly the previous night and during the wedding. Bollar Marine, with its ice-breaker prow of extremely strong steel, would steam one-half mile off Titanic's starboard bow, playing interference among the icebergs for her, as necessary They would maintain 17 knots---fast enough to reach New York by the targeted time, but slow enough to give Bollard's vessel time to react to ice dangers.

Captain Smith was pleased with the progress they were making. He turned the helm over to Murdoch, jesting with him about what he should do if he hit another iceberg. Unaware of the possibility of the ship's return to 1912 and its destruction, Murdoch did not consider the captain's humor out of place.

"I shall be at the reception If even the slightest problem arises, send someone for me."

When Captain Smith arrived, he was given a seat between Messrs. Kaplan and Miller. After introductions, Captain Smith said, "I understand from your son, Mr. Kaplan, that you at one time were a member of the U.S. Coast Guard reserve out of your home town of Glen Cove. Is that correct?" That was enough to get the conversation going.

"What line of work are you in?" asked the captain. Kaplan's response and their subsequent conversation were of interest to the participants, but drifted off beneath the sounds of the orchestra.

Randy was dancing with his new bride and, on occasion, he turned her over to Matt and the two fathers. Dick Bollard, who chose to ride Titanic to New York, cut in on Randy once, and found this gorgeous creature to possess a personality matching her beauty. He was fascinated with her Irish accent, her Victorian attire and her obvious love of life and the man with whom she had chosen to share it.

"Are there more girls like you back in 1912, Sarah?" Bollard asked her.

"Oh, I might be able to come up with a few, Mr. Bollard. All we need do is find our way back there, and I will get on it upon arrival.." They both laughed unrestrainedly at the improbability of its happening.

Randy, alert to how Sarah was getting along, experienced his very first pangs of jealousy. His reaction was to calmly cut back in. Sarah and Bollard were taken by surprise, prompting Bollard to say, "Whoops, here's the boss She's all yours, Randy."

As Bollard left, Sarah noticed Randy's slightly reddened face and said,

"Randy, I do believe you are jealous. I will accept that as a compliment Mr. Bollard is a very down-to-earth and humorous man. He would be a good friend for us if we all lived in the same century."

"Right, Sarah, right." He wasn't so sure he agreed.

After a period of dancing, Captain Smith asked everyone to stand, while toasts were made to the loving couple.

"I would like to start by saying that this very strong couple has chosen to spend their lives together in one or the other century---different cultures, different technological progress, a world apart, but brought together by their love for each other. May they find great happiness, and may they be blessed with many little time-travelers."

Randy's father then rose and said, "I have not known my new daughter in law but a few hours, and in that short time Mrs. Kaplan and I have taken her to our hearts. From what we can discern, she is all of what we could ask for. Here's to the happy couple....may they always feel the love we feel for them, and may God's love be evident to them."

Other similar toasts were proposed, after which the meal was served. A large buffet table held many kinds of cheese, caviar, herring, biscuits and other hors d'oeuvre. At the other end, for those with a sweet tooth and no breakfast, came every possible kind of pastry and fruit. Captain Smith had emptied the larder for this reception.

Randy and Sarah could hardly wait for the reception to be over so they could walk the deck, enjoying the warmth of the sun. Since there would be plenty of daylight left when the festivities ended, they relaxed and enjoyed themselves.

Matt had met an English girl in her twenties, named Elizabeth. She was full of energy and seemed to enjoy Matt's humor. They got along fine on and off the dance floor. This was her first trip abroad, and she was making it with her parents. As much as he had missed Emily, Elizabeth filled his day with laughter and pranks. He thought of how great a companion she would be as a time-traveler.

The boys' parents were having the time of their lives. Consider---a 300-mile helicopter ride, including their Newfoundland fuel stop; a wedding of one of their sons, a ride back to New York on the most famous ship of all time---all with excellent food and weather thrown in, and all on the house. What more could one ask? Both fathers danced with both mothers, they sang together, spoke to many of the famous people aboard, shared the grief they had felt over the presumed loss of their sons. It was a bonding experience for them all.

Sarah spent considerable time with them, answering questions about the early 20th century, her family, the economy of the country, what her education was like, and so on. She patiently answered every question, and displayed pleasure at the interest everyone was showing.

Meanwhile, the lookouts in the crow's nest once again brought the attention of those aboard to the horizon before them. Calling down to the bridge, they said, "Enormous, hull-down vessel slightly off collision course at what appears to be three miles. Difficult to tell due to its tremendous size. Murdoch once again sent Mooney to notify the captain. When they did, Smith advised Bollard and they both went to the bridge. They could hear the tanker's PA system announce, "Shipmates, we have an unusual sight here. The famous Titanic is passing us to port, and along with it the ship that found her wreckage. Believe it! Get your cameras ready. You'll not see a Kodak opportunity like this again soon. Mr. Ripley, are you watching?"

As Murdoch pointed, questioningly, Bollard said, "That is an EXXON oil-carrying supertanker. Most supertankers have gross weights in the hundreds of thousands of tons, compared to Titanic here, which, if I remember rightly, is about forty-six thousand tons. They are as long as 1,500 feet and carry up to nine million gallons of crude oil. Refined crude has replaced coal as fuel for most forms of transportation."

"Captain, it might be best to have Michaels radio the tanker from my ship. I'm sure they are aware of our existence and will have been on the lookout for us."

As they passed the tanker, almost her entire crew elbowed one another on the bridge, cameras in hand. Word quickly spread among Titanic's passengers and crew and the port side rails filled with the curious. "Awesome!" was the word heard most. Wasn't Titanic the largest ship ever built in their lifetime up to this point?

As applause and waving began, one of the onlookers on the tanker said,

"It really is the Titanic! I was sure it was some kind of scam or publicity stunt. But I don't think they'd dress that many people in costumes just for a stunt---there are hundreds of them!"

The enormous ship---1500 feet of it, moved steadily away, leaving a wake large enough to roll Titanic several degrees. The sightseeing guests drifted back to the reception, where the faithful orchestra continued to play for dancing and the champagne issued forth from some unending source. Slowly the ballroom emptied, enabling Sarah and Randy to slip back to their room to change into casual clothing again.

During the reception, Matt had moved Randy's things into Sarah's room, as Randy had requested. This change would introduce them to the first of their many steps toward marital intimacy. They were to find Sarah's modesty reflective of her upbringing in the Victorian age. Using their private bath as dressing room, she forestalled Randy's daylight viewing of her undergarments. Perhaps later, with darkness tempering the experience, her modesty would be somewhat overcome.

The sun was warm for mid-April; their intense feelings for each other augmented by a little champagne. Emotions were running high.

"Randy, we are so blessed. But I'm afraid Time will separate us before we come to know each other totally. Please tell me you'll do something about that."

"Sarah, Sarah, you know how much I love you, and you know I can't be separated from you any more than I can be separated from myself."

"Yes, I know, but this fear just won't go away," explained Sarah.

"Sarah, before we actually met, I heard your voice calling me. Only when God finally brought us to the same place at the right time did we meet and come to know the love we feel.

"If we lose each other temporarily, we will have to be patient until He brings us together in His time. Our prayers will soften the sense of loss we feel. At least we'll be with our families, whose love should sustain us."

"Perhaps, Randy, His time might differ from any we've known -- chosen for a journey, loved beyond loving, we will share it with Him."

Chapter 35
The Arrival

The two ships maintained their speed and position relative to each other. No large icebergs were seen. The calm that enveloped the ship belied the fact that the "Sword of Damocles" hung over it.

As one droll knave expressed it, "It's like waiting for the other shoe to drop."

The Captain, despite his sense of responsibility for what did or was to happen, was most sociable. He kept the food and drink flowing. He reckoned that if the ship were to sink within the next few days, he wasn't about to lose her larder to the sea. The gaming room was kept open, contests of all sorts were started on deck. All-in-all, it was a festive experience---possibly the last most would not likely experience again.

As the sun went down gloriously that evening, Randy and Sarah sat quietly., appreciating its setting not only for its beauty, but for delaying that inevitable moment when they would become truly one. Many on board congratulated them as they walked by, with some of the older ones outwardly expressing their envy. But, what guidance was available to them for this new experience.

A chill wind began to blow as the sun dropped behind the horizon. Shivering slightly, Sarah asked that they go in. Randy, confident of many things, was not self-assured about his role as husband and lover. Many things were taught to those entering marriage; sexuality was seldom among them.

Randy helped Sarah out of her chair, grasping her arm gently. Her brief chill had produced "goose-bumps," resulting in rough, cold skin.

"Pardon me, Randy, the cold must have gotten to me," explained Sarah, noting that Randy had withdrawn his hand almost imperceptibly. Once inside the stateroom, her skin softened as she warmed up. Randy felt he had shared a very intimate moment with Sarah. Sarah felt the same and, wanting to express it, threw herself into Randy's arms and relaxed against him. The beginning of their search for intimacy had begun in a simple way -- tension was broken, their need of each other unleashed. Modesty, reserve, self-concern evaporated as two years of love and desire demanded expression.......!

The following morning, Wednesday, April 18, 2012, began in a dense fog. Titanic sounded her mournful horn, while Bollard Marine echoed at a higher pitch. The chorus was repeated every thirty seconds. Captain Smith knew from previous experience that motor and sailing vessels would have left port the night before to greet the famous ship. The fog presented a hazardous setting for them. It would be very easy for them to drift off course and cross the main shipping lanes slightly south of Titanic's position. This hazard would increase as more boats joined the greeters. Several, having found either of the ships, stayed close in for safety.

As the sun rose in the sky, the fog began to burn off. By noon it was almost completely gone, and the tallest buildings in Manhattan began to penetrate the horizon. The twin-towered World Trade Center stood well above other tall structures.

Randy and Sarah had awakened early to the sound of the fog horns. Lying snuggled under a magnificent quilt, they wanted to prolong the warmth they found in each other. Randy suggested, however, that this was to be a very busy day, and they'd best prepare for it. Reluctantly they began to dress as the modesty of yesterday's daylight failed to return.

"Sarah, I love you so," said Randy.

"I know, Randy, I know." she responded.

"Sarah, I dreamed about those dark angels again last night. They warned me once again not to try to change history. They were most emphatic about it this time."

"Randy, let it go. We face whatever our fate may be, either together or separately. But our love can never be divided. We are one."

Captain Smith had lowered the ship's speed to 10 knots for the safety of the many boats in the area. Most boat owners were not well-schooled in water safety and did not account for drift or their inability to stop quickly. The fog presented another hazard---disorientation. The continued sounding of the fog horns provided some focus for their wanderings.

Randy and Sarah met Matt, the Kaplans and the Millers for breakfast. During the meal there had been much laughter and reminiscences, but in between they had felt themselves being examined by the parents for some indication of how the wedding night had gone. Both of them felt uncomfortable and hoped what was being looked for did not show on their faces.

Randy and Sarah excused themselves to clean up their room and pack their clothes in anticipation of leaving the ship that night. They then rejoined Matt and the parents on deck.

Once seated, Randy said, “I’m waiting for the fog to lift before I ask Captain Smith to let me steer Titanic as far as the Narrows entering New York harbor. I’ve dreamed of doing it ever since we became involved with her.”

Captain Smith’s reaction to Randy’s request was somewhat negative.

“Randy, White Star regulations don’t allow for such. And I am concerned about the ‘small boys’ surrounding us. But, if I stand by closely to monitor your direction, it shouldn’t be a problem. You’ve earned it. You can take the wheel when we reach Ambrose light, take her through Ambrose channel until we reach the Narrows. I’ll have to take over from there. We’ll pick up a pilot before entering the Narrows.”

“Oh, thank you, Captain. Matt, go fetch your life jacket -- your time has come.”

“I’m on the way, ‘Skipper’.”

The ships’ ‘fleet’ of boats was scattered everywhere. Captain Smith calls to Bollard, asking him to announce through his PA that all boats line up behind Titanic in a double line. Many more would be joining them as they neared the harbor. “Also, Mr. Bollard, please take your position directly ahead of us and lead us in. This will be the biggest celebration of the century. There may be something symbolic in the salvage operator bringing the real thing home, still in one piece.”

It was only another 9 or 10 miles to Ambrose light. The New York skyline came into full view, bringing exclamations of all sorts from the observing passengers. An hour later they reach Ambrose. Randy takes the helm, saying in a formal voice, “I relieve you, sir.” Sarah, standing just outside the bridge door, listens for Randy’s voice. This is a great thrill for him.

The string of boats stretches out for a mile behind Titanic. As they reach the Narrows, the pilot joins them, taking a position just forward of Bollard. Randy seems to be doing quite well, his expression like a child with a new toy.

The parade passes Coney Island to starboard, then passes under the Verrazano-Narrows bridge, connecting Brooklyn with Staten Island. Necks bent back to view this extraordinary bridge, then to take in the spectacular buildings of all heights filling Manhattan.

As they enter Upper New York Bay from the Narrows, the world explodes in front of them. Fireworks, tugboats, fire boats with hoses streaming upward, several bands, six helicopters circling, the "Budweiser" and the "Get Met" blimps slowly covering the scene. Hundreds more 'small boys' fill the harbor, most of them sounding their horns or instruments they carry. Many billboard-size banners welcome the 100-year late-arriving ship. The welcome had been a-comin' for 100 years and nobody was going to put a lid on it.

The pilot leads the ships past the Statue of Liberty to port. Many passengers remove their hats out of respect for this internationally know symbol of hope. The young immigrant repeats his comment about meeting his father at the statue. Sarah leaves the bridge and runs to the bow to see New York for what is probably her only time. Randy joins her, they hold each other and, through tears of happiness, become part of the massive celebration.

Titanic is picked up by tugs and maneuvered into a vacant bearth in the cruise- ship docking area along Manhattan's west side. The dock is filled with welcoming dignitaries and the press. Passengers begin to disembark, third class and steerage through the aft doors, 1st and 2nd class the forward. .

As the Kaplans, Millers, Matt, Randy and Sarah step onto the dock, they are rushed by photographers and reporters. But they are surrounded by people from all over the States who have come to meet and greet their ancestors---great grandparents and beyond---whom they have only heard about and never known. Ancestors they'd been told had perished on the Titanic.

Several reporters manage to elbow their way through the crowd, and begin a barrage of questions. Most are told that a press conference will be arranged at which these questions would answered.

Then, suddenly, the gaggle of reporters steps aside as the President of the United States and the First Lady stride down the dock. Captain Smith and the White Star, Harland & Wolff executives hurry to the dock to meet them. The Kaplans, Millers, Matt and Sarah gather with them.

"This is, indeed, a great pleasure to meet people from another time," said the President. It has been most difficult for my wife and I to accept this as truth. But, from what we see to be obvious, the passengers and crew are from 1912. How does this fit with the casualty list published in 1912?"

"Your question, sir," said Matt, "entails an entire treatise on the many dimensions of time. Albert Einstein is the source of most information regarding time and time-travel. It has been suggested that if we young college students could develop a procedure for it, there would be no problem for a government agency to develop and refine it for the world. Like NASA, for instance."

"You may be right, son. I just might recommend that to the Congress. Now, let me meet the young lady from 1912 Belfast."

"Sir, we would have you meet Sarah Carlisle, daughter of Alexander Carlisle, designer of the Titanic," said Randy. Captain Smith married us yesterday aboard ship. It was quite a bash -- you should have been there."

"Thank you for that, but I don't recall receiving an invitation," the President said with a smile.

The First Lady then asked if she might meet with Sarah to discuss clothing styles, which had obviously changed in the intervening 100 years.

"I would love to do that, madam."

A sudden commotion at the end of the dock catches their attention. One of the steerage passengers has disappeared in a matter of seconds, followed by his wife and children, then others around them. Reporters jump back in astonishment as more people vanish. The President's Secret Servicemen guarding him act instantly and rush him and the First Lady off the doc and to their limo. Everything begins to crackle with static electricity -- the ship, the helicopters, the docks.

Randy and Sarah desperately run toward each other, holding hands tightly, hoping to prevent her disappearance.

"Don't leave, Sarah. Don't leave me. I wanted to rescue you!"

Sarah understands what's happening. Her fingers begin to disappear as she consoles Randy, "And you did.....if only momentarily. If it is our lot to meet that iceberg in the cold Atlantic, at least all those poor lost souls, were able to meet relatives they'd never seen. You gave us another day to live. Goodbye, my love."

With that, Sarah vanishes entirely, leaving Randy on his knees and her echoing last words,

"Save us! Save us!"

Within a few more seconds, the ship, everyone and everything that had come through to 2012, had vanished. The great celebration was over. The thousands of articles that would have been written, the hundreds of photographs that would have been taken, now must rest with Titanic two-and-one-half miles below the surface of the North Atlantic.

Randy, still on his knees sobbing, Matt and the parents stood there alone on the dock in total shock. They were unable to move quickly enough to avoid being trapped by reporters seeking to save the media day.

"Why didn't you all go back with them?"

"Where did they all disappear to?"

"Will you ever see your new wife again, Mr. Kaplan?"

"How can they return without use of time-travel equipment?"

These and many other questions comprised the barrage from a disappointed and frustrated press corps. Mr. Kaplan backed them off, saying,

"This is a very emotional moment for my son. You can't expect him to respond to your inane questions. Perhaps, when the boys have recovered from this extraordinary experience they will be more willing to answer your questions. Now, if you will excuse us."

Impressed with Mr. Kaplan's appeal, they reporters slowly backed up to allow them to leave.

Not seeing or hearing from Randy since Sarah and the ship had disappeared and the FBI and press quit bothering them, Matt and Roxy come looking for him. Mrs. Kaplan responded to their knock, saying, "Randy is out in his shed looking at his prisms. He is still very depressed. He has not been eating. We're becoming very concerned."

With that, Matt gets that sinking feeling again and heads for the shed.

When he sees that Randy has taken down the Titanic posters in his windows, he runs toward the shed yelling, "No, Randy! Don't!" Before he reaches the shed, he is blown backward by the sudden lightning-like implosion coming from the room........

Matt and Roxy run to the shed and look into the open doorway. When the smoke clears, they find no trace of Randy. The room is empty save a laser and a letter nailed to the center-post.

Roxy removes the letter and opens it. As she reads it she begins to cry softly and hands it to Matt who comforts her as he finishes reading.

May 20, 2012

To those I love in this century;

Matt, please explain this to my parents. They have been my only love for all my young life, but the unbelievable feelings I have experienced in the past few months, have come forth like a well of pure spring water.

I cannot let go of the love Sarah has for me....or I for her. I've cried every day since I felt her leave me. She vanished as I held her gentle hands, drawn back to that time in which we met.

Please try to understand. My whole world and reason for being now revolve around this angel from another dimension in time. I have no choice, I must follow after her. I realize leaving this way is not logical and I know going without you, Matt, means wherever I wind up, that's where I will remain. Love is stronger than death and I will be with Sarah forever!

Your friend,

Randy

THE END?

Printed in the United States
By Bookmasters